RESCUE INSTINCT

CERBERUS TACTICAL K9 TEAM BRAVO

CERBERUS TACTICAL K9

FIONA QUINN

THE WORLD OF INIQUUS

Ubicumque, Quoties. Quidquid

Iniquus - /i'ni/kwus/ our strength is unequalled, our tactics
unfair – we stretch the law to its breaking point. We do
whatever is necessary to bring the enemy down.

THE LYNX SERIES

Weakest Lynx

Missing Lynx

Chain Lynx

Cuff Lynx

Gulf Lynx

Hyper Lynx

STRIKE FORCE

In Too DEEP

JACK Be Quick

InstiGATOR

CERBERUS TACTICAL K9 TEAM BRAVO

Warrior's Instinct

Rescue Instinct

Hero's Instinct

This list was created in 2022. For an up-to-date list, please visit FionaQuinnBooks.com

If you prefer to read the Iniquus World in chronological order you will find a full list at the end of this book.

RESCUE INSTINCT

Cerberus
Tactical K9

TEAM BRAVO

FIONA QUINN

Cerberus Team Bravo (Caribbean)

- Ares — Team Lead
- **Mace (Austin Mace) and Diesel**
- Ash and K9 Hoover
- Bear and K9 Truffles
- Mongoose Phipps — Cerberus veterinarian — Team Bravo logistics and communications officer

Cerberus Team Alpha (Washington D.C.)

- Bob Palindrome — Chief of Tactical Operations Center
- Tripwire and K9 Valor
- Wife — Major Dani Addams
- Noah
- Montgomery Chasten — Cerberus Kennel veterinarian

Cerberus Logistics (Washington D.C.)

- Kiyana Swabi — Lead, Logistics Team Lima
- Hailey Stapleton
- Fiancé — Ares (Heath Sterling)

Trifalgar Working Group (Maryland-based DARPA-affiliated research group)

- Dr. Guha — Program Director
- Koda Masami — Program counselor
- **Dr. Tara Alvarez** — Research Scientist
- Mother — Terry Alvarez
- Brother — Matteo Alvarez
- Dr. Jim Driscoll — Expedition Team Leader
- Husband — Trevor Driscoll
- Dr. Pria Gupta — Research Scientist
- Dr. Niels Grabner — Research Scientist

Emergency Management, Dominica

- John John — Director of Emergency Services

MAP

THE CARIBBEAN

You don't need to be in a plane crash to know
that it would be bad to be in a plane crash.

~ Zeid Ra'ad Hussein

~

This book is dedicated to the world's environmental
scientists, with my gratitude.
And to my granddaughter, Ivey
May she grow up in a world bright with hope.

1

Tara Alvarez

Friday, Dominica

TARA ALVAREZ BLINKED AGAINST THE VELVETEEN DARKNESS.

Tucked in the back corner of the house she was renting on the Caribbean Island of Dominica; her bedroom was soft. The edges of her furnishings hadn't yet sharpened into focus.

Holding her breath, Tara stilled to absorb the shockingly silent moment of pre-dawn.

It was the elusive time when the nocturnal buzzing and clicking suddenly stopped as the night animals curled into sleep, hiding away from the dangers of the encroaching morning light.

The birds—heads tucked up under their wings with their feathers fluffed for warmth—had not yet shaken off the dew to tweet and chirp, rousing their fellow rainforest dayworkers.

A thin-lined demarcation. A sound horizon.

There and gone again in the space between an inhale and an exhale.

Like watching a humpback whale breaching the ocean in the mist, if Tara happened to be awake and aware enough to catch that moment, it was magical.

Today was going to be a good day, she told herself, in the thickness of her half-awake thoughts.

Today, something *amazing* was going to happen.

She felt her fingers cross as she squeezed her eyes tightly, trying to propel that idea into reality.

It was a reflexive thought and action she'd performed since childhood. And now, all grown up, this was the way that Tara transitioned from night—when anything could happen in her dreams—to day, when she had to be an adult.

The sun wasn't awake yet, Tara told herself, and she shouldn't be either.

Lately, sleep was harder to catch hold of. Harder to cling to. When Tara did grasp some transient ZZZs, come morning, her time in bed often left her stiff-muscled and drained.

Tara desperately needed some sleep to catch up on the exhaustion of trying to sleep.

Punching her pillow and nestling her head back against the cool cotton, Tara hoped for…ten more minutes? Fifteen, maybe?

Nope, not gonna happen.

She rose up through the layers of sleep past her childhood optimism into adulthood.

The tingle of existential dread, Tara's every-morning snooze alarm, jangled her nerves, radiated heat out from her stomach along her limbs to buzz her fingers and toes wildly.

It sure would be nice if she could take a day off from that sensation just every now and again.

Weirdly, this morning Tara's first thought—just before she caught the enchanted moment of stillness—was about a mountain chicken she had seen the day before.

Mountain chickens were actually an endangered frog species here in Dominica and not a bird at all.

So foul, not fowl.

Tara guessed that they were nicknamed "mountain chickens" because they had big meaty thighs. And people who ate frog thought they were delicious. Sort of like chicken wings at a tailgate party, only a terrible culinary choice for species survival.

"Delicious," Tara whispered. She disliked the sound of that word the way some people disliked the word "moist."

Mountain chickens were both moist and delicious, she mused through her pre-caffeinated brain fog. So, *blech*, people should just leave them alone.

Tara threw her sheet back and lay there in a t-shirt and grey striped cotton panties, letting the ceiling fan brush air gently over her heated system.

Tara was now remembering that in her quasi dream—the thing that roused her to catch the magic moment of silence—the frog she had seen on the trail. Though in her dream it was in car-sized frog form. It had looked her in the eye and croaked, "The chickens have come home to roost."

It was terrifyingly Alfred Hitchcockesque.

What did that even mean: "The chickens have come home to roost"?

Something about karma…some action or inaction reflecting back.

Usually bad.

Tara swung out of the bed to go pee, feeling her way through the room without turning on the lights.

Chickens coming home to roost *could be* a good thing.

After all, Tara tried to be a good person. An imperfect person, sure. Room to grow. Ways to be better. But for the most part, she lived a reasonable life with a smile on her face, a kind word on her lips, a helping hand.

Chickens roosting might be okay.

Lifting the lid, Tara slid her panties down her thighs, and plopped onto the toilet.

Tara pushed the mountain chicken out of her thoughts to replace it with, "The early bird catches the worm." Yeah, she preferred that to chicken thoughts. Not only was the phrase proactive and inspiring—up and at 'em! —it also made a heck of a lot more sense.

Right now, worms were what Tara did for a living.

Tara was a glorified worm hunter.

And she loved to tell people that, just to see the bemused, lost expressions that followed.

"Worm hunter. Such a glamorous existence," she muttered.

Yup, ten years of university and the attainment of a doctorate degree to do the exact same thing she did as a five-year-old in her mother's back yard, dig worms.

Tara dragged a length of paper from the roll and tore off the section, wondering if other people talked out loud to themselves like this.

Granted, she was the only human being around. She only saw people on her once-a-week trip down the mountain.

She liked it.

And didn't.

Left to her own thoughts, things could get dark.

"Existential dread."

With a flush and a hand wash, Tara headed back to her room and climbed onto her bed. Leaning over the table, she clicked on the little bedside lamp with a fifteen-watt bulb that eased her into her day.

While Tara might be alone in talking to herself out loud, she certainly wasn't the only one in her research cohort who fought off existential dread.

Tara was part of a government-funded research program headed by Dr. Guha.

Their task?

Find innovative, out-of-the-box ways to deal with climate changes. The diverse group that Dr. Guha had put together all read the same scientific journals. They all had their finger on the same data points. All knew the truth those numbers told.

Existential dread was pervasive in their group.

Afraid of the scientists' burnout rate and having had one of her researchers commit suicide, Guha hired a therapist, Dr. Masami, to try to calm everyone's nerves.

"Do you feel your job makes you prone to anxiety?" Masami had asked Tara.

"Pretty much, yeah." Tara had shrugged.

The first piece of advice Masami handed out to their team was narrow their focus to a single issue. "Don't take on all of the world's problems. Narrow things down as much as possible."

The problem Tara was focused on was polystyrene foam, the ubiquitous packaging used for disposable hot coffee cups and take-out menu orders.

While plastic accumulation already got a lot of attention and funding, polystyrene foam? Not so much.

It accumulated in the landfills where it would hangout for like five hundred years, an ever-growing mountain of disposed foam.

In the lab, Tara had discovered that the chemical components in the foam were the same, in large part, as the root of the doubloon plant—a plant that was only found in one place in the world. Here in Dominica.

Rare and endangered, Tara had to apply for special permission to work around the plants.

"What did this have to do with worms?" people would ask.

The doubloon root was eaten, digested, and turned to fertile soil by a unique species of worm. This worm, thankfully, could also devour other plants and was not on any endangered species list. It made collecting them for study less fraught. And since Tara was removing the worms that would kill off the endangered doubloon, Tara was, in fact, helping to save the species.

Tara had done some initial studies in the lab, feeding the worms polystyrene. On a petri dish-sized scale, there was demonstrable success.

That success was interesting enough to gain funding from the U.S. government and to get the required Dominican permits.

Tara's thoughts about the worms? What if she could isolate the digestive process, the chemicals that could break down polystyrene foam, and she could create a synthetic?

What if the foam could be melted away? Or the biproduct could be used for something else? Something useful, like fertilizer.

The goal was to find a way to make the worms' digestion process scalable and useful.

Yes, everyone who heard Tara say that her job was to "hunt for worms that could digest coffee cups" stilled and stared, not quite sure what to do with that information.

A bizzarro way to live one's life? Tara got that it might sound that way.

But instead of sitting in a cubicle punching numbers into a calculator, people paid her to hang out on a Caribbean Island and play in the dirt.

Hunting worms, sure.

Still.

Worm hunting was kind of glamorous. In its own way.

And with those words, a wave of dread flooded her system. Weirdly more so than usual. Tara's mom would say this was a premonition, and that Tara should pay close attention.

But Tara was *not* her mother.

She didn't believe in premonitions.

Tara pulled her feet in to sit cross-legged with her pillows supporting her back. She dragged her journal onto her lap, the point of her pen landed on a blank sheet.

Masami, their stay-sane guru, said, "Start each day writing down—don't just think them, it's the writing down that makes the difference—three things that you're grateful for. Specific things that happened in the last twenty-four hours and the 'why'." Masami said this trained the brain to look for good when the data being written up in the scientific journals was all bleak.

1. I am grateful that when I was at the waterfall, I discovered tiny diamonds glinting in the sunlight. I was filled with awe and peace.
2. I am grateful that there was a cool breeze last night that kept the bugs away, and I slept deeply until I didn't.

MAYBE I SHOULDN'T WRITE that last part. Does it nibble away at the gratitude?

1. I am grateful that even if my ex is now dating my best friend, Pria—and I will have to see them together tomorrow— I can truthfully say I am happy I'm out of that relationship with Neils and have forgiven myself for being blind and involved with him for so long. Best wishes to both of them.

TRUTHFULLY, this list wasn't coming off as gratitude.

Chewing the end of her pen, Tara thought about that last entry—Neils and Pria.

Tara let herself wiggle around in the sensation.

Nope. No tenderness there. Just relief.

She looked over her gratitude list. Tara should probably be writing something about riotous colors—the lemon-yellow butterflies landing on deep purple flowers or the cotton candy clouds of last night's sunset—but she just wasn't feeling it today.

"This is going to have to do."

There were two more steps to Masami's prescribed morning ritual.

Next up, a ten-minute guided meditation where Tara was supposed to follow her breathing, releasing other thoughts, *centering in the moment.*

Tara tried to grab hold of that childhood cross-fingered ritual as her focal point for her meditation. But that place of optimism seemed as ephemeral as the transitory moment of silence she'd happened upon that morning.

After a few minutes, Tara gave up on meditative breathwork.

Whatever was going on with her and the nightmare warning

from the mountain chicken, trying to follow the breath was making her hyperventilate.

And no one needed to start their day sucking air out of a paper bag.

Did she even own a paper bag? Tara wondered as she started the last component of her required morning ritual, meditation cards.

Masami had told the team to pick decks of cards that *called to them.* The purpose was to give them a different perspective of how to look at that day. Something that would encourage the scientists to consider different points of view—something new to consider so that they didn't fall into "ruts and bad thought habits."

Tara wasn't really into meditation cards. She'd asked her mom what deck to get. And a mom package had arrived with three decks.

Thanks, Mom.

Yeah, she'd told her mom *one.* Whatever. That was fine. Tara would use all three assigning a specific task to each deck.

The first deck, Tara dedicated to the idea of easing her through her existential dread. Though, that wasn't how she defined it in her personal session with Masami. Tara told Masami that this was her outward-facing deck, the one that would give her food for thought about how she, Tara, would interact with the world.

The card she pulled from that deck today was Treasure Chest. Tara grinned as she noted it in her journal: **Today, I found the Treasure Chest. Yay me!**

This was apt.

The doubloon plant that Tara looked for on the mountain was so nicknamed because of its round, yellow-orange leaves and brown veins that looked like the design on ancient coins.

That's why Tara nicknamed the worms she collected "Gold". To her they were as precious as gold.

And it amused her.

Every Friday, Tara went down to the town to mail her weekly *gold*, in a box filled with coconut coir, back to her lab. She had a running joke with the mail guy that she was sending off her treasure chest.

Today was Friday.

Fridays were good days. While down by the shore, Tara had a restaurant meal, window shopped, and handed in her mandated paperwork to the Dominican government. She'd sit under a tree where she could pick up internet and cell reception. There, as she breathed in the salty thickness of the sea air, she caught up on her correspondence. Most importantly—according to her mother—Tara called home to let everyone know that a giant boa constrictor hadn't wrapped her up during the night and squeezed the life out of her.

Her mother had a *very* vivid imagination.

Yup. Treasure Chest was a good omen for today. (Much better than the chicken thing.)

The cards were working. Her anxiety was petering out. *"Brava, Dr. Masami!"*

Tara picked up her second deck. This was a basic tarot deck with water-colored designs. She assigned this set of cards with the task of giving her something to reflect on for the day. Something to chew on while she was digging her worms.

She noted her card in the journal: **Fool.**

"Huh. That doesn't sound good." Tara looked up the meaning in the instruction booklet: The start of a journey, naiveté.

See? If these cards were predictive, it would have been something like Three of Cups—celebration, and the gathering of friends. Pria and the crew would be docking here in Dominica sometime today.

But sure, she could use this card as a way to see things anew.

Okay start of a journey—Tara's friends were taking a few days here in Dominica to work on Trevor's film project—some screenplay he said was inspired by Tara's "treasure hunting silliness". After they were done filming in Dominica, they'd be island hopping for fun, and to fulfill the teams' contractually required time off, that was supposed to shield the scientists from doom and gloom.

This would be a good break from the worm tedium.

Tara might join them on the island hops. She might not. The hesitation was over Neils, her ex, being there.

She'd test the waters and see how weird that energy was once she saw him again. It had been over a year now that the relationship was in her rearview. It should be fine. But it could be weird.

Tara placed the card on the bedside table.

The last card she pulled was from her animal deck.

Tara loved the artwork in this deck. She also kinda liked the idea of inviting an animal to metaphorically walk beside her and give her counsel during the day.

Today, she pulled the monkey card.

"Monkey!"

She read the card's description that accompanied the deck. "Playful. Curious. Mischievous."

Yeah, Tara would focus on her own monkey qualities today. She'd try to find ways to be humorous and have fun. That seemed like a good remedy for dread.

Tara stilled. Did it work? Was this morning ritual helpful?

Yup. Better already.

The birds were singing.

Though the sun hadn't yet shined on her face, a soft yellow glow began to paint the sky.

Tara climbed from her bed with an enthusiastic fist in the air. "The early bird catches the worm. Up and at 'em. Proactive! Doing my part to save the world!"

And then, just because it felt right, Tara bounced around being a monkey until she was breathless. One of the joys of living alone was that she could be as silly as she wanted when she wanted.

Now *that* was something to add to tomorrow's gratitude list.

2

Austin Mace

Friday, St. Kitts

AUSTIN MACE STOOD ON THE EDGE OF THE ST. KITTS CLIFF overlooking the bright turquoise waters of the Caribbean Sea.

His K9 partner, Diesel—a giant of a German Shepherd—sat by his side, lifting his nose to scent the air, salted with dead fish and the rotten egg smell of decomposing seaweed.

It would grow worse with the heat of the day.

Mace's teammate, Ares, clapped his hands sharply to focus the attention of the thirty-odd veterinary students. "Is everyone ready?"

It was early morning, before the first classes of the day.

The students slogged forward to create a semicircle, coffee not kicking in yet. Coming from both North and South America to study on St. Kitts, this group of twenty-somethings all looked like they'd rather still be in their beds.

Maybe today's demonstration would wake them up a bit.

"I'm Ares, commander of Iniquus's Cerberus Tactical Team Bravo." He bladed his hand toward Mace. "This is my number two, Austin Mace, with K9 Diesel."

"Good morning." Mace squinted past the glare of the morning sun. "I want to thank you for your interest in pet rescue and pet sheltering following a natural disaster. Your work in putting together a deployable team is commendable and much needed."

"To that end," Ares said. "Cerberus Tactical Team Bravo is glad to work with you. Our team vet, Mongoose, as you might already know, is a graduate of St. Kitts's veterinary program and will be working closely with you as you build your rescue skills. Mongoose will be your point of contact with Cerberus. If you have any specific questions or concerns, you can reach out to him. Your professor has that contact information for you." He waited for the heads to swing toward Dr. Jeffers then back to him. Then Ares continued. "As an opener, Mongoose thought you might like to see a tactical K9 in action. Was he right?"

The students shifted around, their faces suddenly brightening with interest as they clapped.

"Team Bravo is made up of seven men. Mongoose makes sure the dogs are in top physical condition. The six other men are each paired with a K9 partner. While each dog has a specialty, and can deploy on solo missions, our team's primary task is search and rescue."

"No women on your team?" a female student asked.

"On Bravo right now, we do not," Ares said. "We do have a female on team Alpha."

"But why not?" she pressed.

"It's not because women can't do the job," Ares said. "The main reason is that Iniquus hires veterans for mission-oriented teams, and there just aren't a lot of women coming through the pipeline who are veteran dog handlers. We hope that'll change." He turned. "Mace."

Mace took a step forward. "This is K9 Diesel, my partner. In the military, he would be ranked higher than me. On Cerberus Team Bravo, we show our dogs that level of respect. Since, Diesel is a working dog, I ask that you not pet him or try to catch his attention."

Mace watched as the vet students' focus shifted to Diesel and quickly back away.

"On the Bravo search and rescue team, we have three German Shepherds, including Diesel. All three shepherds are cross trained to special operations spec. They can be deployed to assist any of the Iniquus operations forces as a force multiplier when needed. Diesel has an affinity for water and fast boats."

When Diesel heard his name, he sat up a little taller and looked just that much more regal.

Mace stopped to grin. "We get him out on water evolutions as much as possible. An evolution, as it applies here, means a training mission."

"Did you all come to St. Kitts just to teach us or are you training here, too?" a student asked. "Will we be able to tag along and watch as you train the dogs?"

Ares gestured toward the mountain. "Team Bravo has a compound on the island that serves as a jumping off spot during hurricane season. Our teams, Alpha and Bravo, rotate in and out of the area to train the dogs for rescue in the Atlantic and Caribbean. As to watching the training, there are times when we could use your help. We like to hide people for the dogs to search out. If you're willing to participate," Ares caught Dr. Jeffers eye, "if you could keep a list?"

Jeffers nodded.

"You're an American team," a male student said.

"Correct," Ares replied.

The student tipped his ear toward his shoulder. "Why, then, are you on St. Kitts and not on American territory?" he asked. "St. Croix, for example."

"Geographical positioning. Elevation," Ares said. "There are distinct reasons. We work closely with emergency management on the various Caribbean islands. Training with our partners keeps our skills sharp, and during natural disasters it helps us to work as a cohesive group when lives are on the line."

"We're first, though, right?" another man asked. "Since you're here and all."

Ares rested his hands on his hips. "Our first obligation is to fulfill our Iniquus contracts. Secondly, we assist where we're most needed. The level of need is decided by our command in Washington, D.C. after gathering information from our allied emergency managers and boots on the ground." Ares turned to look over his shoulder at the blaze-orange life raft barely visible in the water about fifty meters out, the length of an Olympic pool. Twenty yards beyond it was the barge. He turned back to the vet students. "Today, we thought we'd move through a water rescue evolution. The scenario is that after a storm, there is a person who has grabbed some debris and is floating in the water. Just beyond the subject is a barge that is unaware of the person in distress. As you can see the barge is the closest way out of the water. There is no visible shore." He nodded toward Mace. "It will be Mace and Diesel's task to get to the subject and get them safely up onto the barge. Other than what he carries in his tactical pack, Mace has no additional gear available. They'll depend on their own skills."

The students moved to the edge of the cliff and looked over.

"He's getting himself and the dog out to that raft to save a guy?" the woman asked, her body posture said she was dubious.

Mace enjoyed their astonishment, the excitement that sparked through the air.

"That's the task," Ares said then pointed to the bus. "Once Mace and Diesel are in the water, we're going to go down to the beach where a boat is waiting. We can continue out into the sea to watch from the water."

A student leaned forward. "And lend a hand." She gave a curt nod.

"Sure," Ares said. "If needed." He caught Mace's eye. "Mace will start at the vehicle." Ares pointed at the teacher. "Dr. Jeffers, if you can wave him in and point out the person you saw floating, we'll have Mace assess, and take action."

The teacher, a slender man with a ring of tightly clipped curls encircling a shiny head stepped forward. He wore crisp-pressed khakis, and a navy-blue gulf shirt buttoned all the way up like a prep-school youth.

Mace gave Jeffers a nod and jogged toward the SUV just out of sight around the other side of the boulder.

Diesel trotted along, pinned to Mace's side, tongue lolling happily. He knew they were going to get to play.

Making this play was the key to success.

The dogs weren't big into the nuances of a task. Mace trained with Diesel to find a person in debris caused by war or natural disaster. The *find* was part of the job. And no matter what state that person was in, the find was defined as a success.

Success was rewarded with joy. High pitched praise. A game of tug. A favorite chew toy.

The satisfaction the dogs got from pleasing their handler, with a job well done, was imperative to a working dogs' ability to do the job.

And that was what Mace offered Diesel. No matter what.

Even in the worst of worse conditions, Mace had to focus his energy on being playful. He couldn't give in to the despair that wanted to claw at his guts when he found the victims.

But too, as he well knew from his years of Iniquus-required mental health support, Mace had to cull space and time to deal with the crap. To ignore the horrors of what he'd seen and participated in throughout his work life, both on the battlefield and now with Cerberus, would give his experiences the power to become closet monsters, grabbing at his psyche, plunging him into despair and existential dread.

"You have to face the demons," the therapist said. "Smile at your anger and say hi. It's yours. You are your shadow side, too."

That was all well and good for Mace, but the dogs didn't get therapy.

The dogs got happy.

Mace opened the driver's side door and signaled his K9 in.

Diesel was a massive German Shepherd, with thick, medium-length fur that was lush caramel and midnight-black. The ring of dark fur under Diesel's almost diabolic shining orange eyes highlighted his intelligence and cunning. His steady gaze spoke of Diesel's missions past, wisdom that had been hard-earned. There was a nobility about him. Not a king that sat on a throne, but a knight that would ride into battle out of loyalty.

Mace had always thought that "Diesel" was a terrible misnaming of this magnificent beast.

For sure, Mace couldn't have asked for a better partner.

Diesel could intuit situations in ways that almost seemed other-worldly at times. They'd look each other in the eye. Agree to a plan. And execute with synchronicity.

Mace always trusted his dog. Always.

Turning the key, Mace rounded the SUV out from its hiding spot behind the boulder.

Jeffers was doing his part with a lot of enthusiasm, waving his arms over his head, jumping up and down in his boat shoes.

With a signal for Diesel to wait in the car, Mace climbed out.

Diesel listened to the command, but that didn't mean he didn't whine his displeasure.

Mace—six foot two, tanned skin and tightly cropped black hair—was dressed in the Cerberus tactical uniform. No matter the weather: combat boots and grey camo tactical pants. Today, he had on the uniform's short-sleeved compression shirt with the blue Cerberus logo over his heart.

"Sir?" he asked, arriving in front of Jeffers.

"There's a person in the water holding debris!" Jeffers ran to the cliff's edge and pointed down. "I believe they're hurt."

The students huddled out of the way.

"Is there a way down to the water? A wharf? Stairs?"

The professor turned to Ares, who shook his head no. Turning back to Mace, Jeffers said, "Not for miles in either direction."

Mace leaned over the cliff's edge to assess. He called out to Ash on the raft, but his teammate purposefully sprawled as if unconscious.

"You must get a boat," Jeffers insisted. "Find people to help you."

"That's okay, sir. We've got this. Thank you." Mace stalked back to the SUV where he pushed Diesel to the passenger's seat.

Slobber on the wheel, running down the window, dampening his seat, pretty much par for the course. At the end of the day, Mace was typically crusty with slobber and dog hair.

Life didn't get much better than that.

Mace swiveled around as he backed the vehicle up closer to the cliff's edge. "I'm going to get the rigging in place," he told Diesel. "Then we go, okay?"

Austin Mace

Friday, St. Kitts

RECOGNIZING MISSION PREP, IT SEEMED THAT DIESEL HAD decided he could lay there and be patient.

Mace called again toward the raft before he lifted the SUV's back hatch.

With no reply, Mace checked his pockets for anything he didn't want to go in the drink. He put his phone in the water-proof bag and secured it in his thigh pocket that both zipped and had a hook and loop closure. Iniquus policy, operators were never more than an arm's reach from their phones 24/7.

Dragging his pack over, Mace grabbed the rappelling bag from inside. Each component—be it food and hydration, first aid, or navigation—was organized into quick-grab bags. Each team member placed the organizational components into their mission packs in the exact same spot. They trained with the exact same equipment. Anyone on Bravo could exchange bags with any brother and be perfectly comfortable with every single item, finding it by feel in the dark and under the worst possible of conditions.

As he pulled out belay equipment and lines, Mace angled his body so the veterinarian students could all see what he was doing.

If this demonstration jazzed them, Bravo might be able to teach the students how to go down lesser inclines and bring animals back up, safely.

If this freaked them out, Bravo would stick to teaching them how to set up mobile animal shelters for the least animal distress and spread of infection.

Better to understand the students' needs and capacities. You can't ask a plow horse to run the Kentucky Derby. That was a bad outcome all around.

When Mace attached his hook onto the trailer hitch, Diesel stood, stomping and snorting. He knew the sequence as well as Mace did.

"Diesel, come, boy, climb."

Diesel didn't need to be asked twice. He clambered from front seat to back, then stood patiently in the cargo space where Mace checked the clasps on the K9 tactical vest. "We're going to go over the cliff and then take a swim. Good?"

Mace checked his end knots and tossed the line over the cliff's edge.

When the rope didn't make it anywhere near the water, the students became agitated.

With their distress swirling the air, Diesel narrowed his focus onto Mace.

Energy arced between the partners as they communicated with thoughts alone. Like having a soulmate. Or as a past girl-friend used to say, "a twin flame." While that term never struck a chord with Mace in a love relationship, it definitely was what Mace saw burning in Diesel's flickering orange eyes. They were in synch. As linked and necessary as an inhale was to an exhale.

Sitting on the edge of the SUV's platform, Mace signaled Diesel to come lay down behind him. Reaching around, Mace attached Diesel's combat harness to his own rigging. "Nice and easy." Mace's voice was brown sugar, sweet and richly soothing. "Here we go, now." When he stood, Mace pushed into his heels, squeezed his glutes, and extended his arms out in front of him to counter the additional hundred pounds dangling from his hips.

As Mace tugged on his fingerless gloves, Ares moved up beside him. He checked Mace's rigging, the rappelling equipment, and then Diesel.

A second set of eyes made for a safer situation.

Of course, this evolution wasn't a whim. This task was calculated at the planning table, assessed on the ground, and practiced in advance. In a real-world situation, they wouldn't have the grace to do the prep-steps. But here, without a life on the line, due diligence was key.

Due diligence was always key, Mace amended. But in the press of the situation, sometimes you had to wing it.

With Ares's thumbs up, Mace gave Diesel a quick scratch by his ear. "Ready to go, boy?" Mace's own heart picked up a beat in anticipation of the challenge.

With the line in his hands, Mace walked backward to the cliff's edge, one hand in front, one hand behind.

Mace leaned back until he was nearly parallel with the water.

The students gasped and huddled.

Mace knew he'd be able to take four steps down the cliff with his feet pressed into the rock, then the lip would curve inward, and he'd be on the rope itself dangling out over the clear waters.

Pulling in a breath, Mace flexed his back muscles. Bracing his abs, Mace let the full weight of Diesel and his own body redistribute to his arms. His legs dropped, and Mace wrapped the rope into his feet.

There was a collective sharp intake of breath from above him.

Thirty heads leaned over the edge.

"You good, boy?" Mace swung his attention to Diesel.

Relaxed and swaying in his harness. Mouth open and panting, a smile curving his lips. Yea, Diesel was good to go.

It made Mace laugh. That dog. No fear. None.

In preparation for his descent, Mace tied off a knot at the end of the rope. When he got there, that would be the assist he needed for the next step of this evolution.

As Mace worked them slowly down the line, Diesel yipped his frustration.

Diesel preferred the thrill of fast roping down.

"We need to discuss your addiction to adrenaline," Mace called past the wind. "Relax for me, buddy. I'll make sure you get your hit." What came at the end of the rope would be his treat.

Diesel turned his head toward the ocean breeze. The wind caught at his fur and flung spittle from his tongue back onto Mace's arms.

"Good job. Relax." Mace inch-wormed his way down the rope with his self-belay equipment. Using all his muscles, Mace countered Diesel's weight that tried to drag his hips out and down.

The faces of the vet students were no longer in his view. Mace knew they'd have run to the bus and were headed toward the dock at the bottom of the hill.

Mace's crossed feet found the knot, and he stood on it, pressing his thighs together, swinging gently back and forth. Catching the rope in the crook of his elbow, clamping in, they waited.

Ares's whistle blare let Mace know the students were on the boat and in place to watch.

"Now's the sugar rush, adrenaline boy." Mace looked down. From here, it was a seven-foot plunge, a safe distance calculated at three times Diesel's height at the shoulders.

At Cerberus's training pool, climbing the high dive, and leaping off the platform was Diesel's reward after they'd swum their laps in the pool.

Squatting like a frog, Mace pulled the rigging around and settled Diesel on his thighs. He unclasped Diesel and gave him a rub behind the ears, waiting for Diesel to calm a bit before the command.

When Mace extended his arm and said, "Diesel, dive." Diesel scrambled his back paws onto Mace's thigh. And though Mace wore the thick tactical cloth, as Diesel launched himself, his claws stabbed into Mace's skin.

Mace kept his gaze unblinkingly on Diesel, his alert whistle clamped between his lips. If Diesel had an issue, Ash would come alive out there on the raft, where he pretended to be the victim, and he'd power over to help.

It was a beautiful leap.

A perfect splash.

It swelled Mace's heart with awe and pride. Always did. It was a fantastic feeling.

When Diesel swam out to clear the area, Mace released the line and plunged.

The weight of his boots and pack dragged him deep. Popped his ears. Compressed his lungs.

Mace tipped his head back to find the sunshine, and with

powerful strokes, pulled himself toward the surface. Mace became drown-proof in SEAL training. He was a frogman through and through. As comfortable in the salty waters as he was taking a morning jog in Virginia.

As he surfaced, Mace gasped in a lungful of air.

There was Diesel, treading water, watching Mace drop in with every bit as much concern as Mace had had for his K9 partner.

Side by side, they swam to the raft where Ash continued to play his role of unconscious victim.

Heaving himself up to dangle over the side, Mace balanced on his hips to reach in, checking for viability. The back of his hand felt breath. His fingers found a pulse from the carotid. Mace pressed down and slipped back into the water where Diesel was happily dogpaddling in circles. "We're going to give him a tow, buddy."

Mace lifted the raft's pull rope. "Diesel, tugboat." Diesel clamped on.

With Diesel powering forward in the gentle waves, Mace gripped the rope with one hand and side stroked with the other. Scissor kicking in the crystal blue water, Mace could see all the way down to the white sand below.

An octopus squirted ink then disappeared into a cluster of rocks.

Things were going to plan.

As expected.

They trained this kind of recovery in the Cerberus pool at least once a week when they weren't deployed on a mission. But it was a bit different when they were pitching into salt water and Diesel's Bravo dog pals weren't lined up on the side of the deck waiting for their turns.

As Mace swam, he kept up a steady cadence of three blasts from his marine whistle, pause and another three blasts. Any cycle of three, anywhere in the world, was considered a distress signal.

At the top of the barge, where he was playing the role of crew member, Bear leaned over the side. "Yo! We see you. Do you need a rescue basket?" he bellowed through cupped hands.

Mace released the rope, flipping onto his back and waving his arms crisscross in the air.

By the time he and Diesel reached the side of the barge, the team above had a rescue basket lowered and ready to heave ho.

The boat carrying the vet students floated in closer. The helmsman cut the engine while the students gripped the side of the boat.

After tying up to the barge ladder, Mace grabbed onto the raft. "Diesel, ramp up."

Diesel swam around behind Mace and, using Mace as his climbing board, scrambled up to lie next to Ash.

Mace threw his leg over the edge. His waterlogged boots were heavy. His soggy pants chaffed his skin and bound his movements. *Yeah, not the most graceful display.* Mace chuckled at himself as he power-lifted aboard and dropped into the bowl of the raft.

"Light as a bull crashing into the proverbial china shop." Ash laughed into his elbow.

"Keep talking, Sleeping Beauty."

Grabbing hold of the rescue basket, Mace tethered that to the raft then maneuvered Ash in. "Dude, you could help a little."

"Nah," Ash said without opening his eyes. "It's best you train for the game you want to play. Some knocked out guy on the raft isn't going to be extra kind and scoot into the basket for you. No magic and pixie dust in the field."

True.

Mace adjusted Ash's limbs out straight and in line, then used the spider webbing to attach him in safely.

Untying the basket from the raft, Mace called, "Lift away!"

"Lifting," Bear hollered back as they winched the basket up the cables.

Holding onto Diesel's collar, the waves lifted and dropped the raft. Mace watched as the basket rose, a strapped down Ash swung gently in the air.

Once the basket cleared, Mace edged the raft along the barge to the ladder. He tethered the float to the bottom rung. Holding the raft flush and as still as possible, Mace commanded Diesel to climb.

Real world? Mace would have waited for the basket to lower for Diesel and then a third time for him.

In this evolution, they'd decided to train for a water exit. There would be times when there was no basket to lower, and Diesel needed to know how to climb a ladder on the unstable platform of a boat in the water.

The team had assessed the wave action today, and decided it was calm enough that this was a go.

At home, climbing a ladder like this was what Diesel did before breakfast. Easy day.

"Diesel, ladder up."

The raft didn't offer Diesel a stable platform to get onto the rungs. He swung his head and caught Mace's gaze.

Mace maneuvered around so that he sat on the rounded raft side like it was a saddle, one foot in the boat, one foot on the lowest rung under the water. He pulled them in tight, then reached for the handle on Diesel's tactical vest. Pulling gently, he commanded, "Diesel, ladder up."

Diesel scrambled onto Mace's lap and once again stabbing his claws into Mace's thigh, he mounted the ladder and started his climb toward Bear who hovered at the top.

Mace wrapped his hands around the bottom rung and started his own climb just beneath Diesel's dripping tail.

Mace's brain wanted to leap forward and think about what came next—hosing off the salt water, giving the rubber pull toy to Diesel for a quick game of tug, high fiving his team. But years of practice kept Mace's thoughts on task. He grounded his focus in the three feet around him.

Celebrations came *after* victories not in anticipation of them.

For. A. Reason.

There was a high-pitched scream of metal against metal.

A shift.

A torque.

The ladder loosened then slammed into the side of the boat.

Mace swung his focus up to find Bear wrestling to keep the ladder in place.

Diesel came flying off backward, twisting in the air.

Without any thought at all, Mace's hand shot out, hooking just the tips of his fingers into the grab handle on Diesel's vest. A hundred pounds of motion.

There was a background of yelling, that Mace pressed away from him.

Mace had lived a danger-spiked life. Since he was a kid, his body had been seeped in adrenaline; he was pickled in it.

Adrenaline could be lifesaving. It could also wreak havoc.

His body knew what to do when the stay-alive hormone flooded his system.

His world became silent as every part of his survival brain homed in on saving Diesel.

Time slowed, giving Mace the processing space he needed. Mace took advantage. He gripped at the ladder as it swung wide of the barge, holding his own weight and Diesel's by the curl of his fingers. Mace squeezed his hand into the grab handle on Diesel's tactical vest.

The momentum was the problem.

Mace missed the point in Diesel's arc that would send the K9 out away from the metal hull. If Mace lost his grip, Diesel would hit the side of the barge, then drop into the water.

A lethal mistake.

Mace assessed the raft. That would have been the softer landing, but it had floated to the length of its rope toward shore, useless.

They were too high over the water for safety.

Well past the seven-foot mark.

Go! Mace's brain decided.

With a twist of his torso, Mace bent his knees and shoved with all of his might, diving straight out away from the boat, dragging Diesel along with him.

"Diesel, dive!" Mace was vaguely aware that his voice seemed steady and commanding and didn't at all hold the terror that coursed through his veins.

Because Bravo evolutions mimicked real-world events, things went wrong.

People and animals could die. It was never a sure bet.

Mace released the vest handle and brought his arms together in front of him. Piking at the waist, filling his lungs with air, he prepared for his own impact.

It was like hitting cement.

In a rush of bubbles and motion, Mace was in the water. He immediately tipped his head back looking for sunlight.

Above him, Diesel peddled his legs.

Mace stuck his hand under Diesel's butt and kicking hard, he powered both of them to the surface. There, gasping for breath, Mace turned and patted his shoulder.

Diesel climbed onto Mace's back, wrapping his paws

around Mace's neck. It was what they trained. Diesel performed like a champ.

Blinking the salt water from his lashes, Mace saw the boat full of vet students cautiously pulling closer.

The teacher threw a life ring,

"The ladder ripped from the barge!" The professor pressed a hand to his chest. "Terrifying."

Mace grabbed hold of the float and kicked over to the tiny three rung stairs of the student's boat.

On command, Diesel climbed on, followed by Mace.

The boat clamored with concern.

Mace waved anxious hands away from both Diesel and him.

"We take you back to the wharf now?" the helmsman asked.

Still breathless, Mace gave a thumbs up that they should go.

With Diesel between his knees, Mace ran practiced hands over his K9's body, checking for any pain spots. "Well, that sucked, hey, buddy?"

Diesel turned to him with a grin and a gleam in his fire-orange eyes. Yeah, his dog thought that had been fun and games.

It was Mace whose heart was ricocheting against his sternum.

4

_____

Tara Alvarez

Friday, Dominica

TWO HOURS INTO HER HIKE UP THE MOUNTAIN, TARA BURST OUT
of the tree line into a clearing and tripped over an unseen root.
With arms thrown wide, she swayed and sidestepped to catch
her balance. Finally, dropping her hands to the ground, butt in
the air, she paused thinking that she was grateful for her yoga
practice and an instinctual downward dog.

Though, truthfully this posture was more like a grizzly bear.

Tara pressed herself back up to standing and sent a glance
around, as if someone were there to see her be a klutz. Reflex.
There was no one in the woods. And if she ever did see
someone in the woods, it would probably freak her out. She was
quite literally in the middle of nowhere, forging a new path,
exploring a new route.

After brushing herself off, Tara did a little jump to click her
heels together, and in her best pirating voice said, "Still workin'

on gittin' me land legs, arrr." Tara brushed the dirt from her hands.

Yes, this what she did to entertain herself. She pretended she was a pirate cruising the Caribbean, looking for buried treasure.

Tara stepped forward, rolling her eyes so hard at herself that she thought she pulled her ocular muscles out of place.

The joke was growing old.

This whole worm hunt was getting old.

With a sigh, Tara stepped up on a boulder and lifted her binoculars to scan the vegetation.

Since this clearing was exactly the environment where she'd found her other doubloon plants, Tara began at the far side of the clearing and worked the space like a grid, making a straight-line sweep from north to south, shifting her waist a fraction of an inch, and starting at the far side of the clearing, followed the line straight down.

And so, she worked until she stopped with a jolt.

Not quite believing her eyes, Tara jumped down from the rock and took a step forward on tip toes, as if any sudden move-ment on her part would shift the landscape and her prize would disappear.

Could it be?

Bending down with and outstretched hand, Tara delicately slid her palm beneath the yellow-gold leaf. "Aye, it's a mighty treasure. Here in the clearing, not one, not two, but three doubloon plants." She pressed a knee down as she put her ear to the soil to examine the circumference of the stem and guess at the maturity of the root structure.

"I've struck gold, I have!"

Wait, striking gold was about the Gold Rush in the West not about pirate treasure. "I've found a pot of gold!" Nope, that was leprechauns. "There is gold in them thar hills." Still Gold Rush.

Tara sat on her heels, pausing to recall any pirate movie that she might have seen—beyond Neverland and Captain Hook—and was a complete blank for any relevant phrase other than "Walk the plank!" and "Shiver me timbers." And neither seemed appropriate for this situation.

"But that doesn't matter. I mean, look at them!" She commanded the bugs and birds in the vicinity.

They were wholly unimpressed with Tara's discovery.

"Well, you might not care, but I most certainly do." She tipped her head back and yelled, "Gold! I've found gold!" Then she tapped the volume button on her phone to crank the tunes while she danced like no one was watching.

'Cause no one was around.

Not even a delicious mountain chicken.

Just her and the worms.

Tara twirled about happily (well away from the precious doubloon plants, lest she land on them and destroy an endangered species). "Yeah, baby! Yeah, baby! Whoop. Whoop." She lassoed her fist overhead.

At the end of the song, Tara threw herself onto the rock, breathless and laughing at the idea of what someone would have thought had they happened on that scene.

Arms wide, embracing the sun as the rays pushed through the weave of her cotton top, Tara tapped the volume down as a new song queued up. She considered the music on her play list as friends, her day-to-day company.

"Solo celebrations kinda suck," she admitted. "But as promised, I keep trying, Dr. Masami." Tara rolled onto her belly and tucked her head into her folded arms to hide from the sting of the bright mid-morning rays.

Dr. Masami told the team that they had to search out fun. "Fun balances bleak" was the phrase she'd used.

They'd all had to sit through a half day's lecture in discovering what "fun" meant to them. "What's fun to Neils might not be fun for Tara," Masami had said.

Wasn't *that* the truth.

But she and Pria had a ton of fun. Jim and his husband Trevor Driscoll when she got together with them. Those three fellow Trifalgar scientists (and Trevor) had been out studying algae in the Indian Ocean where they'd had each other to bolster morale.

Yeah, on the whole, Tara loved her Maryland-based research group; she just didn't see any of them often.

"Laughter greases the cogs in the fun engine." Dr. Masami had baskets full of pithy phrases. She'd reach in, grab a handful, and scatter them about like a flower girl at a wedding.

Though on a "sucks to be Tara" note, Masami had said, "Fun is almost one hundred percent a group endeavor. Alone, one can perhaps experience peace, or contentment. Fun? That was harder to find without the sizzle and spark one got in community. Even a community of two."

Tara mumbled into her elbow. "The only people I'm around are the people I meet down in town. Though, granted, the mail guy plays along with the whole treasure theme I've got going on. I probably break up his day from the normal stamp sales and box weighing."

Truth be told, though, Tara had been the sole researcher here in Dominica for seven months, she didn't know many other people on the island. It wasn't that they were unfriendly, it was that Tara lived a hermetic life as far away as one could get on this tiny island. And her work had her lying on her stomach, digging in the rich volcanic soil, not walking on the beaches, and hanging out at tourist spots.

Sure, Tara *could* go down in the evenings after she was done for the day, but the road back was barely a road at all. It was more like a section of cleared field that some worker mowed every few weeks or so.

Yeah, there was a decidedly creepy quality to driving home in the dark with her utility vehicle pitching her back with the steep incline, making the lights shine on foliage rather than the roadway. It was a game of roulette guessing where the road was in front of her.

There was the grandmother, Mrs. Joseph, in the house on the way up to Tara's rental "Parrot's Perch".

Mrs. Joseph lived with her daughter and her daughter's three kids—all boys, aged eight, five, and not quite two.

Tara had met them on her first and only hike down to town when Tara was trying to figure out just where she could start picking up even a glimmer of cell phone service. It turned out that Tara could make out about a half of a bar once she reached the paved roads. It got better the closer she moved toward the government buildings.

That five-mile hike down the mountain was a heck of a lot easier than the trek back up.

Mrs. Joseph had signaled Tara over to rest in the shade of her porch. They'd rocked and talked. Mrs. Joseph chatted about things that Tara might find helpful. The restaurants that had authentic food versus the restaurants that catered to tourists. She told Tara where the nicest beaches were and where she could go to listen to traditional music and see the islanders dance. And best of all—after Tara showed Mrs. Joseph a picture of the doubloon plant on her phone—Mrs. Jones pointed out a large specimen at the edge of her property and told Tara she was welcome to dig worms there.

It was a lovely visit. And when Tara left, Mrs. Joseph handed her a basket of sun ripened vegetables and cut flowers that she'd had ready.

This started the seven-months-long basket passing ritual that Tara relished.

Tara would take the empty basket from her house on Fridays as she went down to town to do her weekly errands. There, she'd buy yummy treats at the bakery. On the way up to Parrot's Perch, Tara would stop off and hand the basket back to Mrs. Joseph with a thank you.

Only the basket was, invariably, just part of an exchange. Mrs. Joseph would have seen Tara drive down the mountain and have a basket of fruits and vegetables waiting on her porch for Tara. And also, an invitation to dinner.

Tara often wondered if Mrs. Joseph could see how lonely Tara's world was.

Isolation was tough.

How did they do it, the lighthouse workers sequestered on their bleak islands in days of old? The men who went out into the wilderness to trap furs all by themselves?

Did it make them crazy?

Conversation, Tara had discovered, was a perishable skill. Tara was sorely out of practice. She had to pay attention to what words she formed on her lips. Out in the rainforest, Tara could say aloud anything that popped into her head.

Not such a great idea when people were around.

Words were a minefield that Tara carefully tiptoed through when she was chatting with live people rather than plants and the occasional mountain chicken.

It was nice to be welcomed into the Josephs' kitchen.

It was lovely that Mrs. Joseph taught Tara some creole cooking methods with the rich aromatics and the light flaky fish.

Tara didn't usually cook. She was a bowl of cereal kind of chef. A nibble a sandwich leaning over the sink kind of gal. But Mrs. Joseph, mmm, Mrs. Joseph could make a feast out of a coconut. She even kept the peppers aside because Tara couldn't handle even the mild heat that they gave the baby.

On those Friday evenings, the eight-year-old would try to teach Tara the rudiments of cricket.

But for the most part, Tara just liked to sit on the porch as the sun melted away and rock the baby, feeling his heavy head on her chest, listening to the sounds of family.

Tara *missed* family—both her birth family and the family of her heart that she'd pieced together through her academic and now professional career.

Leaving the Josephs' house always made the loneliness bite a little more sharply. Made the bleak just a little grayer as she took her scientific journals, that she'd collected from her post box, back to her own home.

There, she'd read the newly discovered devastating news about the environment.

"Bleak. Bleak. Bleak," Tara squawked.

Pushing herself up, Tara scolded. "Can you hear yourself right now? You're like a cow chewing cud." She grabbed up her pack. "What you need are some new ideas in your head."

She'd have to watch this new habit of talking aloud when she was around Pria and the others this week. "Because you sound nuts." She sighed loudly.

"All right, break time's over. Time to get back to work."

This wasn't sustainable. Tara was exhausted. She figured that it was a combination of the sleepless nights and that she was expending tons of energy on trying to keep it together.

Both Tara's mother and her older brother Matteo had been concerned about this very situation and had tried to talk her out of coming to Dominica alone. Tara had explained that funding was funding, and the grant she was working under simply didn't stretch to include companionship.

"Isolation is a death nell"—not Dr. Masami's exact words.

The good doctor only picked uplifting, bright copper penny words.

"There's that movie about that guy who survived an airplane crash only to find himself stuck on an island. Alone. For years. With only a volley ball named Wilson for company. He didn't even have a fun mail guy like I do. And he certainly didn't have a once-a-week Joseph family visit."

Tara swiped her phone to pull up an app that she used to document the plants she found. Recording her finds, like the location of the mountain chicken yesterday (though, surely that had changed) was a key step for the island's scientific researchers.

Tara would take the pictures, then start the two-hour trek back to her house. She checked her watch; she should be there by noon.

There, she'd snarf down a quick PB&J, grab Mrs. Joseph's basket, gather the box of worms she'd put together to mail back to the lab, the file of paperwork for the Dominican government about the plants she'd found, and be in town by one—that was the plan.

Such a productive day.

Lying back down on her belly, Tara looked through the lens to line up the shot. In this first photograph, she wanted to capture the proximity of these three plants. Tara hadn't seen that before. Typically, the plants stood alone.

This camera app she was using not only documented the GPS location but also the compass degrees and the angle of the shot. If someone had the picture, they could get back to the very spot where Tara took the photograph, line up all of those data points with the specifications imprinted on the image, and find three beautiful, lush, and endangered doubloon plants.

She'd print these off and add them to her paperwork. These

photographs were part of the data required for Tara to maintain her governmental permissions.

Tara decided to set the timer and go pose with the plants.

Yup, celebrate the small things.

This wasn't small, though. Three doubloon plants in one clearing? This would keep Tara busy for at least a week. At that point, she could decide to go island hopping with her friends or maybe she would just fly home to Maryland.

Maybe she was just done with all of this.

That was feeling kind of right to Tara.

She'd give notice to her landlord when she went to town today.

If she needed more worm specimens, she'd come back after the rainy season.

Rounding from behind the camera, Tara quickly squatted beside the doubloon plant. One knee on the ground, she threw up her version of a gang sign and her tough gal face—which was kinda ridiculous.

The camera flashed, and Tara shielded her eyes, squinting at the rock behind the camera.

Hallucination?

Was that a…monkey?

"Hey, there." She sing-songed. "What in the heck are you doing here? Monkeys don't belong on this island. Are you lost?"

The monkey sat down companionably and gave her what might be interpreted as a wave.

Weird.

"Are you someone's pet? Are you lost?" Tara slowly stood. "Are you from the vet school? Did you escape?" She took a tentative step forward. "I don't know what to do here. I mean, we don't know each other. I don't want to grab you or anything." She took another slow step forward. "Are you a nice monkey? Were you raised by someone?" One more step. "Are you a wild monkey?"

Tara didn't know anything about monkeys except that when a species showed up where that species didn't belong, it could create environmental havoc. There was enough of that going on in the world.

The monkey was fingering the strap of Tara's bag, and Tara decided the monkey was up to no good. "That's mine." She used her most commanding voice and clapped her hands.

The monkey let go of the strap.

"Go now, shoo!" Tara flung her arms wide, making herself big like she'd been trained to do around bears. It's all she had in her bag of tricks, no one had ever trained her in how to deal with an errant monkey. "Go!"

The monkey bared its sharp-looking teeth and hissed menacingly.

Tara jumped back. "Rude thing." Looking around for a stick to defend herself, Tara found nothing useful.

The monkey reached out for her phone, and Tara screamed a high-pitched scream, rushing forward without a single thought about the dangers posed by the monkey, until the monkey bared its teeth again at her and hissed violently.

There was a threat implied in that hiss.

The monkey turned and dashed off to the trees.

With. Tara's. Phone.

Tara gave chase. Of course, she did. That phone was her volley ball, Wilson. It had her music. Her photo album. It was her once a week "I'm not dead on the side of a mountain" phone call to her mother.

Her mother! *Oh, holy hell.* Tara had to get that phone.

With her bag slung over her shoulder, Tara crashed through the vegetation, chasing the monkey. She didn't get far before the scoundrel scampered up a tree and disappeared from sight into the dense canopy.

Tara sat there for a long moment, straining to hear if the monkey dropped her phone. But with the soft mounds of vegetation, it would be a miracle to hear it.

The phone was on, Tara reminded herself. If there happened to be cell service in this part of the island, she could just go back to the house, boot up her computer and tap the "Find my" button to track it down. But unless some miracle happened—wait, Tara thought, it was newly charged. That could last a couple days.

She had her wake up alarm set on high. At night, Tara was in the habit of leaving her phone in the bathroom, so she'd be propelled out of bed and didn't keep hitting snooze button come morning. Unless the monkey knew how to turn off a smart phone, Tara could come out tomorrow morning before the alarm and follow the sound.

And while she thought all of that, she knew it was a lost cause. There was no way that Tara was going to make a two-hour hike in the dark of the morning in the off chance that she'd hear the alarm go off and the phone would be in a place that she could access it.

New plan: Buy a new phone in town. Have them reload my stuff. File for the insurance. Call mom.

It wasn't the end of the world.

It was just a slap in the face when Tara was already having a mentally-struggling day.

I'll figure it out, Tara thought as she pulled her backup GPS tracker from her bag.

After setting a pin in the app so she could find this clearing again, Tara pulled up the pin for Parrot's Perch and started her trek down the mountain.

She was all kinds of pissed off.

5

Tara Alvarez

Friday, Dominica

WITH HER CAR PARKED OUT FRONT, TARA WALKED INTO THE empty mailroom lobby. She smiled. "Hi, Mr. Francis."

"And here she is right on time."

The door's bell tinkled behind her as another patron came in.

Tara pushed her box of worms carefully packed in coconut coir onto the counter.

Mr. Francis lifted it. "Your treasure box is heavier than usual. You must have found a lot of gold."

"I had a successful week." She watched as he weighed the box then started to fill out forms by hand. "Why are you doing that old school?" she asked.

Without looking up, Mr. Francis said, "Tuesday a ship dropped anchor on the sea cables."

"What does that mean?"

"It means that we lost the internet. No cell phone calls off the island."

Shit, her mom was going to be out of her mind.

Would her mom look up the news and discover Tara's call didn't go through because of a communications issue not a "Tara has fallen into the volcano and can't get out" issue?

And her phone, Tara wouldn't be able to get that replaced until the network was functioning. "Do they know when it'll get fixed?"

"They say this Sunday, so perhaps some time next week. Hopefully, when you come down from Parrot's Perch, next Friday it will be all right."

When her friends got in, they'd have satellite phones, Tara thought. That might be later tonight. Her mom would be freaked. "Hey, Mr. Francis, I need to call the United States. Do you know someone with a satellite phone?"

"My friend Thomas at the marina has one to communicate with boaters. He talks them through repairs when they're out on the water. Are you trying to catch up with your friends. They come today, correct?"

"Good memory."

Mr. Francis tapped the side of his head.

"My friends are getting in later tonight. They're staying at the Blue Horizon. I needed to call my mom for my check in before that."

"The Blue Horizon? Swanky," he said, reaching for the stamp pad.

"Is it?"

"Yes, very nice. But if you want to contact your mother, just go to Thomas. I'll text him to make the introduction."

She canted her head. "The cell phones still work?"

"On the island yes. No internet. Just cell tower. Let me give you his number."

"Thank you but my phone was stolen this morning."

"Stolen, no." Mr. Francis stopped his work and blinked at her. "Stolen?"

"It was a monkey incident." Tara sighed.

Mr. Francis pulled his chin back with a look of confusion. "I don't follow. Is this something about your friends? You told me they will film bringing up the treasure in Hidden Cove, correct?"

"Yes to filming the treasures being brought up. But sadly, no to this being part of that project. This was a real monkey in the real rainforest that popped up out the blue and stole my phone."

"No." He clicked his tongue with a shake of his head. "There are no monkeys in Dominica."

"So I thought. But apparently, I was wrong."

"When it stole your phone, you were close by? Why did you not grab it back?"

"It hissed at me. Bared its teeth."

"No. The monkey was aggressive like that? Normally, they run. The vervet monkeys on St. Kitts and Nevis are shy creatures. Perhaps it was a rabid monkey."

"Rabid?" Tara's eyebrows flew up to her hairline.

"I'll call emergency services and let them know that there may be a diseased monkey. Everyone should be made aware."

"Oh, uhm yeah, thanks, Mr. Francis. You can tell them it was up on the mountain above my house at Parrot's Perch. I have it pinned on my GPS because I had just found three doubloons."

"Three? Wow. Very good. It was a very lucky morning for you. There will be a lot more gold to dig."

"Exactly, I was really excited. But then, the monkey…"

Mr. Francis frowned. "I'm sorry for your misadventure."

"Thank you."

"Listen, after you make your phone call at Thomas's, go a block down the road and you will see my friend George."

"George."

"Yes, he has security supplies. He will have a solution for you. Even if it isn't a rabid monkey, it might have those monkey pox. It's in the international news, monkey pox, very painful. Sometimes deadly. Most definitely, you should not be up on the mountain alone. It can be dangerous with a hissing monkey on the loose."

"Yes." Tara slid her palms down the side of her shorts to wipe off the sweat. That had been a closer call than she would have imagined. "You're right. So, Thomas at the marina, then a block further down and see George."

"Correct." Mr. Francis lifted her box. "Now, this is properly insured, I will get your gold safely sent out. Even though the computers are down, it's not a problem. I don't want you to worry."

"Thank you. Can you take credit cards with no internet?"

"Cash. But there are no ATMs functioning."

Tara opened her wallet. "It's okay." She handed out the Eastern Caribbean dollars and waited for her change that she pocketed.

Offering up a wave, Tara said, "I'll see you next Friday."

Turning to leave, Tara plowed right into a man who caught her by the elbows as she lost her balance, trying to stop her forward momentum.

His silver hair was caught back in a sleek ponytail. His white linen shirt smelled of salt air.

"Agh. I had no idea anyone was right behind me." She stepped back. "Are you okay? Sorry, I was caught up in my to-do list."

"No problem." He let her go and with a slight bow said, "Have a good day."

Tara swung through the door, pausing outside of the post, taking in a deep breath. *Stupid monkey*. This phone situation was going to cause all kinds of problems.

Walking up the main road, Thomas's was easy to find.

The bell tinkled as she walked into the store.

"You're Tara?"

"I am. Hi. You must be Mr. Thomas? Mr. Francis sent me."

He pushed a phone across the counter. "This is what you needed. Do you know how to use it?"

"I do."

Mr. Thomas pointed out the door. "Go out to the end of the dock, that's the best place to get reception."

"Thank you." Sliding her straw hobo bag up higher on her shoulder, Tara went out to make the call. It connected fairly easily, but her mother didn't answer. It went to voice mail.

Weird.

Tara's mother was always sitting right there, waiting for her call. Tara checked her watch. Twenty minutes early. "Hi Mom," she said as the phone beeped to start the recording. "There is an internet cable issue on the island. I'm calling from a satellite phone. But nothing's wrong." *Liar.* "I'm perfectly fine." *More lies.* "I know I'm a few minutes early with this call. It's because I'm borrowing this phone." *And I'm rambling.* "Pria gets in tonight. I'll meet her sometime in the afternoon tomorrow. That's Saturday. I'll call you from her phone then. K? Love you!" and she hung up.

Something felt off about that call.

Tomorrow, if she didn't get her mom, she'd call Matteo. His wife could be having their baby or something and, of course, Tara would be impossible to contact with the news.

Mr. Thomas was standing in the open door when she wended her way back. "Success?"

"I got through to leave her a message." She handed the

phone back then pulled her bag around to dig out her wallet. "I really appreciate it. How much do I owe you?"

"It was less than a minute? That will cost me a few cents." He waved his hand in the air. "Don't worry."

"Well, thank you." She looked up and down the street.

"George?"

"Yes, sir."

"Francis told me about your monkey problem." He tipped his ear. "A block that way."

Tara raised her hand and walked on.

Island gossip was faster than any emergency messaging system.

And sure enough, there stood Mr. George, waiting for her.

"Tara?"

"That would be me. I have—"

"A monkey problem. I have just what you need. Come." He waved her inside and over to the counter. A long thin box was set out. "This is a system that will warn you of an approaching monkey." He tapped the top.

"What?"

"Infrared fencing. It has a 150-decibel alarm. You carry it in your pack—it's light weight—and when you get to where you dig the gold worms, you simply set it along the perimeter at a safe distance. The farther out the better."

"Like an electric dog fence?"

"No. For a dog fence to function the dog must wear a shock collar. You must not get close enough to the monkey to put on a shock collar."

"No." She shook her head for emphasis. "I wouldn't want to do that."

"These are stakes that send out a beam of light. You extend the polls telescopically. Once you sink them into the ground, they will be about shoulder height. The beams are about six inches apart, so even a clever monkey couldn't pass through without setting off the alarm."

"Okay."

"You must be away from a tree line where the monkey might swing in from above. With these set in place, if the monkey approaches you while you're focused on your digging, then the alarm goes off, so you have time to get prepared."

"Okay." Tara pulled the box over and looked at the description. "And say the monkey sets off the alarm." She looked up to catch his eye. "What would I do then?"

Mr. George pulled out a tall can of bear spray. "You shoot him with this."

She picked it up and read the label and pulled her brows together. "You have this around for all the bears on the island?"

"Normally, we wouldn't carry this product." He tapped the lid. "But it came in with our shipment accidentally. They said to keep it. So, there you have it."

"For rabid monkeys."

"There are no monkeys on the island. But now that you've seen one, and Francis thinks it might be rabid, there could be a market for this product if I cover over the word 'Bear' and put 'Monkey Spray' instead."

Tara nodded. "Very entrepreneurial."

"Thank you." He gave her a slight bow.

"All right, I'll take both, I guess. And if I'm hiking up to do my field work—"

"Carry the bear spray in your hand. Monkeys can drop down from above."

"But they wouldn't, right? I've never heard of such a thing." She scowled. "I'm not a zoologist, but that doesn't sound like normal behavior."

"For a healthy monkey, no. I wouldn't think so. But for a rabid monkey?" He shrugged.

6

_____

Austin Mace

Saturday, St. Kitts

MACE MADE HIS WAY ALONG THE BUFFET IN THE INIQUUS complex's dining room, loading his plate with fresh fish and vegetables, eggs, and biscuits.

Ares lifted his chin in Mace's direction then tipped his ear to the seat next to him.

The dining room was comfortably island elegant, designed to receive government officials or others in the emergency field. In the evenings, this was the room where the team liked to unwind with storytelling and cards, cigars, and island rum.

On clear mornings, like this one, the view of the sunrise through the floor to ceiling windows would be incomparable. He'd have to wait another hour or so.

Mace sidled behind the chairs, making his way toward the head of the table when his phone jangled with his friend

Matteo's ringtone. Setting his plate down, and giving Ares a nod, Mace stepped out onto the balcony for privacy.

Matteo never called unannounced. And never at zero six thirty. He texted to make sure that Bravo wasn't dangling out of a helicopter over a cavern somewhere. That Matteo skipped that step made Mace's heart pound. Matteo's wife was close to giving birth and had been having complications.

"Yo." Mace exhaled, moving away from the open French doors with the billowing sheers that kept any bugs at bay.

"Dangling from a cliff?"

"That was yesterday morning. You caught me at a good time. Is everything all right?"

"Hard to say." Matteo's voice was entirely too gruff for Matteo.

And that pushed Mace's concern higher. "Bethany? Your mom?"

"Mom's right here. And yes, she's the reason for my call."

"Give me that phone." That was definitely Mrs. Alvarez. She sounded like the spitfire mama bear that Mace had always known.

"Austin."

"Yes, ma'am."

"Matteo tells me that you're down in the Caribbean."

"Yes, ma'am. We're training in St. Kitts."

"Tara is working south of you in Dominica."

"Yes, ma'am. Something about worms, right?"

"Yes, the worms that are up in the mountains." She exhaled as if she were blowing out birthday candles. "I am a little bit freaking out here."

"A little bit?" Matteo said from nearby.

"I can't get in touch with my Tara."

"Can you tell me a bit more?" Mace walked down the balcony to the library door. He stepped through the white curtains and strode over to a computer, sliding into the seat. A few taps of the keys, and Mace had brought up the emergency management website. If anything was going on down in Dominica, be it a police report or a weather system, it would be listed there. With his phone pressed between his shoulder and his ear, his fingers flew over the keyboard, hunting for information. "Where is she staying on the island?"

"Tara lives alone in a little house up on the mountain side."

"There's no internet connection or cell service up there. You could only get hold of her if she was in town." Bravo had done training missions on the island. The land mass and vegetation made radio signals almost impossible except for line of sight, and the tree canopy made satellite phones hit or miss.

Mace saw that the last entry from Dominica into the system was days ago.

He flipped to a database that was a wider net of communication from emergency services over the Caribbean.

"Exactly. Tara goes to town *every* Friday," Mrs. Alvarez said. "We have a video chat *every* Friday."

"It's only Saturday. Could it be she got held—okay, wait. I see the problem. Mrs. Alvarez, I'm looking at the news that's shared by emergency personnel in the region."

There was a gasp.

"No, ma'am. It's nothing that bad. There's a technical difficulty. A ship threw its anchor into the sea in exactly the wrong spot. It severed the underwater cables. The island has no internet connection."

"What?" she asked. "The phones go through satellites like I get my television, right?"

"No, ma'am. The telephone signal runs through cables that lay at the bottom of the sea," Mace explained.

"But if it's a cable, Austin, that would interrupt phone calls all over the area and here Matteo called you with no problems."

"I'm...let me scroll. Yes, So I'm on St. Kitts. St. Kitts has three cables coming to the island and the lines that were cut are south of us. We're closer to the United States, we wouldn't be affected."

"Oh."

"It doesn't happen frequently, but every few years you hear about it. Dubai a while back had an anchor sever the cable. It left over fifty million people without internet. And more recently they had an incident in the English Channel. It's not great when it happens, inconvenient, but it's fixable. I'm looking here on the emergency communications site, it says they think that this will be repaired by tomorrow."

"Sunday."

"Yes, ma'am." When Mrs. Alvarez didn't respond, Mace added, "Look, Tara probably came down the mountain the way she always does, probably went into town, discovered that she couldn't get a line out."

"No bars?"

"I'd have to do some investigating, but I would think the cell service on the island is still functioning, just off the island."

"But what if there's an emergency?"

Mace tried to imagine an island-wide emergency. "Like—"

"The volcano blows."

"Isn't it dorma—we'd see a volcanic eruption on satellite images. Our D.C. headquarters would have scrambled Bravo. We'd be ready to drop in and lend a hand. There definitely wasn't an eruption, or earthquake, or other natural disaster."

"That can be seen on satellite pictures, anyway."

"We would know if something big was happening. There are people on the island with satellite phones. All the boats would have them, for sure. Emergency services has them. If there were an island-wide emergency, we'd know," he reiterated.

"I know you're trying to soothe me, Austin. I'm sorry, I don't feel any better." She blew out again. She used to do that when they were kids. Matteo and he would do something crazy —jump off the roof of the garage into the pool—and there would be Mrs. Alvarez, as if magnetized to her kids' dangers. She'd take a moment and blow, getting hold of her emotions before she spoke to them.

And then, boy, were they spoken to.

Mace was treated the same as Matteo. If Matteo was scolded and given chores as punishment, so was Mace. And Mace was always grateful. It was something to be scooped up by a friend's mother who was willing to expand her brood and treat him as family.

From a lifetime of experience with Mrs. Alvarez's mother's radar, her blowing like that sent danger messages along his nervous system.

Tara—Mace hadn't seen her since she was five years old, clinging to her mom's neck and sobbing, her little hand waving good-bye as Mace left to go live with his dad after his mom's death.

Matteo and Mrs. Alvarez had kept Mace up to date over the years of all of Tara's accomplishments. But he hadn't seen her since he left Indiana for Rhode Island. Mace had been invited for all the big family events—the graduations, Matteo's wedding—but Mace had always been deployed. They knew he couldn't get back, but it was nice to be included.

"I'm being a mom," Mrs. Alvarez said tightly. "And I'm *freaking* out. Maybe it's just the cable. That could be it. I'm handing you back to Matteo. I have to go do something. Go for a walk to burn off this energy. I've been a wreck since she missed her normal call-in time."

"Yes, ma'am."

"Hey," Matteo said.

"Did you hear what I told your mom?" Mace asked.

"Mom had you on speaker." Matteo lowered his voice to a whisper. "Hey, man, mom mentioned the missed phone call, but she's had nightmares about Tara being in danger all week. And my mom has a gift for knowing when loved ones are endangered."

"Yeah, I know."

"She's been calling me every day about her latest dream, nothing specific just generally that Tara is in life-threatening danger. I came into town to be here to support Mom when she got the call from Tara on Friday, thinking there would be bad news attached. But then Tara never called."

"This is the first time Tara's missed her check in?"

"She protects Mom. Tara calls at exactly the same time each week, to the minute. And has for seven months now."

Mace had already made up his mind. He was heading for Dominica as soon as he hung up the phone and could get things coordinated.

"I didn't read your text about being in the islands until this morning." There was a pause. "Look, Bethany is going to go into labor any minute now or I'd fly down to Dominica to check. When I saw the message, I thought I'd pull in that favor you owe me."

"That must be a pretty big favor I owe you—why do I owe you?"

"You remember when that chick—"

"Yeah, I remember. This *isn't* a favor. If you're worried about Tara, I'm worried about Tara." And he was. "I'll get a plan together and head that way right now. Text me anything you've got—home address, phone, friends, any island contacts she's mentioned. Places she likes to hang out."

"There's no address. She's rented a house called the Parrot's Perch. That's basically it. Her mail goes to a PO box. Tara works on the mountain alone. She's mentioned a family that gives her vegetables, they're the only other house on the road up the mountain. But I'll look through mom's phone and find anything else Tara referenced." There was a pause. "Hey man, this is my little sis. She's a brat, but she's my brat. I appreciate you doing this, brother."

"Heads up, I'll be calling you with updates from my satellite phone. It won't be my normal cell number."

"I'm looking at mom through the window. She's standing under the tree. When she starts clutching at her heart…"

"She's never wrong."

"Yeah. That's a sure sign bad is on the horizon."

Austin Mace

Saturday, St. Kitts

AUSTIN SLID ONTO THE CHAIR NEXT TO ARES.

Goose was slathering a slice of bread with a thick coat of gooseberry jam. "Everything okay?"

"Did you know that Dominica got its comms cables sliced? They have no sea cables functioning on the island. No internet."

"How'd you figure that out?" Goose asked. Mongoose Phipps was born and raised on St. Kitts. His father, a businessperson from Florida, was the tie Goose needed to become a naturalized American citizen. The U.S. Army benefitted from Goose's veterinarian degree. Assigned to duty with their military working dog program, Goose deployed around the world wherever K9s were doing their jobs. Goose's specialty was keeping the highly trained, high-energy working K9s in top shape.

Now, Goose worked with all the Cerberus dogs, but he was attached specifically to Bravo.

"I got a call from a good friend of mine just now. His sister, Tara, is in Dominica. The family didn't hear from her for her weekly safety check-in." Everyone on the team knew what it meant when a fellow soldier failed to call in on schedule. Antennae went up. Plans were put in place. "I pulled up the emergency sites on the computer to see if anything popped up as concerning, and that's what I found."

"When do they think they'll reestablish the connection?" Ares asked, slicing into his steak.

"Don't know. They say Sunday," Mace said. "But which Sunday is the guess. We're on 'island time'." He caught Ares's gaze. "Since it's my day off, I need to take some time and go down and check on her."

"Her family's that worried even after you explained about the cable?" Ares asked.

"I am, too. Tara's resourceful. She's world traveled—remote places, not London and Paris, more like the Amazon rainforest and Borneo. Tara knows her mom would freak if she didn't find a way to make contact. I can't imagine that she didn't try everything in her power to get a message out."

"Carrier pigeon? They take a while to get to the U.S." Goose took a bite and stilled as he savored. "You can only get gooseberry jam like this on St. Kitts. I miss this so much."

"The boats down at the docks, at least, should all have sat phones," Ares said.

Goose dropped his bread to his plate, wiped his hands, then pulled his computer from where it rested on the chair next to him. Opening the top and letting the computer scan his retina, Goose did a search. "Dominica is four hundred and seventy miles, that's out of range for the heli. It would take a full day by boat. It's an hour straight flight."

"I'll rent a plane." Mace shoveled up a bite of eggs dripping with cheese. "Down, eyes-on, and back." He took the bite. Mace figured he could grab his go bag and be over to the airport within an hour. Mace had friends there from past training stints on the island. They'd hook him up.

"How about we push your day off out until Monday?" Ares asked. "You take the floatplane with Bear and Ash. While you're checking on your friend—Tara, is it?"

"That's right. Tara Alvarez."

"Ash and Bear can go shake hands with John John. Take the dogs. Let Ash fly back tomorrow morning. We need everyone to get in some rotations on the plane and the dogs need to be comfortable making water landings."

While Mace shoveled up his food, Ares pulled his phone from his thigh pocket, sending texts to the hangar operator, and to put Bear and Ash on notice they'd be wheels up this morning. Time to shake a leg.

"What's your friend doing on the island," Goose asked, "vacation?"

"She's a scientist with Trifalgar Working Group."

"That's a DARPA affiliate," Goose said.

Ares canted his head. "Now, how would you know that?"

"It was in a brief a couple days ago. Kiyana wanted us to have a heads up."

Kiyana Swabi was on Iniquus's Tactical Logistics team. When Goose was fulfilling a logistics role for Bravo, he was Kiyana's point of contact. Logistics liked to keep a finger on the pulse. Keep an awareness of which team was in the vicinity of which clients.

"Logistics is tracking a group of Trifalgar scientists who were out in the Indian Ocean." Goose took a sip of coffee. "A handful of them are headed to the Caribbean this week. And there's a storm that looks like it's gathering into something significant in the Atlantic. It's one thing to do search and rescue on an island that got blown. A completely different beast if they're in a small vessel outside of the U.S. Coast Guards' area of responsibility and lost in open waters."

"Then it's on us," Ares said. Ares's phone was dinging with responses to his texts. "The plane is being pulled around to the dock and will be ready within the hour. They're filing your flight plans, and they'll contact emergency management in Dominica to meet you with a customs agent." He lifted his attention from the screen. "Goose, paperwork for the K9s?"

"It's always updated. I just need to print it off. I'll do that right after breakfast." Goose ducked his ear toward the food line. "Ash and Bear got the message. They're piling their plates full."

"Back to that boat of scientists," Ares said. "We have a line of communication with them, right?"

Mace asked. "Logistics was putting a pin on the board in case they need support?"

"Exactly, logistics is aware." Goose rubbed at his nose. "I'm not worried about the weather. Not until late July. I contacted Noah back at headquarters." Noah was on Cerberus Team Alpha. He held a degree in meteorology and was a good man to have in their corner to clarify what information Bravo was given from their military and governmental sources.

"Noah said that European models have that weather cell heading up the East Coast as a tropical storm. The issue is that the number of our protectees in the area is up significantly this year. And Noah says this hurricane season when it gets going will be no joke."

Ares nodded. "Command has the issue on their long-term radar. With the uptick in natural disasters hitting in previously safe areas, it places more of our clients in danger zones for their work assignments. One of the ways Command is adapting is to develop a K9 Team Charlie. They're putting out feelers for handlers to staff the new team."

"Their specialty?"

"Same as Alpha and Bravo, mixed training to head into any disaster or to peel off in support of the Iniquus forces."

"We'll need at least one more vet." Goose swiped his napkin across his face. "Chasten and I are at capacity."

Ares gave him a nod over his coffee mug. "Trip's wife just found out she's pregnant." Tripwire was on Team Alpha. Last year, Trip pulled Major Dani Addams, an Army veterinary surgeon, off the side of a cliff in a bomb cyclone. Soon after, they'd decided that they wanted to weather all the storms life had in store side by side and were married.

"Good news." Mace grinned.

Ares signaled the staffer for more coffee, then turned back to Mace. "Possibly for us, too. Command is negotiating to bring her on."

Goose nodded. "When do they think that could happen?"

Ares was right, year over year the storms weren't just getting more frequent, their power and devastation was increasing. With the two Cerberus teams in place, Alpha and Bravo often felt like they were behind the eight ball, packing up and jumping off.

"Dani's still got her contract with Uncle Sam to finish up," Ares said. "That's all I know."

Ash and Bear sat down with nods as greetings.

The table was quiet as the men dug into their plates. Years of military life taught the men to get while the getting was good.

Mace was anxious to get moving toward the floatplane.

With the last bite swallowed down, Goose leaned in. "I was just thinking. You said that your friend is with the Trifalgar Group? I don't know if all those researchers are under the

DARPA umbrella. I'll look her up and see if she's an Iniquus client. What's this woman's full name?"

"Tara Magdalena Alvarez." Mace pronounced slowly.

"And what's her field of research?"

"Worms, last I heard." Mace rubbed a thumb along his jawline. "I really don't think she's connected to DARPA. I can't imagine a security-worm connection."

"It's a stretch," Goose acknowledged. "But I'll put her name through the database anyway. If she's on our list, Iniquus has a responsibility."

List or not, *Mace* had a responsibility, this was family of the heart. He would do anything for Mrs. Alvarez and Matteo.

8

_____

Austin Mace

Saturday, Dominica

THE LANDING WAS LESS THAN GRACEFUL. THERE WAS A FEEL
for putting a plane down in open waters and that feel was
perishable. He needed to get some training in.

Ash did it as easy as walking. He was born and raised in
Juneau, Alaska, where the only way to connect to the greater
world was by plane or by boat.

Ash jumped out to tie them to the dock.

"I thought John John was retiring," Mace said, nodding
toward the man who was standing at the end of the dock, hand
over head, waving. "He's in uniform." Mace lifted his hand in
response.

Bear dragged a pack closer to the door. "His number two
had a stroke. They pulled John back in to maintain the institu-
tional knowledge."

"Sorry to hear that."

"Hey man," Ash said. "Ares told us to go work with John while you make contact with Tara. Do you think that's a good plan, or do you think you need us to go with?"

"I have no idea what's going on here." He accepted the pack that Bear handed him and passed it on to Ash. "The island's tiny." The next pack Bear handed out, Mace set on the dock. "Let me run up to her place and have a look around." And honestly, Mace thought that Tara might not appreciate a team of geared up search and rescue professionals and their dogs knocking on her door while she lounged around in her pajamas trying to enjoy a lazy Saturday. "I think let's work the plan. I've got my sat phone. I'll call down if anything looks off." The third pack was his. Mace dragged the straps over his shoulders and adjusted the weight.

They leashed the dogs and jumped them down, giving the K9s a moment to shiver off any stress and get a feel for their new environs before walking toward land.

After shaking hands all around, John said, "While customs check your paperwork, tell me about the dogs you have here."

Ash put his hand on his German Shepherd's head. "This is Hoover. He's cross trained for tactical deployment. That means we can get him over cliffs and fast rope from helicopters. Though, his specialty is urban search and rescue. He's a pile sniffer. When all you've got is a mound of rubble and crossed fingers, he's your guy." Ash pointed over to where Diesel lay between Mace's feet. His regal head lifted, his eyes blazing orange. "Diesel is also tactically trained. He can trail the bad guy in a hot situation."

"Hot dogs?" John tipped his head.

"Yes, sir," Ash said with a lopsided smile. "Hot means bullets flying. In a disaster situation, Diesel can alert Mace to things that might go boom—gasses, explosives, chemicals, trip-wires. That keeps the team safe. If a specific person is missing, let's say they were disoriented by the disaster and wandered. If we have a good scent source for that person, Diesel can track them down."

John looked down at Diesel. "Yes, that last part I knew. He is a miracle dog, I tell you." He leaned over and blew a kiss toward Diesel. "I was with Mace in Haiti. We were speaking with their emergency manager. An earthquake struck. 4.0—not large enough to make the news, but," he raised a finger into the air, "enough that it caused structural damage." He gestured toward a grinning Mace.

Mace loved stories that praised Diesel. And John loved to tell a story.

Leaning against the signpost, John settled in. "Mace, and his good boy Diesel, came upon a mother who had been pulling her son to the school in a wagon. The mother was knocked unconscious when a portion of the streetlight fell. She was fine but the child—a six-year-old with Down syndrome—was missing. The mother was holding his shoe, standing in the middle of the street screaming. While I helped to calm her down, Mace held the shoe for Diesel to scent. Diesel splayed his legs out," John was using his whole body to animate his story, "to get his nose down to the ground and guess what? He found that child. Found him! The boy had made his way through the park and was splashing in a water fountain. We provided field medical care to the mother, returned her son, and moved on to help others. Amazing to watch the dogs in action." John pushed his hands deep into his pockets as he bent over Diesel, again. "I wish to pet you, my dear friend. But I know this is not allowed. But I speak of you often. You are a hero dog." He turned to Bear who was adjusting the collar on his Labrador. "And who have we here?"

Bear missed the question as he focused on a small cut, he found on Truffle's ear.

"Bear is our team curmudgeon," Ash said.

That, Bear obviously heard. "Curmudgeon, huh?" Bear stood and patted Ash's shoulder. "Good on you. I see that Word a Day calendar I got you last Christmas is really paying off." He back handed Ash's chest. "Keep working at it. Pretty soon no one will call you a knuckle dragger anymore."

"Why is this man named Bear?" John asked, Mace. "There's a story?" He looked over at Bear. "I was named with the first and last names exactly the same, John John. On an island where most of us have surnames that are the same as many people's first names, my mother thought it would be less confusing for folks. I like to collect the stories behind other people's names and nicknames. Mace," he bladed his hand in Mace's direction, "is a disappointment. I thought there would be a good story there, but it is merely Austin's last name." He looked around at Mace with his eyebrows held high. "You disappoint me."

"Apologies." Mace chuckled. "There's not much of a story for Bear either, I'm afraid," Mace said. "He loves to eat blueberries and take naps. That's about it."

"Yeah, that's it," Bear said.

"And who is this Labrador you have here?"

Bear looked down at his K9 who lay with her feet crossed daintily. "Her name is Truffles."

John's brows drew together. "Like the fungus?"

"Eh, well more like the pig that sniffs the truffles," Ash said. "But when we tried to call her 'pig', she became indignant."

"Indignant." Bear nodded. "Another power word. Yup, with that calendar, there's a marked improvement."

John grinned at their banter. "She doesn't look like a pig." He squatted in front of Truffles. "Do you sweetheart?" he baby-talked. "Truffles sounds like ruffles, very ladylike, indeed. But ladies can also be brave, and strong. You're setting the standard for beauty. Such a good girl." John stood and kicked his legs so his pants would slide back down into place. "So, what does she do that's different than Diesel and Hoover?"

"The true story," Ash said. "Bear got his name because Bear and K9 Truffles are our cave team. Be it a natural cave or debris from a disaster, both of them like to be in dark tight spaces where any sane person would refuse to go. Truffles likes any place where she's wriggling through debris on her tummy."

"And Bear likes the solitude for his naps." John grinned.

"Here we go." Mace nodded toward the customs officer making his way back over to them.

"All is in order," the official said, pressing the folders into Ash's hands. "Enjoy your stay."

"Come." They turned and followed John's outstretched arm, pointed to his headquarters across the street.

The teammates lifted their go bags and slung them onto their backs.

"Your flight was good?"

"We're practicing with the floatplane," Mace said, as they jogged across the street ahead of an oncoming car. "And after the landing I made coming in, I know I'm going to have to do some jump up and downs to get the feel again."

"Very different than landing on land," John said. "But of course, in a disaster, one is not assured that there will be a better place to land other than the water. There may very well be no docks nor runways." John pressed the door open and held it wide as Bravo moved into the entry. "I read just the other day that they needed to reroute planes from London because in the recent heat wave, the runways were melting."

"Crazy, huh?" Bear asked.

"And getting crazier each day," John agreed. "We are very concerned by the changes in the atmosphere. After Maria stripped our island naked, we vowed to make Dominica the most resilient island in the Caribbean. You see my headquarters?" He spread his arms wide. "It will withstand most anything. Category five storm, tidal wave. Volcanic fire."

"Are you expecting the volcano to blow?" Ash scowled.

"A funny thing for a man named Ash to ask." John chuckled. "Who knows. What I know is that we have as many rivers as there are days of the year. We have a boiling lake. And, we have nine, count them," he held up his fingers, "nine active volcanoes, my friend. Now, the last time we had an eruption was back at the times of Christopher Columbus. This does not bring me comfort." He waggled his finger. "Dominica is like a woman heavy with pregnancy. At some point, what is inside the belly of the earth must come out."

Bear raised his eyebrows. "Just not while we're here, okay?"

"If this were to happen, I would be sitting on your plane in the passenger seat, waiting for you to fly us to safety." When John laughed his beard danced on his chest. John looked down and lifted it for the men to see the ends were blue. "It's blueberry gelatin."

"What now?" Mace asked.

"My granddaughter made me promise that when I retired, she got to make me a blue beard. Since the pirate movie was filmed on our island, she is pirate crazy." He twisted a hand by his ear. "You know, we have just given permits to a crew who will be doing two days of filming here. They are making a fiction movie about modern-day treasure hunters who find the Queen's Treasure, and while elated by their sudden wealth, it ultimately is their ruin. It's an indie short film not Hollywood, this time. So, I didn't tell my granddaughter. She'd probably want me to get face tattoos to celebrate." He laughed richly at his own joke.

It was an infectious laugh, and the team chuckled along.

While Mace enjoyed the comradery, his mission was to find Tara and, if all was okay, facilitate a phone call to her mom. That "if" was burning a hole in Mace's chest. "Hey, I'm going to let you all catch up and do some initial planning. I'm going to see about a vehicle and go find Tara."

"Ares said she had missed a check in." John pressed his knuckles into the tabletop. "Where is she staying?"

"A house called Parrot's Perch. I don't have the address."

"Ah yes, the researcher. I know of her from the permits that she's obtained for her work alongside endangered species. Worms, isn't it?"

"Yes, sir."

"There is no address for that house. Let me show you." John held up a "wait here" finger then moved into his office. He returned unfolding a map. Spreading it wide, John made a circle high up the tallest volcano. "This is where she is living, Parrot's Perch." He drew another circle. "This is where we are." And a third circle. "This is your hotel, which is just a block down the road in the other direction. From here," he moved the pen back to the headquarters, "follow the main road around. You will see a mango-colored house across from a gas station, yes?"

Mace nodded. "Got it."

"Fifty meters farther, you will see a grass road that winds up the mountain. Eight kilometers on the grass road, bumpy ride, steep incline. At three kilometers, there's a small farm on the left. Five more and you will see the sign hanging on the right. It's hard to see the house though. Turn at the sign anyway and past the trees there it will be."

"Remote," Bear said.

"Very. But her worms are up there in the clouds and the volcanic soil." John folded the map and handed it to Mace. "If you have trouble finding it, come back down, and I'll go up with you. I just have a meeting now. But in two hours I am free." He held up a finger and walked away. A moment later, he was back a set of keys in his hands.

"In that front parking space, there is a SUV for you." He handed Mace the keys.

"Thank you."

"Are you here long?"

"We're leaving out again in the morning if all goes as planned."

John nodded. "You are welcome to use the vehicle during your stay."

"Thank you, again." Mace tossed the keys up and snatched them out of the air. With a glance around the group, he said, "I'll see you all later. I'll call if needs be." He turned toward the door, Diesel at his heels.

"No calls." John lifted his voice as Mace pushed the door open. "There is no cell phone service on the mountain only in town."

"We have sat phones." Mace patted the bottom of his go bag.

John shook his head. "The tree canopy is extremely high and very dense. Even a sat phone becomes problematic."

"Smoke signals then." As Mace raised his hand to sign good-bye and let the door swing shut behind him, Mace could hear John's laughter. He was a good man.

But Tara's being on that volcano alone and possibly hurt with no way to communicate, yeah, that was no laughing matter.

9

Austin Mace

Saturday, Dominica

MACE FOUND THE TURN OFF ONTO THE ROAD UP TO PARROT'S Perch by a stroke of luck. It wasn't an easy climb. This was definitely side-of-the-volcano terrain. It drove nothing like the rugged mountains in Afghanistan, the grass making his tires slip and spin.

Mace had the windows rolled all the way down and Diesel had spent the ride leaning out his side, sniffing all the new scents, having a great time.

The vegetation on either side of them was thick and snarled. It was the kind of landscape that slowed a search to a snail's pace as the team crawled under, over, and around. At least Mace didn't see any rhododendron or sweet briar, the bane of their practice searches in Virginia.

Mace's time in the Navy was spent in the water and in the sandbox. Line of sight was to the horizon. Most of the scary was either buried in the form of an IED or aiming down at him from a rooftop.

Since he'd joined Cerberus, his training and missions had been focused on urban disaster where Diesel would sniff out anything that might become a hazard to his teammates.

Nobody wanted an unexpected BOOM.

He'd admit it, this terrain wasn't where he liked to be. He wasn't a fan of creepy crawlies, or anything that slithered and hissed. Mace would take a midnight shark-infested ocean over green and sunlit almost anytime. His training was his comfort zone.

This?

Mace couldn't see three feet to either side of him.

But he could definitely see Tara loving it out here. Mace was thinking about the time when Tara was three and four years old, he was eleven and twelve—Mace thought of her as a nature child, one with the natural world.

Mace had very distinct pictures of Tara at that time

She liked climbing trees and lying in the grass. Curious. Brave.

Maybe a little too curious and brave at times.

Mace remembered vividly holding Tara in his arms at his mother's funeral.

There were a bunch of strangers at the graveside from his dad's side of the family. People Mace had never met before. They'd come to get through this hassle of Mace's mom's sudden death as quickly as possible and back to their lives. They packed up the house, throwing almost everything away. Mace got to have three suitcases and that was it as he moved from middle America out to Rhode Island.

At the time, if anyone had asked him where Rhode Island was on a map, Mace had no clue. Far away was about the most he could wrap his head around. Yeah, he'd just turned twelve.

Mrs. Alvarez was there at the funeral, too. She was there constantly from the time Mace found his mother on the kitchen floor until the moment the car drove around the corner.

Too old to be coddled, Mrs. Alvarez just stood close. He'd leaned into her, wishing he was smaller and wasn't supposed to be the tough guy his dad said he had to be. He wanted to cry and mourn.

But no one from his family was in mourning. They were inconvenienced.

Yeah, just when he thought he was going to break, Tara, dressed in her fairy princess wings, crawled into his lap and sobbed into his neck. He was able to duck his head into her soft curls and cry silently. As long as she was there, he was given a little space to turn the valve and let a little pressure off, hiding behind the semi-transparency of the fairy wings.

He remembered his gratitude.

He remembered her saying, "I'm so sad about your mommy. I'm so sad you're leaving." It was simple and sincere. And it meant the world to him that this little kid was giving him such a huge gift. The gift of space.

That day, Mace couldn't look for touch and kindness in an adult. Or his friends. He had to be the tough guy. Silent. Stoic.

But a fairy? He was allowed to take comfort there.

And he did.

Tara let him carry her around most of the day. And when someone tried to pull her away, she became an anaconda around his neck.

To this day, Mace couldn't see a little kid dressed up in wings without thinking of Tara.

He couldn't see a butterfly without thinking of his mother, beautiful, graceful, gentle-souled. But an addict. She tried so hard to beat it. But the drugs were so much stronger than she was.

Last evening, Mace was getting his miles in along a quiet road up the side of the mountain in St. Kitts. Tiny white butterflies were so prolific that it looked like snow was falling on the wildflowers. He'd said aloud, "What's up, Mom? Are you trying to tell me something?" The memory of Tara's wings with their rigid wires holding the mesh wide, stabbing at his face as he cried at his mother's funeral came and went in a flash.

That phone call from Matteo this morning hadn't been that much of a surprise.

Thirty years old. Unimaginable. A woman living her adult life. Yup, mind blowing.

What would Tara look like now?

She had been in family holiday photos, photos of her visiting from school that Mrs. Alvarez texted to him. But Tara was usually a drape of long black hair, the flash of a smile.

Why hadn't he focused in on her?

His vehicle bucked and balked at this last bit of the climb, pulling Mace's attention back to the present situation.

As he rounded a curve, he spotted a portion of fence. A post held a swinging sign, a parrot carved into the wood was painted in bright primary colors. "Parrot's Perch."

"We're here."

Diesel swung his head to pant toward Mace.

"There's a utility vehicle," he told Diesel. "That makes more sense. This beast is ridiculous on this path. Had I known, I would have hunted up my own side-by-side to rent."

Diesel's tongue hung long—the heat and humidity amongst the plants was palpable.

"Okay, slobber monster, this is the correct place. Let's go see what there is to see."

Throwing the gear shift into Park, Mace quietly opened the door and stood, one foot on the ground, the other still on the floorboard, taking the pulse of the space. "Does this seem okay to you?" he asked Diesel. "Feels…empty." He swept the scene. "One way to find out. Come on, let's go knock on the front door."

Diesel scrambled over the front seat to jump down beside Mace. As usual, Diesel wore his tactical vest when he was off Iniquus property to show folks this was a working dog. Hopefully, it would keep everyone at a good distance. Not that Mace didn't trust his dog. He didn't trust folks near his dog, was all.

"Not that there's anyone around," Mace muttered under his breath.

Diesel's nose went up into the air, scenting the breeze.

Mace was going to give Diesel a moment to settle. He'd watch Diesel's posture. Mace had no idea what he was walking into—a typical day or a hostage crisis.

Or anything in between.

Diesel had a way of pulling the correct emotion from the ether. He was like a mood ring that Mrs. Alvarez had drawn from her jewelry box to show him from when she was in high school. He'd slipped it on his finger, and it had turned immediately black. Mace pulled it off as quick as he could. He didn't want Mrs. Alvarez to know how dark he felt inside that day. When Mrs. Alvarez slipped it on, the ring turned yellow. That seemed correct to him. Sunny even when the storm clouds brewed on the horizon.

Wow, he'd forgotten about that. It was what, twenty-five years ago?

Mace focused on Diesel. In this moment, his dog was interested but not braced.

Patting his thigh to signal Diesel to his side, Mace made his way up the stairs to the door. He tapped lightly as he looked through the glass. No lights. No movement. No disarray of overturned furniture and drawers emptied onto the floor.

He knocked louder.

Waited.

Jiggled the knob.

Nada.

He moved to another window and looked past the sheers.

The front room was lived in. Piles of novels. Some art supplies. A computer...

That looked fine.

He walked along the wrap around porch with its table and chairs overlooking the vista. A hammock hung beam to beam.

At the next window, Mace looked into the bedroom.

The bed was unmade. A journal and pen lay on the pillow. There seemed to be some picture cards on the bed sheet. Shoes kicked toward the wall. A nightgown thrown over the chair.

Nothing concerning.

He wished he'd asked what exactly Tara was doing here. Research covered a whole lot of ground. And he didn't see any scientific instruments. Digging worms didn't add a lot of context.

Why would a biophysicist be in Dominica?

Why would she be isolated out here without a lab?

Moving a little further along the deck, Mace found the back door was open, the screen keeping the mosquitos at bay. He tried that knob.

He was in.

Huh.

Should he be in?

Yeah...he didn't know what to do here. Leave a note and a phone number?

"What do you think, Diesel? What's the play?"

Diesel padded through the little house that was flush to the ground in front and rested on stilts in the back as the incline fell away. Sniffing surfaces as he went on a tour of discovery, Diesel snuffled and chuffed his way. He spent most of his time exploring the bedroom and sniffed around the nightgown and bed. He came to a standstill with his muzzle resting on the sheets looking at the cards.

The first was a painting of someone scattering seeds.

The second was watercolor of a coyote who looked none too friendly.

The other was a picture of a person blindfolded and bound. Swords, shoved into the ground, made a ring around them.

And there was her journal lying there. Spiral bound, it lay open, a pen splayed across the page with today's date in neat numbers at the top right of the page, like a school assignment.

Mace wasn't going to pick up the journal and read it, but the date at the top of the page gave him the impression that, as of this morning, Tara was fine. Though, anyone could have written this. After all, the last Mace had seen Tara, she was just learning to scratch out basic letters

Mace turned his head to read the curly script.

SEEDS AGAIN. **I hope this means I find more gold!**

8 of Swords, ain't that the truth?

The coyote, though…trickster. Yesterday, the monkey, and now we're upping the mayhem a notch?

Breathe.

INTERESTING.

Cryptic.

And invasive for him to look.

A glance toward her bedside table and there were three boxes of meditation cards. He remembered cards like that in Mrs. Alvarez's bedroom.

He wasn't here to snoop. He was here to verify that Tara

was A-Okay and deliver the news to her mother. Eyes on, that's all he needed.

While his conscious brain had said that this check was the very least he could do for a lifetime of kindness, his gut had another message. *Danger brewing.*

His body had been braced for bad since the call, though he'd tried to write it off for the most part as contagious emotions.

Just like laughter can spread through a group of friends, so too could the icy feel of dread.

The last place you want to be is in the middle of the ocean, swimming next to someone having a panic attack. Best thing to do under that circumstance? Swim away.

Panic kills. Even if it's second-hand panic.

Focus. "This morning she was fine," he told Diesel. "Hey, hey, hey, let's not drool on the bed. No one wants to sleep in your dried-up slobber. Especially someone who hasn't even met you. Manners, okay?" Mace gave the room another glance. Yeah, nothing here said scuffle. It was neat and peaceful.

She had found gold?

"Diesel, what do you say we track her down and say hey."

When Mace said "track," Diesel went from curious to go-mode.

"Nightgown or pillowcase?" Mace reached for the pillow and then thought, *nope, too intimate*. Same with the nightgown.

He found a sneaker under the bed. Good enough.

"Diesel, scent." Mace held the open shoe out to Diesel who stuck his nose into the scent source and chuffed it in, letting his brain learn his task.

When Diesel sat down and focused on Mace, Mace commanded, "Diesel, find."

As usual, Diesel moved around the house sniffing away. It was a small house—great room, bedroom, bathroom, deck.

Diesel stopped at the footstool; an open science journal lay with a neon-yellow highlighter. Mace picked it up and read the section that Tara (presumably) had found interesting enough to mark up.

A STUDY PUBLISHED in the journal Nature & Climate found that nearly 90% of all marine life would be extinct by 2100 if greenhouse gas emissions remained constant. This time period will shorten with each increase in temperature, making it possible to have no marine life in the oceans as soon as 2050.

WAIT.

He read it again, letting his eyes scan further into the paragraph. 90% of all marine life…unless the carbon dioxide levels were seriously contained.

What would the 10% be that got left?

He imagined maybe some of the Frankenstein's monster-looking beasts in the far depths of the ocean. Maybe some algae? Other than the food chain, he didn't know how marine life worked.

On land, Mace thought it would be the cockroaches that survived.

Maybe bed bugs.

In the water? Mace thought maybe it would be lobsters. He thought he remembered reading that they were older than dinosaurs.

"Come on, Diesel." Mace opened the door. "Tara's not in the house. Let's go see what she's up to. Diesel, find."

Diesel barreled through the door and down the steps. He

spent some time with the random trails around the house and the side-by-side vehicle, figuring out which one was newest.

Mace jogged down to the SUV and grabbed his hiking pack. He pulled a plastic bag from the side pocket and tucked Tara's shoe inside.

He hoped it was Tara's shoe...

If it wasn't, then they'd gather intel and move along. Mission: find Tara and relieve Mrs. Alvarez's worries so she could get some sleep. Easy day.

10

Austin Mace

Saturday, Dominica

OKAY, NOT SUCH AN EASY DAY.

Diesel plowed through the vegetation.

If he squinted, Mace could kind of make out a trail of broken limbs and scuffed leaves, but it was new and not well traversed.

It didn't look like there was a fight along the way. Again, not his bailiwick. Tracking outside of tunnels and buildings wasn't in his tool kit. Diesel had a lot more training with this. Mace made a mental note that he needed the more experienced trackers on his team to work with him and build more rainforest skills especially if they'd be working more and more in this region.

An hour of tracking went by, then two.

Of course, when Diesel homed in, he was focused and unwavering on his goal.

Mace in turn was focused on his K9 as he managed the logistics. When they left Parrots Perch, Mace had put a digital pin in the GPS at the vehicles, he could trace his way back. And push comes to shove, if they got lost out here, all they had to do was aim down the slope. Eventually they'd arrive at the coastline. It was a tiny island.

Mace was thankful that this was June, the longest days of the year. Still, it would be better to get off the mountain before dark.

But the idea that he'd turn around and a few more steps he would find Tara trapped by a fallen tree or lying there with a broken ankle? Mace would go as long as Diesel had a scent trail.

Next time he found a break in the canopy, he'd call his teammates and keep them apprised.

Though it had taken hours to get this far, Mace saw from the readout on his GPS that they were only about two miles from Tara's house. It had taken so long to get this far because of the thickness of the vegetation.

Mace looked up from his GPS to find a damned big snake dangling from a branch directly in front of him. He jumped back.

Detour.

Diesel turned to watch over his shoulder as Mace moved around the outside of the tree. There was laughter in his eyes. If Diesel were a Bravo brother, he'd be throwing shade about now.

They moved out of the tree line to a waterfall and river. John John said there were enough rivers on the island that he could walk in a different one every day for a year. It was about time they crossed one.

It looked blissfully cool after this trek. It would be a pleasure to strip down and dive in. The air here was thick with moisture, it lay on his skin and made him feel oily.

Diesel stilled at the shoreline. He was flummoxed.

The breeze and water interrupted the trail.

Mace pulled out his sat phone and tried to get a signal, but it was a no go, still too much overhang.

Whistling for Diesel to follow, Mace jumped rock to rock to the other side. "I'll tell you what, boy, you find Tara for me, and we'll take a swim in that pool under the falls on the way back."

Mace pulled the bag with the sneaker from his pack to remind Diesel of the scent and let his snort it back into his system.

"Diesel, find."

With his eyes bright with excitement, Diesel dashed up and down the shoreline chuffing air over his olfactory sensors until he picked up a scent, then he raced into the brush.

Mace sprinted after him.

Nose to the ground, then up in the air, head on a swivel, then back on to the trail, Diesel's body language said he was locked in and getting close.

It always felt miraculous to Mace when he saw Diesel in go mode.

And Diesel was really moving now.

Mace had to push hard to keep his K9 in view. Bursting through a curtain of vines, he found Diesel lying down, paws together nose resting on his feet, whimpering.

This was Diesel's signal for a tripwire or booby trap.

Here?

Mace scanned.

Improbable.

Mace slowed, crouched, and approached, keeping his posture low. "What have you got there, boy?" he whispered.

They'd stopped just past the tree line. Ahead, the vegetation and rock outcroppings were about knee-height. Mace pulled out his binoculars and scanned for a possible illegal cash crop that Tara might have tripped upon accidentally.

And while that sent a momentary jolt through his system, drugs didn't make a lot of sense unless someone was cooking meth. Man, he hoped he wasn't sneaking up on somebody cooking meth. Meth heads were known for setting some heinous mantraps in the woods where Bravo trained. Cerberus was always cautious when they worked in the parks and wilds around Virginia.

Searching along the dirt in front of Diesel, Mace didn't find any telltale signs of being disturbed by digging. Mace lowered to Diesel's level and followed his K9's gaze as Diesel looked along in either direction, insisting with his whimpers that something was there.

Mace reached into his side pocket for the unscented baby powder that he used to check wind direction. Maybe Diesel was smelling something rolling down from the summit.

Squeezing the bottle to send a puff of powder into the air, there in the shadow of the trees three very faint red lines, each about a foot apart, hovered in the air and disappeared as the powder settled to the ground.

"Son of a gun."

Mace held out his hand and squeezed again. "Sure, enough, an infrared fence."

Mace stepped well back of the fence line and pulled out Diesel's reward cloth. He spent a few minutes playing tug with Diesel and praising him with high pitched praise, spoken softly so that his voice wouldn't carry to whoever it was that felt they needed to be warned of approach way out here in the middle of nowhere.

Why in the heck would someone think this was necessary

out here? Mace looped the question through his mind as he scrambled around for an explanation.

And why would Tara's scent lead them here?

If Tara was on the other side of the infrared, that was where they needed to be as well.

The distress in Mrs. Alvarez's voice came back to him. She felt in her bones that Tara was in danger.

This didn't look good.

With Diesel by his side, Mace worked the powder wherever there was enough shade to allow him to see the faint lines. Finally, he got to a space where he could see his way over. A log leaned into a fork in the tree. Mace shimmied up, edged to the side, and made a circle with his arms.

"Diesel, pass through," he commanded.

With a wagging tail, Diesel gracefully ran up the log ramp and leaped through Mace's arms, just like they did back at the Cerberus training grounds where their trainer, Reaper Hamilton, put the dogs through all types of possible scenarios. Mace had never considered this one, and yet here it was.

Diesel landed lightly and turned for his next command.

Mace held up a fist then a flat hand, sit-stay.

That leap was easy enough for Diesel. This was going to be a bit of a challenge for Mace. Not the height but the distance. It seemed that the system was set up just out of reach of tree limbs. Perhaps, it was for just this reason; it would keep most people from climbing up and jumping over.

Mace decided he'd have to mimic Diesel, diving out, then he'd have to tuck and roll. That was it. There weren't any other options.

Pulling off his pack, Mace tossed it out to land on the other side of the alarm system.

Mace stood, swinging his arm into a diver's stance, his

focus aimed at a grassy spot between the rocks when he heard a shriek ring out, loud and long.

The next thing he knew, Mace was on the other side of the infrared fence, swinging his backpack into place, and sprinting over the terrain in the direction of the scream.

Clambering over the rocks, up an incline, and there he stopped on a dime.

In front of him was Tara. Unmistakably, Tara.

She was hugging herself with her head thrown back laughing.

Mace sat down to let his heart reseat, Diesel lay down beside him, chin resting lightly on Mace's knee.

Tara, oblivious that someone was watching her, was singing at the top of her lungs and dancing—ridiculously.

Booty shaking, legs kicking, back bending, gyrating.

Mace sat on the flat rock and watched what he would describe as the exact opposite of what he'd feared.

This was pure joy.

Pure abandon.

Diesel was panting with his stinky breath, and Mace reached out to massage his neck, hoping that Diesel wouldn't bark and call attention to them. Though this side of voyeuristic, Mace needed a minute of time to adjust.

He had been chasing the image of a five-year-old child up the mountain.

And this, this was a *woman*.

Long, shiny black hair.

Sleek athletic legs.

Curves that…

And the most magnetic thing about Tara was the abandon and joy on full display.

Mace was drinking in this scene.

Drinking in her image.

Storing this away for the times when he was parched for something hopeful. That happened quite a bit when the team was deployed and finding the victims of mass disaster.

"Look at that, Diesel. My wood fairy has morphed into a goddess."

And the fluid twirls turned into a wide-legged twerk.

Mace caught Diesel's gaze. Diesel's lips curved into a smile and his panting made him seem like he was laughing. "Yeah, that's not very goddess-like." But completely Tara-like.

Familiar and yet brand new.

It was a head trip.

Mace should call out and let her know he was there…

Nah.

This was too good to interrupt.

As her song wound down, Mace wondered, why the infrared fence?

She flopped down on her back and caught her breath, then rolled, crossing her arms below her head and closed her eyes, kicking her legs in the air.

When Mace watched her dance, his whole body stirred with recognition and some primal energy that surprised the hell out of him.

Tara was his best friend's little sister.

Period.

He needed to wipe any of those wolf thoughts right out of his system.

As Mace watched her lying there, peace washed through him, a sense of coming home.

Baby Tara would do that so long ago. She'd play so hard that she'd curl up in the crook of a tree trunk and fall asleep. Mrs. Alvarez would send Matteo and Mace to go out to find her.

As boys, the two of them used to like to find a branch with a few leaves on the end and break it off. They'd tickle her bare feet until she woke up giggling.

Mace wanted that, the tinkling sound of nostalgia.

"Diesel," he whispered. "I'm going to go down and say hello."

Grinning at his plan, Mace looked around. There were no trees within arm's reach of the infrared fence.

Instead, Mace broke off a few long strands of tufted grasses.

Leaving Diesel in a down-stay, Mace snuck forward, reached out the grass and tickled the bottom of her foot.

It surprised the crap out of him when she shrieked and pulled her legs in tight. Her eyes widened.

Then, pain seared his senses.

Pepper spray.

Unmistakable.

As Mace back peddled to get out of the chemical cloud, he heard Diesel barking frantically, begging for a release command to come and protect his partner.

"Diesel, stay!" Mace yelled into his elbow, hoping not to suck anymore of the spray into his lungs. He needed to keep Diesel from breathing this crap.

Whatever the hell Tara had sprayed at him was worse than anything that he'd had shot in his face in training.

"Tara," he gasped out, his elbow shielding his eyes lest she spray again. His mucous tissues were on fire. "Tara! It's me, Austin Mace."

"What?" Her voice was sheer horror. "Austin? Holy hell. What have I done? Why are you here? How did you find me?"

Mace hunkered over, coughing up phlegm. "What have you got on me?"

"Oh…Ah…It's bear spray. Capsaicin. I…I…I thought you were a rabid monkey."

11

Tara Alvarez

Saturday, Dominica

Tara dropped the can. Hands to head. Eyes wide with disbelief. The only thing her shocked brain could grab onto was, "We have to get you to a hospital."

Austin pressed one hand onto his knee and held the other up as if to ward away another attack. "It'll take at least three hours to get me down the mountain and to the nearest hospital." Austin gasped, stepping upwind from the capsaicin plume that visibly lingered in the humid air. "Water." He coughed and spit. His eyes were streaming.

Tara scrambled around to get to her pack. Dragging her water bottle from the side pocket she unscrewed the top.

When she tried to press it into his hands, Austin pushed the bottle back. He reached down to tug his shirt off, flinging it away from him.

Holy shit.

Tara stood frozen on the spot, questions stumbling over each other looking for an answer.

Why was Austin here?

How had he found her in the middle of nowhere?

How could she help him?

But most of all, Tara was caught on her *holy shit* thoughts.

Tara had seen pictures of Austin all along his timeline. She'd watched him mature into a high school graduate, a Navy sailor in his Class A whites. She'd seen him in camo paint and in a wetsuit as a SEAL, but she'd never seen him as a shirtless man.

Shirtless Austin Mace was drool worthy.

She watched the drool drip from his chin as he hacked up a lung.

Not what she meant.

"Look what you've done to him, Tara," she said aloud still trying to process the scene.

Tara reached for Austin's hand. "Water," she said loudly, pressing the bottle into his fingers.

Austin stood tall, then leaned back prying his eyelids wide as he emptied the bottle in a gush.

And Tara got to take in the wide circumference of his biceps, the powerful expanse of his shoulders. The ridges of his abs with a dark goody train into his—

"More," he called.

Yes, please. "What?"

"More water." He bent forward and coughed up another glob of mucous as Tara grabbed up the can, her eyes scanning the "In case of accidental dispersion" information:

"Rinse for minimum of twenty minutes under cool running water," she read aloud. "I've given you all I have with me."

Austin swung his finger around. "My pack is near my dog." He coughed, then called out, "Diesel, speak."

Over by the edge of the perimeter where she'd staked her infrared fence, Tara heard a deeply resonant bark.

Damn that ineffectual fence. It hadn't work at all.

"Austin, listen to me." Tara quickly gathered her things and pulling on her socks and boots. "There's no way you have enough water in your pack to flush this off you. And you'll need that drinking water to get off the mountain. You can't ingest the river water, there are too many bacteria. But you can flush with it. There's a water fall nearby."

He nodded through another hacking spree.

His face was red as if burned. She could see the demarcation around his neck where his shirt had protected his skin.

Tara reached for the shirt, but it was so toxic with fumes, that she dropped it again. That was *not* coming with them. She'd collect it a different day.

"You're going to let me lead you to your dog." She raised her voice so he could hear her past his coughing. "Then I'll take you to the waterfall. That'll fix you right up."

Without waiting for his go ahead, she grabbed his hand and pulled. Warmth radiated from his palm to hers and up her arm. It was the strangest sensation, tingly.

Capsaicin?

She led him in the direction she'd heard the bark. There sat a regal German Shepherd, his orange eyes burning bright. As he eyed her, Tara felt like he was taking her measure, to see if she was a good guy, or if she was the bad guy who'd just burned the heck out his handler. "Hi puppy. Hi good boy," she baby called.

He stomped his foot, vocalizing his concern in whines and yips as they approached.

"Diesel, friend," Austin commanded. He squeezed Tara's hand making another wave of tingles flow up her arm. "Tara, can you hand me my pack?"

Slowly, tentatively, Tara reached her hand past Diesel's open mouth to catch up the black strap. "Good boy. Nice boy."

The K9 nose chuffed in the scent on her arm, and he seemed to switch gears from warry to oddly proud as he lay down and relaxed.

Tara dragged the heavy backpack closer, then bent to pick it up, pressing it into Austin's other hand.

He let go of her while he swung the pack onto his shoulders, and the warmth and comfort she'd found in his grip disappeared. She wanted it back. Tara reached out and took his hand again. "Let's get you to the water." She scooped her GPS tracker from the side pocket of her own pack, tapping to find the flag she'd pinned for the waterfalls she'd discovered the other day.

As they stepped forward, Austin patted his thigh. Diesel swung around to walk next to him.

Three more steps and the alarm shrilled at a hundred and fifty screaming decibels.

"Oh, so now you work," she muttered angrily.

The buzzing, tweeting forest came to a startled halt. "Sorry," Tara called out. She wasn't going to dig the remote from her pack to turn it off. She'd set the timer at thirty seconds; the fauna would just have to deal for that amount of time.

Tara plowed forward. And soon enough the alarm stopped. It took a few minutes for the startled wildlife to rev up again, and then it was none too pleased. The scolding was cacophonous.

As they walked on, Austin's coughing and spitting was coming less frequently. And the ringing in her ears dissipated.

She squeezed his hand. "Hanging in there?"

"It's easiest to lead someone in single file. They're less likely to trip or fall in a hole."

"That makes sense." But she wasn't sure how to lead someone that way.

"I'm going to hang on to your pack, okay?"

Not okay, no. "Whatever keeps you safe. If I were walking alone, it would be about twenty minutes to the falls. Not very far. Well, I say that but, twenty minutes with your eyeballs on fire will feel like an eternity." *Babbling.*

Tara made a concerted effort to keep her mouth shut and put her whole focus on following her GPS tracker.

"I haven't checked in on you." Austin's voice was gruff from the hacking but still held a note of contrition. "Did you get any spray on you? Are you hurt?"

"I'm just stunned that this is happening. I had a perimeter set."

"I know. This is completely my fault. I breached your line. Apologies."

Tara scowled. "How did you know? What does that mean you breached my line?"

"Diesel tracked you from your house. And indicated."

"Whew, boy. This is a lot to take in."

"I was in St. Kitts," he explained between coughs and spits. "This morning, your mom called. When she didn't get her regular Friday call from you, she thought you were in danger. Diesel and I tracked you up the mountain. There was an infrared fence. I didn't know if it might be someone up here doing something illegal. I was just trying to make sure you were okay and not you know…kidnapped or something."

"Kidnapped and held in the Dominican rainforest? You have a SEAL brain."

"Quite possibly."

Tara could totally see her mom calling in the cavalry. Embarrassing as hell. And yet, a half-naked Austin was holding onto her backpack. Mixed bag of emotions going on for her.

"How much bear spray did you use on me?"

"Uhm. The whole can?"

"A whole can stops a charging grizzly."

"Or a rabid monkey."

"There are no monkeys in Dominica."

"Fat lot you know."

"I'm afraid to ask. Obviously, you thought you needed a heads up about something. Were you expecting to be attacked?"

"Not by a person. I don't deal with the same kind of evil you deal with."

"You deal with evil?"

Tara grinned at the overtly silver backed ape-ness of his tone. "Uhm. No. I mean, I guess in the grand scheme there are the people who put profit over planet. I consider them evil." She lifted up a branch for them to pass under. "That feels passive where what you did with the military was active. Throat slitting. Eye gouging."

"Blowing shit up."

"Matteo told me you liked that best."

"So, the story behind the bear spray was a monkey?"

"A monkey stole my cell phone. That's why I called my mom from the satellite phone yesterday. I left a message telling her I'd try calling again today when I meet my friends for dinner. But now that I'm saying that out loud, I remember that my mom has a spam filter on her phone."

"One too many 'Our records indicate that your car is out of warranty' phishing calls?"

"Exactly. She has an app that filters out phone calls from unlikely places."

"Like Dominica."

"I would guess. My cell plan is in Maryland. And my phone number is in her contacts."

"Infrared fence and bear spray. Smart. Well done."

She curved their unwieldy group of three around a curtain of vines. "Mmm. Maybe a little too well done. How are you doing?"

"It burns pretty badly. I'm not going to lie. How about you tell me a story and keep my mind on something else."

"We're not far now." She looked down at the time to destination calculator. "At this pace, ten minutes according to my GPS."

"Story?" He coughed up what sounded like a glob of phlegm and spat it into the distance.

"I'm trying to think of something that…okay, I've got one. You were a SEAL, and you know that the Navy trained aquatic animals, right? They thought that whales and dolphins could be useful partners, sort of like how they use military dogs."

"I'm not sure I ran into trained dolphins. I was a frogman. That's as close as I got to working with animals. Other than my K9 partners that is."

"Diesel's a good boy." Tara let her hand tentatively trail down to Diesel's head to give him a scratch behind the ears.

"Yes, he is."

"So, I had a friend in grad school who was doing an experiment on weaponizing a crow."

"For the military?"

Tara stepped forward. "Duck," she called out.

When she piked in front of him, sticking her butt out, Austin's hands moved to her hips. Tara wondered how she could prolong the sensation of warm vibrations that flowed through her. "Three steps." That was the most she thought she could get away with.

This was such a weird day.

Tara thought she'd need a long soak in the tub to try to figure out what was going on. The shock of seeing Austin for the first time since she was what—five? Wittingly harming another human being. And mostly, why her system lit up wherever Austin touched her. All of it seemed to overload her electrical system and was making her short out.

She came upright again. "Okay, we're good."

"Why would your friend want to weaponize a crow?"

"It was his thesis. And that's when I learned that experiments in the wild can have unintended consequences."

"Yeah? Start there, what were the unintended consequences?"

"No, I'm not starting at the end of the story and backtracking. Do you read the last chapter in a book first? Watch the last five minutes of the movie then go back to the beginning? That's cheating."

"Fair. Okay start at the beginning. Thesis project...your friend says, I know what I'm gonna do, I'll weaponize a crow. And this isn't like carrying actual weaponry, correct? Like a carrier pigeon with messages in wars of yore?"

"Wars of yore?" She switched to her pirate voice. "Arr. Ye olde battle pigeons?" She coughed and switched to her normal voice. "No, it was much more insidious."

"With consequences."

"Exactly. It began with my friend befriending a crow. He would bring food every day and sit and talk to the crow. Smile. Be friendly. It took a long time to build their rapport, but eventually, they were pals."

"Okay."

"Then my friend was out there one day feeding his crow friend and having a conversation when his lab accomplice came up and pretend punched my friend. My friend pretended to cry, and the crow started clawing at this accomplice's face. The accomplice ran away."

"Okay."

"That was the experiment. Would the crow defend a friend? Answer, yes. Now, on to the unintended consequences. The problem was that crows can memorize the human face and remember it for years. This poor accomplice would be walking around campus and the befriended crow would attack him. This was just some undergrad, mind you, that got some extra credit for helping with the experiment, a completely innocent guy. But from that consequential day forward, not only the befriended crow but all the crows in the flock would target this guy for retribution."

"What now?"

"They learned what his car looked like, and they chose that as their toilet. Every day they'd all go over and poop on his vehicle. Or snatch his hat. Or fly at him screaming, talons spread. It got to the point where the poor guy walked around campus hiding under an umbrella. The flock kept it up year after year—they didn't forget him over summer break. Eventually, he graduated and moved away."

Austin bent over laughing, then coughed up more phlegm and spat it out.

As they paced forward, Tara checked her GPS. "We should be at the falls in the next minute or so. I can hear the water. This is a stump. Step high and over." She turned and caught his elbow, guiding him. Going for the tingle. Okay, that could become addictive. "Can you see at all?"

"I'm trying not to get air on my eyeballs. It's pretty intense. Squinting like this I get the major shapes."

She stood in front again, and he took hold of her pack. "Would Diesel get you out of here if I wasn't helping?"

"Following our scent trail down the mountain, he'd keep me going in the correct direction, get me around obstacles. I'd have had to crawl on the ground next to him. On the way up, we jumped over a shallow river with a waterfall. I think that's where you're going now. I'd get that far and be able to fix myself up. But this is a good experience to have."

"What?"

"I'll to talk to Reaper—our trainer—about this situation and see what he says. Our dogs are highly intelligent. If we aren't always teaching them new skills, they get bored and mopey. This might be a good thing to train."

Pushing through the wide-leaved plants, Tara arrived on a rock outcropping. "Here. We're here." She maneuvered him over to the waterfall. "Probably easiest if you get into the pool. It isn't deep. Up to your hips, maybe. Then just walk under the falls. The velocity isn't too intense. I'll time you."

He sat down and shucked his pack.

"I'm so, so sorry," she whispered.

"Today, as I said, was entirely my fault. If I had stood at a distance and called your name, there wouldn't have been an incident." He unlaced his boots and tugged them off. His socks. "It taught me a lesson that I'm sure will serve me well." He stood and put a hand on his belt. "I'm wearing boxer briefs. Would it be okay if I got out of the pants before I get in the water?"

"Of course, take them off. I'm not modest by any means." Yes, in fact, Tara was modest, but, hey, she just needed Austin to be comfortable, right?

And now she got to see the length of his legs and the shape of his thousand-squat-a-day butt and thighs as he stepped into the water.

She plopped down to pull off her own boots. "I, uhm, think I lost the thread of our conversation. Let's get you positioned under the waterfall." She tugged at her socks. "We can both cool off," she whispered to herself, stepping into the shimmer of water.

12

Tara Alvarez

Saturday, Dominica

TWENTY MINUTES UNDER THE WATERFALL GOT AUSTIN together enough that he could get down the mountain without her assistance. Which was fabulous…and disappointing.

Most of the hike was in silence.

Pacing ahead of Austin, Tara kept fishing around in her brain for a topic. But honestly most of her friends were in the same field, so they had science to talk about. And all she had from her own life's experience over the last seven months was worm related.

Worms just weren't normal-person conversation fodder.

Through the foliage, Tara could now see the red roof of her house. They'd be down in a few minutes, and she finally remembered something to say. "Matteo told me your dad passed. I'm sorry."

"I'm not." He said it so softly that she barely caught it.

"Oh." She walked a few steps. "That must be its own bad feeling. It sounds like you missed out on an important relationship." She pulled in a breath, feeling awkward. "Heck, my dad left when I was a baby, so what do I know about fathers?"

"It's fine. My dad and I didn't see eye to eye."

He didn't seem to be put out, so Tara decided to ask. "How so?"

When Austin didn't reply, she added. "One story to help me understand."

"Okay." They walked a few paces. "The first one that comes to mind was a day when Dad and I were driving down the road in his work van. We passed a guy who was hitchhiking. It had started to rain. My dad pulled over."

"That was kind of him."

"I was surprised as hell. It would be unlike my dad."

"He was big like you?"

"Yes."

"Strong like you?"

"Yes."

"So, he wouldn't have been worried about picking up a hitchhiker in the rain."

"He wasn't afraid of anyone or anything."

Like father like son, she smiled and nodded. Since Tara was leading the way, Austin would miss the smile, but since he could see now, he'd catch the nod.

"I remember a flash of lightning and the thunder just sort of rolled across the sky. The guy got up to the passenger side door and put his hand on the handle. And my dad put the van in gear and drove on down the road. I stared out the back window at the hitchhiker feeling ashamed. The sky opened and dumped on that guy. I remember the temperature dropped suddenly from T-shirt weather to me shivering in my seat. I couldn't imagine how miserable that guy was out there."

"Could have been life threatening wet and cold like that with no shelter."

"Worse than that. Dad gave that guy hope, and he snatched it back."

"Purposefully?" Tara's brows knitted together. She couldn't imagine. "It wasn't a mistake?"

"No mistake."

Tara clenched her stomach muscles. "Was he physically abusive toward you?" she whispered.

"Nah. That would have taken too much energy. No, he never physically hurt me."

"But emotionally?"

"Let's just say that I developed some callouses. I'm not sure if they serve me or not."

"Balance this out for me because my heart is aching for teenage-you. One nice thing that happened after you moved away."

"That's an easier one. Did you know that every year on my birthday until I left for the Navy, and it was no longer possible, your mother baked me a cake?"

"What?" She stopped and turned to look at Austin.

"Every year. My favorite cake with my favorite-colored frosting. She froze it and sent it overnight to my neighbor's house, old Mrs. Tate. She's dead now. She was ancient when I moved to that neighborhood."

Tara held her breath. "Did your dad ever find out?"

"Mrs. Tate said that some things were sweeter when they were kept secret. How your mom made contact with Mrs. Tate and worked that out with her, I never knew. Didn't think to ask at the time. At Christmas, even though I was a teen, there was always a stocking with little things she thought would bring a smile—candy, gift cards, a letter. She'd send me phone cards so I could call Mateo whenever I wanted. She just wanted me to call from Mrs. Tate's house was all. She showed up for the ceremony when I finished bootcamp."

"I remember her going."

"Yeah, she's a very special woman, your mother. I still talk to her at least once a month when I'm someplace that has a phone. You didn't know any of that?"

"No." Tara turned and moved through the tree line. "I knew you and Mateo talked. Mom never said."

Diesel had his nose to the ground and pushed in front of Tara. They must have reached a spot that overlapped the direction he and Austin took as they made their way up the mountain, and he found the trail.

"I remember your mom," Tara said in return. "Flashes of her—curly hair, cigarette. I remember her standing at the mailbox in a blue coat, laughing. She was pretty. She always wore lipstick."

"Yup. Long, long time ago."

They were in her yard, up to her front steps, and with a twist of her key, they were through her front door.

"Why don't you come in and get cleaned up and rested before you try to drive. I want to make sure you haven't damaged your eyesight before you tackle that road of mine." She smiled.

"Probably a good plan."

"The bathroom is through here. I can toss your clothes into the machine. I think I have a t-shirt around that'll fit you."

"I have a change of clothes in my pack. I just didn't want to put them on until I got hold of some soap."

"Still, let me wash your things so you can pack them to go back to St. Kitts." Yeah, it wasn't lost on her, Tara was trying to delay his departure. She pushed the bathroom door wide. "The next time I'm up at work, I'll collect your uniform shirt for you." She wriggled past him in the hallway. "I'm going to get you some dish soap while you get the water going."

"You know about dish soap?" He moved into the bathroom and sat on the toilet to untie his boots.

"Cuts the capsaicin oil. Yes," she called over her shoulder, moving toward the kitchen.

"You've been sprayed before?"

She bent over to grab the soap from the cabinet. "I've studied a lot of chemistry."

"Ah, yes."

He was in the shower when she got back.

The shower curtain was opaque white from the chest down, clear at the top. There stood Austin Mace in all his glory, looking straight at her as he rubbed shampoo into his hair, the bubbles sliding down his pecs.

That view was going to seed every sex dream she had for the rest of her life.

Tara cleared her throat then slid her hand into the shower to hand him the degreaser.

"Appreciated."

Moving to the linen cabinet, Tara snagged a towel and laid it on the sink. "Listen, I have some friends who came onto the island last night. They were doing research out in the Indian Ocean and are borrowing a colleague's boat, doing some touring in the Caribbean for vacation."

She bent to gather his clothes.

"This is with the Trifalgar Working Group?"

Tara paused hugging his clothes to her chest. "How would you know that?"

"Iniquus has contracts with DARPA affiliates. We go in and scoop them up if there's a disaster scenario. In order to know who might need help, we keep track of their locations. Trifalgar scientists coming in from the Indian Ocean was a bullet point on our area report."

Tara was suddenly horrified. "How many of your team came with you? Am I on that list?"

"They were checking on that when I left, so I don't know if you're covered by a security contract or not. Two of my team-mates came with me to Dominica with their K9s. I went in search of you. The other two are conferencing with emergency management to plan a training session. Now that I know you're safe and sound. I'll have Iniquus call your mom from the States to let her know you're okay. I'll reach out to them as soon as I get back to the hotel."

"Thank you. When I left a message for her yesterday, I said I'd try to call again from my friend Pria's sat phone tonight."

"That would probably be good."

"Are you here long?"

"We'll fly back to St. Kitts in the morning to join up with the other members of our team. There are seven team members down in the islands."

"Ah, well, if you'll be here over night. Do you and your two teammates want to meet my friends?" She bit her lip and crossed her fingers behind her back. "Right now, the gang is out scoping out the site where Trevor is shooting his movie tomor-row. We're planning to meet up for a late dinner. I would love for you all to join us. It's the least I could do, invite you and your teammates to make up for today."

"My fault, remember? Please stop beating yourself up. That sounds good to me. I'll have to work something out when I get back to the hotel. We have the K9s."

"They're staying at Blue Horizon near their dock."

"Same."

She should leave the bathroom and have this conversation when he was dressed. And yet, her feet weren't cooperating.

"We're meeting at the hotel restaurant, Tikki Torch at eight thirty." She forced a step toward the door. And with her back to him, Tara finally got the courage to ask, "Real question here, Austin. My mom called and said she hadn't heard from me." She put her hand on the knob and twisted. "You knew about the cable." She pulled the door open. "You could have just said, 'let's wait a few days and if you don't hear from her once the cable's fixed, I'll call the authorities on the island and have them check it out.'"

"I could not have done that. No."

"But—"

"No buts. Pick another topic."

Her eyes stretched wide. Wow. Cement.

"Okay." She stepped into the hallway. "I'll stick your clothes in the washer." Then pulled the door closed.

"Tara, I apologize for my tone," he called out. "It's crazy seeing you after all these years. Grown up. I guess it's bubbling up a timeline of memories I thought I'd packed away."

"It's okay, I'll see you when you get out."

Such different viewpoints.

Tara was thinking hot and bothered thoughts, *come out of that shower, and take me to bed,* thoughts.

And in return, all she seemed to be doing for Austin was opening old wounds.

Now, didn't that just suck?

13

Tara Alvarez

Saturday, Dominica

After Austin and Diesel left, Tara lay on her bed, watching the fan cast shadows as it slowly spun overhead.

Coyote, you trickster card, next time I see you in my morning's pick, I'll pull the pillow over my head and hide under the covers all day long. No venturing out for me on coyote days.

That's what she wanted to do now—stay in bed and push away the inner dialogue that had her reviewing everything that had happened that day.

Tara was worried about Austin's eyesight driving back to the hotel. When he left her house, his eyes were blood shot and red rimmed.

He was stoic; Tara would give him that. He hadn't hollered once.

Tara had moved one of Mrs. Joseph's peppers from the fridge to the countertop about a month ago, then, without washing her hands, had inadvertently touched her eye. Just that had made Tara scream in pain. Mrs. Joseph poured goat's milk over her face and that calmed things right down.

Until that moment, Tara had forgotten the magic of goat's milk. Didn't matter, she didn't have it in her fridge to offer up as capsaicin balm.

He was *so* nice to her.

So…brotherly.

No, that wasn't right. Her real brother, Matteo, would have shouted his head off at Tara.

Austin was so big-brother's-best-friendly.

Or maybe, he was so "your mom was kind to me, and I'm doing a payback".

It was probably a combination of the last two, but it had nothing to do with her. Austin hadn't seen her for over twenty-five years and would only know about her through second-hand stories.

Twenty-five years. Wow, that was a long time.

Didn't matter, Tara obviously still had a crush on the guy. She was still tingly, hot, and bothered from seeing him.

The alarm jangled on her nightstand, telling Tara it was time to head down to Blue Horizon to hang out with Pria until dinner with the gang. With a groan, she reached out to slap the old-fashioned wind-up clock that came with the house as a part of the décor. She looked forward to getting a phone (when the internet lines were fixed, and she could access her account) and a less jarring alarm tone.

Tara wasn't sure her ego was up to seeing Austin again and being treated like Matteo's little sis.

～

TARA HAD MOVED from the bed at her house to the bed in Pria's hotel room. She leaned back against the headboard and hugged one of the pillows. "The other two guys that Austin's got with him are named Ash and Bear."

"Ash and Bear?" Pria sat cross-legged on the comforter, dragging a brush through her long black hair. "Unusual. Are those family names?"

"All I know is Ash has K9 Hoover, and Bear has K9 Truffles. I've never met them. Austin, on the other hand, I've known all my life." Tara shook her head. "Not all my life. I knew him when I was tiny and then he moved away. But Mom made sure that Austin and Matteo stayed close."

"Besties." Pria smiled.

"Do men say besties? Austin was a SEAL. They have some other term." Tara looked at the ceiling. "Swim pals? No, that's not it. I forget what Mom told me."

"And he's here in Dominica because?"

"Of my mom."

Pria jutted her face forward, scrutinizing her friend. "What was that?"

"What?" Tara held her eyes wide and innocent.

"You're bright pink."

"I am not," Tara scoffed. "It's warm in here."

"You're flushing like a 1930s movie star who's going to faint from falling in love."

Tara rolled her eyes. The last thing she needed was Pria in a mood, sticking her nose where it didn't belong. "Stop."

"I most certainly will not." Pria squinted at Tara. "What is going on with you? Who is this Austin guy?"

"Like I said, friend of my brother's."

"Better yet." She wrapped her arms around her knees and grinned. "The forbidden little sister trope."

Tara held up a finger. "Stop. And I mean it. I'm just embarrassed. Matteo and Mom must have pulled the poor guy out of bed with a crack of dawn phone call."

"Wait, I don't know what's going on here. Your mom? And don't military guys get up then anyway? Five o'clock drill sergeants becoming a habit?"

"He's out of the military now." Tara grabbed a second pillow to hug. "Okay, Pria, picture this—Austin, Matteo's best friend, was hanging out on St. Kitts. Mom got all freaked out about the communications challenges with the internet cables severed and calls him in a panic over my safety. Austin jumps in a plane and flies to Dominica, figures out a vehicle, and hoofs it up the side of a mountain by the time I was finishing lunch. I was lying there in the sun—trying to do a Dr. Masami, really-this-angst-is-joy-mind-bender act—when Austin tickled my bare foot. Startled, I flipped over and blasted him full in the face with an *entire* can of bear spray."

Pria's hands squeezed her cheeks. "You did not."

"I most certainly did." Tara rolled to her side and propped her head on her hand. "This supper tonight is me trying to make up for that. If his face looks burned to shit, that was my doing. Please don't say anything to him. Maybe it'll look like a sunburn."

"No wonder you're blushing. Yeah, sorry for the misunderstanding. I'd be mortified, too. I mean 'hide me under a rock, you couldn't drag me to dinner with a herd of horses' kind of embarrassed."

"Thanks for your support and understanding," Tara deadpanned.

Pria pressed her palms into the mattress. "Well, you certainly can't go to an apology dinner looking like that."

"Like what? Comfortable?"

"Exactly. You're going to have to get polished up as

penance." Pria danced her way over to her closet. "I like this song."

"No, to the polishing. Yes, to the music."

One at a time, Pria assessed the dresses in her closet, then slid each hanger to the side.

Tara wondered how many suitcases Pria had brought up for their week's stay in Dominica.

"So where did this surprise encounter go down," Pria asked, "your house?"

"Out in the field."

"Wait." Pria turned to look at Tara. "How did he find you in a rainforest?"

"Diesel is a tracking dog and followed my trail."

"Oh yeah sure, the hunky ex-SEAL and his wonder dog hunt you down quite literally, thinking they were coming to your rescue, and you spray them in the face." Pria turned toward Tara. "I'm assuming he's hunky. In my imagination, he's Thor."

Yes, he was hunky, but Tara decided to ignore that last part. "I didn't spray *them*. Diesel was away from the stream."

"Thank goodness for small favors." Pria turned back to her hunt through the closet.

"Amen." Tara climbed from the bed and went to stand near Pria, pressing her back against the cool wall, waiting to see what Pria would come up with.

Pria had excellent taste.

When they'd been roommates all through under-grad then grad school, Pria had styled Tara, which was probably how Tara ended up in a relationship with someone like Neils. Neils was always much more materialistic and concerned about outward appearances than Tara was.

One good thing about dating Neils was that Tara got the opportunity to see how other people lived. From that, Tara decided that she was content just being out in nature. If she had enough money to pay bills and travel, that was all she wanted.

Tara framed the time she dated Neils as a *growth period*.

Pria pulled out a neon orange dress, holding it up for Tara's inspection.

"No. That's entirely too bright for my comfort. It would look great on you. On me, I'd look like a traffic cone."

Since it was going to be in her face over the next week or so, Tara decided to go ahead and get the Neils-Pria dating situation out in the open. She started awkwardly with, "Why do you like my ex?"

"He's pretty," Pria said distractedly.

Tara tucked her chin and raised her brows. "To be honest, I don't like pretty boys. Not all—but in my experience most—feel entitled."

Pria pulled out a cocktail looking dress, scowled, and put it back on the rod. "You dated Neils for three years."

"True. But not because he was pretty."

Pria paused her search to look at Tara. "Is Austin pretty?"

"Too manly to be called pretty. Rugged maybe."

"Yummy?"

Suddenly, Tara felt territorial, and she didn't want Pria to hear it in her voice, so she moved the conversation back to the ex. "I dated Neils because he was smart. Athletic. Curious. I just didn't realize that his curiosity meant sleeping with every woman he came across. He swore we were monogamous."

"Even when you went away for months on end?"

"We did...we...I thought we had a system for taking care of our needs. Regardless, if I was in town, out of town, heck just next door for an hour or two, he was finding some woman and banging one out."

Pria held out a dress that looked like a tropical garden. A square neckline, poof sleeves, and a baby doll cut to the skirt.

"I knew Austin when I was five," Tara said. "I don't want him to think of me as a preschooler."

Pria pressed the hangar into Tara's hand, and Tara held it against herself. She looked down. "It's really short," Tara said as Pria turned back to the closet. "Maybe something else?"

"Looking…And just so you know, it wasn't you specifically that made Neils act that way. He's still a player. I think he's slowed down a bit. He'd have to. We're out on the research vessel most of the time. I'm the only woman."

"Mmm."

"I don't care if he has other partners," Pria said. "People say I should, but I don't."

"You do you."

"Mostly, that's how it works." Pria laughed as she bent over and picked up a pair of pink sandals. "But sometimes I like someone else to do me." She popped her brows at Tara.

"And with that, this conversation is done."

"I think that dress is the best we're going to do," Pria said fingering the hem. "It looks different on. The fabric is like butter. It'll skim your curves and float in the breeze. Just try it." She reached for Tara's elbow and turned her to the bathroom. "Moving on from sex. What are you looking for in a guy these days?"

"Kindness."

"That's it?" Pria flipped on more lights as she followed Tara into the spacious bathroom.

"It covers most things." Tara hung the dress on the curtain rod. "Kindness to the planet, to animals and people, kindness to self, which means taking care of one's mental and physical health."

"Nothing else?"

Tara reached down and pulled off her tank dress, hooking it on the towel rod. "Courage."

"Yup."

"And curiosity." Standing barefooted in her matching lacey bra and panty set, Tara knew Pria would notice. It was the style Tara called her "date night foundations," too itchy for everyday wear.

"Though curious in a kind way," Pria said. "Not in a Neils's sexually curious way."

"Exactly." Tara pulled the other dress over her head as quickly as she could. But when she'd wrestled the skirt down, the laughter in Pria's eyes told Tara she hadn't been fast enough, and Pria knew that Tara was hoping for a little attention that night.

It was generous of Pria not to poke fun. "Kindness, courage, and curiosity. That's it?" she asked.

"My top three."

Pria popped her eyebrows. "From what you said about Austin riding to your rescue, he seems to have those qualities."

"Yes, and I'd be down with seeing if we might fit as a couple." She smoothed the fabric down, then gathered her hair, and turned for Pria to zip her up. "He, though, last saw me when I was five."

"He was kind back then?"

"And courageous and curious." When the zipper was up, Tara turned to face Pria. "I always dressed up like a butterfly when he was around so he would think I was beautiful and graceful."

"You thought the word graceful when you were five?"

"Looking back, that was what I tried to convey."

Pria left the room and called over her shoulder. "How much older is he than you?"

"Seven years? Seven and a half?"

"That's not much."

"Now, it's not. As a thirty-year-old woman, thirty-seven in a man is good. But I was five when he was twelve."

"Yeah. That would be wrong." Pria came back in with a pink necklace that matched the shoes that she'd dumped on the floor. She extended it to Tara.

Looping it around her neck, Tara examined herself in the mirror and decided she liked the look. She bent her head to clasp it. "And I had known him since he moved in next door when I was three. Out of diapers, mind you, but still peeing down my leg on occasion."

Pria shrugged. "Some men are into that."

"You are so gross."

"Earlier today…what kind of vibes did he give off?" Pria pressed her hip into the counter. "Is he interested in you?"

"Nope. It's the same as it always was. Unrequited. I'm in the permanent 'my best friend's little sister' corner. I think there's some bro code about such things."

"So I'm told."

"Or there's always the possibility that I'm not his type."

"Have you seen his type? Who does he date?"

"When he was thirteen, he was dating Rosie Testin. When they kissed, I used to cry. She lived two doors down. But then Austin's mom died."

"When he was just thirteen? Wow. Tragic."

"Overdose."

"Shit. That's rough. What happened to him?"

"He moved away to live with his father in Rhode Island."

"But he's Matteo's best friend? Still to this day?"

"Absolutely. He's going to be Matteo's kid's godfather."

"Bethany hasn't popped yet?"

"Any minute."

The music stopped. "This is an all-island news alert. A vervet monkey is being tracked in Dominica."

"Changing the subject to Trevor's project for a second," Pria said.

Tara held a finger to her lips. "Hang on. I want to hear this about the monkey."

"Authorities are advising all residents and visitors in Dominica be on the lookout for a vervet monkey. Reports indicate that a group of criminals are functioning on various Caribbean islands. After catching baby monkeys on St. Kitts and Nevis, this group is training the monkeys as thieves. The criminals are focusing on tourists, however, until authorities trap the monkey in Dominica, please secure all electronics including phones and cameras, as well as small purses and wallets. If you see the monkey, call the non-emergency number to alert the police. Rumors of illnesses such as monkey pox or rabies have not been confirmed. Authorities believe that disease is highly unlikely. However, do not approach the monkey. Call the authorities. Thank you. And now for a drumbeat to get your feet moving, let's enjoy some reggae."

"That's the monkey that stole my phone," she told Pria.

Pria moved out of the bathroom. "I saw a monkey in the lobby when we were checking in."

"The monkey is in this hotel?" Tara was sitting on the toilet strapping on Pria's sandals happy that they wore the same size. "Did he have a phone with him?"

"Not that I noticed."

Pria showed up dressed in a sleek black sheathe and gold flipflops.

"It makes sense that he was here, though, surely the thieves would train the monkey to go where the tourists hang out." Tara stood in the shoes, balanced herself, then twirled. "What do you think? Cute?" Tara looked in the mirror and smoothed the front of the dress. "I can totally rock this dress."

"Not with your hair like that you can't." Pria moved to the

counter. "This dress calls for curls and makeup. Balance it. You can't be happy from the neck down."

"I'm happy all the way up." Tara batted her eyes with a pasted on cheesy smile. "If I curl my hair, I'll be late for dinner."

"A few minutes. We'll save you a seat." Pria plugged the curlers into the wall.

"But you don't know the men. That would be weird."

Pria reached across Tara, dragging her makeup bag over and began to fish through. "Do you know the men?"

"No. Just Austin."

"I'll keep Austin entertained. He'll be the guy with the dog. Right?" She laid out a blusher, some eyeshadow, and a lipstick.

"Possibly with facial burns."

Pria caught Tara's gaze in the mirror. "You owe the guy a clean and pleasant you. Not Jane of the jungle." She held up a mascara. "Brand new. Take it with you when you're done. I have another one on the boat." She zipped up the bag. "I'll be the hostess with the mostest.

I'll sit near Austin and figure out just why, when your mama put up the bat signal, lover boy jumped on his boat—"

"Plane."

Pria canted her head. "Yellow amphibious plane? There's one down from our boat at the dock out front."

"I didn't see it. All I know is that Austin piloted in, and Ash is going to fly it back. Everyone needs to practice. Let's be clear here." Tara's voice turned stern. "Austin is my brother's best friend. *Not* lover-boy. Please, Pria. He was so nice to do this for my mom, don't make this uncomfortable for him."

Pria stood there, mouth hanging open.

Picking up the brush, Tara looked past her elbow. "What?"

Pria shook her head and clamped her jaw back shut.

"Pria, what?"

"Nothing." She pressed her lips together and smiled. "You look totally cute. I'll see you down there in what? Twenty minutes?"

"Yeah, yeah. Twenty. You'll be nice?"

"Extra special nice with whipped cream and a cherry on top."

Pria slid her key card into her purse and left.

With a scowl, Tara stepped out of the bathroom and stared at the closed door.

What the heck was that last bit about?

14

Tara Alvarez

Saturday, Dominica

FROM THE LOBBY, TARA COULD SEE TREVOR TELLING A STORY like only Trevor could. His full-bodied animation was the result of years on the stage.

There went his hand, rolling like an ocean wave. That was invariably followed by a—yup, there it was—hip bump.

Pria was the recipient.

If Trevor made that motion in the air any man, woman, or child needed to be ready for the hip bump that followed.

To Tara, it was an act of inclusion, pulling the listener into the dynamics of the conversation. A moment of happy. A micro dance break often injected into fraught moments and sometimes followed by, "We're all gonna die, better get our party on."

Trevor held a Master of Fine Arts degree focusing on screen plays. He didn't want to do it professionally. His inheritance from his grandparents said he never had to enter the rat race. He simply took joy from writing and filming.

Their little pack of friends circled Trevor like vultures, feasting on his *joi de vivre*. They needed his optimism. Trevor was a vacation. A yang to the gang's yin.

Next to Trevor stood his husband, Dr. Jim Driscoll. Theirs was a May-September romance. Jim was the Trifalgar expedition lead, and he wore the responsibility with grace.

Jim was bald with startling white lines that radiated out from the corners of his eyes, drawn onto his face by squinting into the glare as his skin tanned under the open-ocean sun.

Trevor couldn't get his husband to wear sunscreen though he tried his best. The threats of future skin cancers were small worries for Jim. He hadn't yet found a sunscreen that he could tolerate. He said it was like wearing a whole-body condom. And he had married Trevor and dedicated himself to monogamy because he despised the feeling of condoms.

Taking another step forward, Neils came into Tara's view. He looked older. And not in a good way. Like he'd been left under the broiler a little too long and had become leathery. Tara stood there and assessed.

She was delighted to discover that she didn't feel what she had been afraid she would feel—nostalgia.

What she felt was indifference.

As long as Pria stayed happy that was. Now, if Neils hurt Pria, Tara's apathy could swing in a different direction.

"Another step, Tara, you're doing fine," she told herself.

From behind the potted plant, her heart hammered at the sight of Austin.

Austin Mace dressed for dinner was a treat to behold. Dark blue slacks, a pressed white shirt. Tanned skin. His cropped black hair had just enough length on top to have a tousled, easy-going feel. The kind of hair she could slip her fingers into as she kissed him.

Nice fantasy. Now let it go.

Tara filled with relief as she saw that Austin had no visible signs of capsaicin burn.

Austin and another man—either Ash or Bear—circled the table and pulled out chairs where Pria gestured with an open palm.

Pria guarded the seat next to her with a purse. Austin would be sitting directly across.

As Tara advanced into the open, Austin turned to catch her gaze, assessing her with a smile and a nod, and maybe a bit of confusion, then focused back on Jim. "In the Indian Ocean, did you find what you were looking for?" he asked as he sat.

"We did." Sitting at the head of the table, Jim slapped his hands together and rubbed them with enthusiasm. "I can't wait to get back in the lab to analyze our findings."

Tara made her way to the seat Pria was patting. She offered up a little finger wave to the group. Turning to the man she didn't know, Tara smiled. "Hi, I'm Tara."

He put his hand to his chest. "Ash."

Tara, slipped into her chair and pulled a napkin across her lap as Trevor said, "You're without the pooches. Pria said three men, three dogs."

"Bear had some paperwork," Ash replied. "He's ordering room service and managing our dogs."

"It gives you a bit of time to relax," Jim said. "Are you on the island long?"

"We flew in today," Ash said, "and we'll fly back out in the morning."

Jim leaned back in his seat. "Quick turn around."

"We're in the Caribbean training and wanted to check in

with our counterpart in Dominica Emergency Management," Austin said, without mentioning his rescue-Tara mission. "With the cables cut, we wanted to know if we could be of any service."

Pria squeezed Tara's knee and sent her a conspiratorial eyebrow waggle.

Tara lifted her glass of water and held it in front of her lips so she could hiss, "Stop."

"You all work closely?" Jim asked.

"With the small island communities," Ashe said. "It's good to have mutual support during difficult times. Iniquus holds contracts with various clients in the region. Training together and having cohesion is important."

"Why did you come for such a quick visit?" Pria asked with an innocent bat of her lashes.

"My mother called Austin." Far from feeling sour about Pria's bating, Tara thought it was good that they'd just get this out of the way. "When I didn't make my weekly check in phone call—"

"The cables being down," Austin added.

"Mom thought I might have been swallowed up by quicksand, or something."

"Which, in your case is reasonable," Pria said.

"True." Tara adjusted her napkin on her lap.

"There's quicksand on the island?" Jim asked.

"No." Pria leaned in to see Jim's face. "It's just that Tara was sucked into quicksand before."

"Are you being serious right now?" Ash asked. "I've never met anyone who was in quicksand."

Tara held up jazz hands and grinned.

"It was our sophomore year." Pria turned to Tara. "You ruined my favorite sweater."

"I bought you a replacement."

"Which I liked but didn't love."

"This is actually a thing?" Neils tipped his head, and Tara tried to ignore the satisfaction she felt from his great vanity—his hair—now showing signs of balding. "You fell in quick-sand? Why don't *I* know this story?"

"Tara's full of near miss stories," Trevor told Ash and Austin. "You just need to dangle a topic in front of her, and she'll tell you something harrowing. She's part cat."

A blush rose up Tara's cheeks. "I'm allergic to cats." Yes, she'd had her fair share of odd happenings. She was incredibly lucky to have survived them all. Unscathed, for the most part.

Tara hadn't decided yet if surviving her adventures meant she was charmed or if her odd collection of experiences meant she was cursed.

"How many of your nine lives have you used up, do you think?" Neils asked.

Neils. If only the 1980s fashions with their padded jackets were still a thing, maybe he could hide the chip on his shoulder. "Shh. I will not allow you to jinx me." Tara pointed over his shoulder. "Here's the server."

The waiter placed a platter of hors d'oeuvres at each end of the table.

Jim announced he'd ordered starters for everyone to enjoy. He turned to Trevor and said jokingly, "La yum."

"Delicious." Trevor reached for the tongs and began to fix a plate.

Jim focused on Tara. "Okay, Tara, let's hear about the quicksand."

"No, thank you." She smiled.

Jim sat back and crossed his arms over his chest and in his very best Henry the VIII accent said, "I am the leader and as such, I *demand* a story."

"My liege." Tara circled her hand in the air and gave a

deferential bow. "It basically goes: I fell in quicksand and broke up with my then boyfriend."

"Where was this, Borneo?" Austin asked.

"No. Virginia. I was on a foxhunt of all things."

"Why don't I know this story?" Trevor asked.

"Because it's a stupid story. Quicksand isn't like you see it in the movies—well this wasn't."

"I saw a meme about that." Trevor wrapping his hand behind his neck. "It says something like 'Saturday morning cartoons made me think that quicksand was going to be a much bigger hazard in my life.' And then I had to get Jim to explain what a Saturday morning cartoon was. Apparently, when Jim was a kid, the parents would sleep in, and the children would roll out of their beds and sit around in their pajamas, watching cartoons on enormous box televisions, eating cereal out of the box."

Jim pressed his lips together as Trevor called attention to his age compared to everyone else at the table. "Tara, the story?" Jim raised his brows.

"Yeah, Quicksand isn't like what you see in the Saturday morning cartoons, which are available on cable, by the way, and they're pretty funny. My personal misadventure began with an invitation to a foxhunt." She skated a hand out. "Not real foxes. A fox scent was dragged around. There were hounds and trumpets. People in top hats on horses. It was picturesque."

"You were riding?" Ash asked.

"Not on a horse. We were in a car with eight people crammed in, trailing the hunters. Just us and the back view of the horses. It went on for a very long time. *Very* long. The people in the car were using this as an occasion to drink alcohol. It was quite a lot of alcohol for nine in the morning. Eventually, the driver—that would be my ex—stopped the car and said, 'Everyone relieve yourselves.' So, dutifully, I got out with the others. Women went down the slope on one side of the road. Men went down the other. The women were just squatting, right there in the open. They were friends. I figured this was their level of intimacy, which I didn't share. I, modestly, went behind the bush. Very quickly, I was up to my shins in quicksand. I couldn't pull my feet out. When I tried, I sunk lower. It took me until I was up to my knees, to realize my predicament. The first thing I did was to struggle my pants back up."

"Priorities," Pria said. Reaching up to adjust the tiny gold nostril hoop that added to her exotic flare.

"Absolutely. Can you imagine the mortification? Anyway, I did the best I could to dress as I screamed for help. The women did nothing but point and laugh. The men didn't arrive to help."

"No?" Trevor's brows pulled together.

"They thought we were pulling a gag. Eventually, when I was up to my hips in mud, I convinced everyone that I was in quicksand. That's when a horse and rider trotted up and offered to tie a rope around me and drag me out, like a heifer that fell in a ditch."

Trevor gasped, "You didn't let them do that, did you?"

"No, that would have been like being drawn and quartered." She leaned in to see Jim. "And my liege, I wasn't of the mind to be thus tortured."

Jim chuckled. "Rightly so."

"In my first-year dorm, one of my group of friends' favorite brain cleansers was a survival board game. I had played enough times to know that quicksand has enormous suctioning force. You can't be pulled out of it." She looked around the table. "You know, I'm very grateful for that game. It's helped me escape my share of near disasters."

"And Tara is nothing if not a near disaster," Neils deadpanned.

Pria dipped her fingers into her water glass, reached out her arm, and flicked droplets at Neils. "Be nice."

"This is in Virginia?" Austin reaffirmed.

"Yes, the area we were visiting was perfect for it. Quicksand forms when sandy sediment, in a confined space, is saturated with water especially when there's clay underneath. That year, it had been a very rainy April. I was down in the bowl of land I'd crouched in. At any rate, once in, the way to get out is never to be pulled. You could tear your legs right off from the strength of the suction you'd create. I just needed them to lay a log in front of me and hold my hands while I wiggled and lifted bit by bit."

"Did you escape with your pants?" Neils asked.

"I did. But they were covered in mud. My date didn't want me in his car, but we were too far from the mansion for me to walk back. So, he put me in his trunk, leaving it open, of course. Now, it was April, mind you, and a very chilly morning. I had been in the quicksand for well over an hour."

"You were probably hypothermic," Ash said.

Tara touched her nose and pointed it at him. "Exactly. Another man on a horse arrived. He happened to be a doctor." Jabbing a finger into the air, Tara lowered her voice to imitate the rider. 'This woman is hypothermic. She must be warmed at once.' And he handed my date a horse blanket that smelled very strongly of wet wool and old sweat. My date handed it to me."

"In the trunk?" Trevor asked.

"Yes. Everyone else climbed into the car and warmed themselves with the heater."

"What?" Trevor gasped again.

"Trunk," Tara said. "Ah, but the nightmare wasn't over, yet. We get to the mansion, and they don't want me to go in."

"Mud," Jim said.

"Exactly."

"Your life was at risk." Trevor's voice was indignation piled on indignation.

"To be fair, the owners had to weigh my life against the possibility to damaging their seventeen-hundreds-era wooden floors. The floors won out. I was sent to an outbuilding that had a tub. The car people wanted me to get into a hot bath. But they were all there, hanging out and drinking."

"You would never undress in front of strangers," Pria said.

"I was purple with cold, so I stripped down to my panties and shirt and climbed in."

"Modesty taking a back seat to death," Jim said.

"Exactly. So then comes in my then-boyfriend's ex, who, by the way, looked exactly like me. So much so that everyone called me her name the entire time I dated that guy."

"Eww," Trevor said.

"Exactly," Tara said. "And this woman decided that since she was a physical therapy major, that she should sit by the side of the tub and cup the hot water in her palm and pour it on my shoulder."

"But why?" Pria asked.

"No clue. So," Tara continued, "warm from the water, and not offered something else to put on, I hid behind a blanket and pulled off the rest of my clothes, wrapped my naked self into the borrowed blanket, and went to the car barefooted with my clothing—including Pria's destroyed favorite sweater, so sorry, Pria—in a garbage bag. The then-boyfriend drove by the lawn where the hunters had come in and had gathered for brunch. Boyfriend parks, turns off the engine, pockets the keys and goes to eat."

"With you in the car, naked in a borrowed blanket recovering from hypothermia," Jim said.

"Exactly." Tara was aware of how many times Austin had now heard her say naked. And if he were ever to picture her naked, this story was not the image that she wanted him to conjure.

"But he brought you a plate, at least?" Trevor asked.

"Hardly." She sipped her water and set it back down. "After a while, he got back in the car and drove me home. And that was that."

"You broke it off then, right?" Trevor asked.

"Of course, I did. No one in their right mind would stay in a relationship with a such a blazing narcissist. And there you have it, my liege." She bowed her head to Jim. "Getting sucked into quicksand, for your entertainment and dining pleasure."

The table clapped.

Tara risked a glance at Austin. His face was still bright with amusement.

"Tara," Jim said. "Promise me that you'll come with us on our island-hopping tour. We miss you and your amazing collection of stories."

"Thank you. I'll have to see. Emotionally, I think I'm at capacity. And after hearing from Sammie last week, I want to get out of the region sooner rather than later."

"We've been considering her findings, too," Jim said shifting his mood from bemused to concern. "I promised Trevor this time in Dominica to shoot the screen play he wrote. And then, we'll reassess. I want to read the new data that comes through. The last thing we need is to be out on the sea and get caught in a hurricane."

Tara turned to Ash and Austin. "Sammie is a friend of ours who is an oceanic climatologist working in the Atlantic."

"Her team," Jim explained, "developed a drone—so remote controlled from a ship. The drone is shaped like a surfboard and has a rudder system that allows the scientists to maneuver it through the water into the path of violent storms. They're tracking a system out in the Atlantic, now."

"That storm is something our team is watching, too," Austin said.

"The genius of this water drone is that the meteorologists have been flying planes to gather data for almost a century," Jim explained. "We have a fair idea about how to interpret that data. Still, it's hit or miss with the different modeling. Sammie thinks that the information that's needed is from the water."

"What is the equipment monitoring, exactly?" Ash asked.

"Temperature," Jim said. "Energy."

Neils looked over at the entry as a server came through. "Am I sitting at a table of geeks or what? Waiter!" he called then looked around the table. "If we're going down this path of science and doom, I need a drink. Who else wants one?"

Jim ignored Neils, but Tara stuck a finger in the air as a plus one. A drink after the day she had seemed logical.

Austin's brow was furrowed as he focused on Jim. "What is that Atlantic team saying?"

Jim adjusted himself in his seat. "The water's already as hot as August when the most intense storms gather over the Atlantic. The surface energy is already strong. This is their second year using the technology, and the comparative difference year to year has them alarmed."

Austin gave Jim a nod. "I'd appreciate it if you could give me Sammie's contact information," he said, "to see if my company, Iniquus, can purchase their research information."

"Iniquus is projecting a difficult season," Ash added. "That's why Cerberus Team Bravo is in the region, training and prepping."

"How does that work exactly? I see your teams at mass disasters on the news. It doesn't seem like a workable business model," Neils said. "Who's paying you?"

"Our teams keep tabs on the people that have contracts with us."

Tara leaned forward. "Iniquus is tracking all of you. They knew you'd be here before I mentioned it."

"Seriously?" Jim scowled. "Why?"

"DARPA," Tara said, referencing the U.S.'s Defense Advanced Research Projects Agency.

"We have government contracts, private industry, a lot of universities," Austin said.

"For natural disasters?" Pria asked.

"Or kidnappings, war, and unrest," Ash said. "We just evacuated a U.S. based company from Nezdolannyy."

"They got bombed down to rubble," Jim said. "Completely uninhabitable. Were you there for that?"

Tara sent a wide-eyed horror face toward Ash and Austin.

"The first couple of days," Austin said. "But we cleared everyone under our protection who wanted to get out. To answer the question of how we're paid, insurance held by our clients pays for our rescue services. After all our clients are cleared from an area, we have the team and equipment in place, so as a charitable arm of the company, we stay, free of charge to the community, and help during the initial critical time while other rescue organizations are gearing up and getting into place."

"How do you get there first?" Jim asked. "Everyone has access to the same news."

"Sometimes they have to wait for a road to be cleared or the airport runway and ports to be repaired," Austin said.

"You don't?" Jim asked.

"Our team is tactical," Ash said. "We can fast rope from helicopters, parachute in if needs be."

"That's why you came in on the floatplane?" Tara asked. "Land on the water? Throw an anchor wherever?"

"Not wherever," Austin said. "We try to avoid the sea cables." He sent a mirthful smile to Tara, then turned his attention to Jim. "Since your group is on our client list, out of curiosity—if it's not classified—what is your team studying in the Indian Ocean that would be affiliated with U.S. military research?"

15

Tara Alvarez

Saturday, Dominica

THE TABLE OF DINERS BEHIND THEM SCRAPED THEIR CHAIRS back as they got up to leave.

Jim waited for them to move on, Tara assumed so Austin could hear what Jim had to say about their work.

"DARPA is funding our research ship. We're just shy of fifty people onboard. Twenty-eight crew members, technicians, and engineers. Then there are twenty scientists. Separate groups focus on different questions." He tipped his head toward Neils. "Neils and I are looking at how to use algae to solve all of the world's woes." He popped a piece of buttered bread in his mouth.

"My husband wants to light the world with microalgae," Trevor said then clamped a hand over his mouth looking around furtively, as if he didn't want anyone to know.

Tara wondered why.

"And DARPA is involved?" Ash asked.

Pria shifted in her seat. "I'm working on bioluminescent masking technology for future *clandestine* operations." She pulled her shoulder forward, ducking her chin to shield her face, like a spy in an old-timey spy film.

"Masking like camouflage?" Austin asked.

"Right. That's Pria's expertise," Jim said as Pria adjusted her chair to let the busser come in and reset the table behind her. "But as a general explanation, there's a Hawaiian bobtail squid. Evolutionarily, it has developed the ability to hide its shadow. For DARPA, they're pretty close to having ways to camouflage large items like helicopters, for example, they have a special-ized cloth that they're testing. Downed crews can throw the cloth over their birds, and they're supposed to disappear if the enemy is at a distance. To some extent they can even replicate an invisibility cloak of sorts by using cameras to take video of what's happening behind someone and projecting them out in front. The wearer is basically a walking movie screen for what's happening behind them. One of the problems with the masking technology is—"

"That even if you hide the object or the person, they can cast a shadow," Austin stilled his knife as he sliced into his plantain, looking jazzed by the concept.

"Exactly," Pria said, popping a forkful of greens in her mouth.

Ash turned to Pria. "But this squid doesn't throw a shadow? And you think you can figure this out?"

Pria held a hand over her mouth to answer before she swal-lowed. "Hope so. That's the goal. I think I can do it with algae."

"Interesting," Austin said.

"Did you know," Trevor asked, "that at Trifalgar Working Group's main facility, they have a car that runs on algae oils?"

"That's part of our task," Jim explained. "Neils and I are on the team trying to find a way to replace the need for petroleum products. For example, our lab is developing algae into polymers that can replace plastic in 3D printing." He spread his hands wide. "I'm telling you algae is our future. We even have food scientists trying to develop algae that is marketable."

"There's big palatability issue." Trevor made a yuck face. "Very big issue there." He picked up his napkin and swiped it over his lips. "It's worse than valerian tea, and that tastes like wet dirty socks." He leaned forward. "Sorry for your appetites."

"As I have learned over many a dinner that turned bleak," Jim said, "algae topics are not an appetizing subject."

"So, you're taking a break from your research," Austin asked. "How did you pick Dominica?"

"To see me, of course." Tara smiled.

"True." Neils sawed into his octopus. "There's nothing more exciting than watching Tara dig up gold worms."

"Tara's right," Trevor said. "As soon as she took up residence in Dominica, she started sending us pirate messages. And I got a wonderful idea for a film."

Austin swung his gaze to Tara.

She covered an eye with her hand and said in her best pirating voice, "Arrr, ye land lubbers, it's time to walk the plank."

He snorted. "That's right. I remember the pirate movie was filmed here. And that's what your story's about, pirates?"

"It begins with a feint," Trevor explained. "People will *think* this is a story about sunken treasure. That's what we'll be filming tomorrow. Pria, Neils, and Jim are my actors."

"This is fiction or based on something historic?" Ash asked.

"It's a combination of a few events we'll be filming," Trevor said. "I don't want to give the gist away."

"I don't mind spoilers," Austin said.

Trevor was delighted. "Okay, so there's a whole thing about

the tragedy of sudden wealth, right? People imagine that they're rubbing Aladdin's lamp, and everything will suddenly get better. But it usually leads to tragedy. People who win the lottery, more often than not, find it ruins their lives. In my film, the successful finding of the treasure will ruin the lives of the entire crew, and everyone will die a tragic death." Trevor grinned.

Tara looked up to see four men focused their way. They pointed to the newly cleared table behind theirs, the only other terrace seating with a view of the night ocean.

One of them was the ponytail guy. He'd changed from his earlier pink pants to Kelly green. Same blue flipflops. He had a European vibe to him that wasn't unusual for the island.

He stopped and gave her a slight bow.

Tara smiled, offering a contrite finger wave.

As he slid into his seat with his back to Pria, Pria leaned in to whispered. "Tara, do you know that man? I thought you only knew the postal guy, and the Josephs."

There was no reason in Tara's mind to whisper at the table. While in her little gang, it would be fine, it felt rude in front of Ash and Austin. "Someone I ran into today. Besides the Josephs and the mail guy, it's just me and my hunt for doubloons." She held up her hands. "Don't pity me. I'll be home soon."

"You've gathered enough of your gold then?" Trevor asked.

"For now, at least. I may come back and dig after this rainy season passes. Trevor, what I really want to hear about is what you've planned for the *Onward, Ho!* tomorrow," she said, adding, "Whoever named that vessel, clearly didn't think the punctuation all the way through."

"Or he did and liked the play on words," Neils countered from behind his scotch.

"Pulling up treasure, even in the context of my project, has a paperwork process," Trevor said. "When the Dominican government signed the permits required to do this legally, we borrowed our friend's boat. He does coastal analysis in the Caribbean, which means he's all set up for our needs with dredging equipment. Sand vacuumey things and specimen trays."

"He's vacationing in our mountain-view cabin just off the Appalachian Trail as an exchange," Jim said.

"Fair trade. If you're on the sea you want the mountains. If you're in the mountains, you want the sea." Trevor rolled his eyes then gave his head a shake. "Humans always want Christmas in July."

"In this phase of the project, have you found the treasure already?" Ash asked. "Or will you be filming the search?"

"Oh, it's been found. We'll be pulling up the Queen's Treasure tomorrow." Trevor grinned.

"Where is this?" Austin asked.

"You know the place that they call Champagne Reef?"

Tara leaned in to explain. "Tourists like to snorkel there because the volcanic gasses make it look like champagne bubbles or diamonds in the water."

"Or so people think," Trevor said. "But the *real* reason is that there are *real* diamonds. Diamonds from the Queen's Treasure scattered there after the ship tried to outrun a hurricane back in 1715 during Queen Anne's wars."

"There are diamonds in the waterfall just up from my house. I showed them to Austin but of course—"

"I couldn't see them. I got something in my eyes."

Pria smiled. "We've been practicing to do this for a while. This really is going to be so much fun."

"You all deserve it after all the research work you've been doing," Tara said.

When she felt eyes on her she turned to find Austin looking straight at her, a smile in his eyes. Warmth. Tara was in danger of falling back in love with Austin Mace. Knowing he thought of her as Matteo's little sis, and Mrs. Alvarez's baby girl, those feelings would just be a future knife in the heart.

Who needed that?

Tara sent him a wink since she didn't know what else to do to break the connection. And reached for her glass.

"You're not going?" Ash asked.

"I'm almost out of time digging my gold. I need to take advantage of every non-rainy day. I'll come down the mountain tomorrow night to join in the celebration."

As Austin leaned in to whisper an explanation of the gold worms to Ash, Tara caught the eye of the server and tapped her glass.

A car stopped outside of the narrow restaurant, its radio blaring a dancing beat that vibrated base notes through Tara's bones.

Pria leaned in to talk into Tara's ear. "You can't hold your booze. One drink. One is your limit."

"Normally, true." Tara's lips were a little numb after her Mai Tai, maybe Pria was right. "Today is an exception."

"Are you still upset that you bear sprayed Austin?"

"It's honestly not that." Tara closed her eyes.

"What then?" Pria pressed.

"It's Austin. It's odd to sit near him. He is after all my first true love." The drama of the day, her drink, and Tara remembering she hadn' anything more than the bowl of cereal this morning and the dinner salad she'd picked at, she was definitely lightheaded.

The car driver turned the music up a notch for the chorus.

Pria shook her head and leaned closer. "What did you say?"

Tara sucked in a deep breath and raised her voice into Pria's ear, "Austin Mace was my first and only love."

Pria froze, eyes wide.

It was in that moment that Tara realized the car had driven on, and she, Tara Magdalena Alvarez, had just yelled that out in the middle of the restaurant terrace for all to hear.

If mortified had an exponent, that would be the correct descriptor.

Pria sent an over-wide smile around the table. "Tara has developed the habit of blurting whatever nonsensical thing comes to mind out loud. She's only around humans once a week. She's not...always..." she swallowed as she fished for the right words, "filtering for public consumption."

Tara's face heated past the blush stage as she stared at her lap. For a moment she wondered about the science behind spontaneous human combustion, and she thought that circumstances such as these might just be the catalyst.

Then Austin came to her rescue. *Of course, he did.*

"When Tara was four years old, she was the prettiest butterfly I'd ever seen. And she gave the best hugs." He caught Tara's eye. "Your loving me at a challenging time in my life was important to me, too. I've never forgotten." He raised his glass of water in a kind of salute. "It's really great to have caught up with you today."

Tara was in a deep dark well and had no idea how to climb out, even with Austin's lifeline.

A fairy in netted wings and glitter glue dancing through the forest with a frog in her hand? That was *not* where she wanted his mind. She wanted him to see her as a woman. Here and now. Grown up. And ready to be kissed.

With an abundance of courage, Tara looked up to apologize. But her lips wouldn't unseal. She gave a little shake of her head.

"I remember my first love. I was three years old," Pria offered, wrapping Tara's hand in both of hers under the table. "He invited me to play in his plastic backyard pool, Andre

Vlasenko. Black curls, soft eyes. Such a tender age to have one's heart broken by his stupid dad relocating." Pria laughed. "Ah, first loves…"

Tara was so thankful for her friend's tone.

This was a joke, a set up for a story. Tara could do a story. "My first love," she tipped her ear toward Austin, "is also—I'll have you all know—my first and only knight in shining armor story." Her lips curled into a smile. She cast a conspiratorial flick of her brow. "Once upon a time, when I was a tiny princess wandering the forest alone, Sir Austin Mace rode to my rescue and saved my life."

"Oh!" Pria turned to assess Austin. "It really is a knight in shining armor story, then. How did you do that? Do you remember this?"

"If I'd been in shining armor," Austin replied. "We would have both drowned." He leaned in toward Tara. "Is that what you're thinking of?"

"Yes." She let her gaze travel around the table. "You see, as a child I thought of myself as Mother Nature's beloved daughter. Royalty. A butterfly princess."

A chuckle warmed the table as her friends nodded.

"I would flit through the woods and commune with my subjects. Only, on this terrible day, I thought I was speaking to my regiment of warrior bees. They wanted to stage a coup and overthrow the spirits of the woods. I approached their hive with gifts of weeds that I'd gathered as a peace offering, so they would be nice bees. But they retaliated my intrusion." She slashed her hand across her body, raising her arm as if brandishing a sword. "I was so angry that I was stung when I had approached as a friend, that I picked up a stick and tried to hit the bee that attacked me."

Austin's face clouded.

"How old was this butterfly princess?" Trevor asked.

"She was four," Austin said quietly.

"I missed the bee and hit the hive like a kid at a birthday party whacking at a pinata."

Gasps rounded the table.

Tara shut her eyes as she remembered. "The pain was instant and searing. I was covered in bees." She felt the panic and pain rise in her memory. She hadn't thought about this in years. "Suddenly, I was lifted and flying through the air. I was screaming from the fire of it. Then, my jaw was pressed shut. My nose pinched. And I was a mermaid, under the water. Cold. So cold and beautifully soothing. I tried to open my eyes. But they were fat and heavy. I came out of the water, and I heard Austin yelling to me that I should take a deep breath."

Tara opened her eyes to find Austin focused unblinkingly on her.

"And because I trusted Austin more than anyone in the world, I did as he said." She pulled in a breath and pressed a fist to her chest. "And I passed out. When I woke up, I was in the hospital. Austin had saved my life." She broke the connection between them. It was too emotional, and tears blurred her vision.

She forced herself to look around the table. And swallowed.

Austin picked up for her. "Her brother called 9-1-1 while I was bobbing in the pond with Tara. And I got to take an ambulance ride to the hospital. For an eleven-year-old, that was pretty cool."

"Ambulance?" Trevor clutched his hands over his heart. "How many times were you stung?"

"Me? They estimated fifty stings." She turned. "Austin, you had what thirty?"

"Only twenty-five."

"Only." Tara's lungs were so tight that she couldn't inhale.

Austin reached across the table and caught her hand. Her

finger tingled and warmth radiated up her arm, into her chest, and her lungs released. She could breathe normally again.

He gave her hand a squeeze, then let go.

Pria picked up her glass. "Tara is here to save the world from polystyrene because Sir Austin Mace ran to the rescue." She stood as she lifted her glass. "Here's to Sir Austin Mace—his courage and gallantry!"

All of her friends stood and lifted their glasses toward Austin, in truth and jest. "His courage and gallantry."

Tara was appreciative of the curtain of bodies that hid her for a moment while she got herself back together.

"See?" Pria was overly glittery as she tried to deflect attention away from Tara's overwhelming emotions. "I told you," she said as she took her seat. "Tara has a thousand stories like that. They're easy to fish out with the right bait."

It had been a real threat to her life. Unlike the quicksand, that misadventure in the woods had been the biggest risk Tara had ever faced. And when it was happening, Tara hadn't doubted, not for one nano-second, that Austin would come racing to her rescue. It was an instinct with him.

What did it mean that he was suddenly showing back up in her life now?

And with that thought, her friends' phones buzzed.

Everyone looked up startled.

"We must be back online." Jim pulled out his phone. "That was fast. The hotel said they didn't expect it to be corrected until Sunday."

Tara leaned in to read Pria's screen.

DR. GUHA: **Everyone breathe. You have a task. Work your task. All of us are out there planting our seeds. That's all anyone can do.**

16

Tara Alvarez

Saturday, Dominica

TARA HATED WHEN HER MEDITATION CARDS WERE THIS LITERAL. One of this morning's cards had been the eight of swords—having your hands tied. It represented terror, anxiety, and psychological issues.

Hour after hour, all day long, in various shades and forms, didn't that card describe her life?

It happened with alarming consistency that the cards were right. To the point where her mother said, "It's a family gift. Or family burden. It's hard to say for sure. A bit of both, perhaps. You'll learn to live with it."

"What do you think it is?" Pria whispered.

Her question was left unanswered.

Bravo glanced around the table then their gazes swept the room as if searching out hidden threats around the sides of the pristine white columns and the potted plants.

"Our director," Tara explained. "We're about to read some piece of science that moves us a step closer to the point of no return in terms of Earth's habitability. She does this so we have a moment to clench our stomach muscles to take the blow."

"Before that news comes in, since we have a connection..." Austin swiped his phone, then handed it across the table to Tara, "Do you want to do a quick video chat, so your mom knows you're okay?"

Tara accepted his cell phone with a smile and scooted off the terrace into the grass where she'd have some privacy.

"Tara!" Her mother's expression froze into that scanning-assessing look that mothers get.

"Yup. It's me. I'm fine."

"Yes, you look beautiful. You're wearing makeup. And your hair is curled. I've been so worried."

"I know. I'm sorry."

Tara could see her mother's stress. "Momita," Tara soothed. "Thank you for your concern. If I were really in trouble, you could have saved my life. I appreciate you."

"I'm not trying to intrude."

"Of course not, mommy. You never have. Truly, it's good to know someone's out there being my guardian angel."

"He's there now, Austin? This is his phone number. When he called earlier this afternoon from the satellite phone number, he said you needed to buy a new cell phone."

"Yes, ma'am. There was a mishap. No big deal. I have insurance. When we sat down to eat—Pria and her gang are here, too—they got a text from headquarters, so we knew the cable must have been repaired. Austin lent me his phone. Now that the internet's fixed, I can get my phone replaced. Monday, when the shop is open, I can. It'll be the same number. But you can call Pria's number or this one to get me between now and then. Austin isn't leaving until the morning."

"Oh, well, if you're sitting down to dinner, you need to head back. Thank you so much for letting me see your face. I'll sleep better tonight. I've been having nightmares about you all week.

"I'm sorry."

"You know how I am. I just need to check that all my little ducklings are safe. Now, go. Have fun. Give Austin a kiss for me and tell him how much I appreciate him."

"Love you."

"Love you more."

When Tara disconnected, she felt oddly unsettled. Nightmares all week? About her? Focused on that, Tara wandered over to Austin's side of the table. "Mom said to thank you again and sends you this kiss." She bent down. As her lips brushed his cheek, her entire body lit up.

She put the phone on the table and slow walked back to her seat, rolling her lips in to stop the buzzing sensation.

As she sat, Austin pressed his fingers into the very spot she'd kissed. With a rub, he looked over at her.

Was that curiosity in his eyes? Could he have felt the same thing?

Maybe she'd left a little drool on his cheek, such was her day.

Everyone stilled as the Trifalgar scientists' phones buzzed, again.

"That'll be the reason for the heads up," Trevor said.

Tara bent over Pria's phone as they read, cheek to cheek. When she looked up the scientists were all blanched. Tara used her napkin to dab sweat from her lip and brow. "Crap."

Austin caught her eye. "What's happening?"

"This is what would be called a table of scientists experiencing a moment of existential dread," Neils said.

"Okay, I can see that." Austin's tone toward Neils said he'd had about enough of the guy's attitude.

Jim laid his phone on the table and focused on Ash and Austin. "On January fifteenth, there was a volcanic eruption under the water near Tonga. That blast was captured on satellite imagery and is calculated to have shot forty miles into the air, the highest on record. That plume is the issue. It was a combination of gases, steam, and ash."

Tara leaned across the table to catch Austin's attention. "Water vapor is a greenhouse gas. It traps heat, raising Earth's temperatures. And for the next few years, it will also worsen the ozone."

"Then things will improve?" Ash asked.

"The problem is," Neils said, "the domino effect of the higher temperatures."

"The ocean temperatures aren't just straining the marine life," Jim said. "The elevated temperatures are creating more frequent monster storms, like the ones Sammie is studying with her water drone."

"I bet we'll be needing a new cat six designation soon," Neils said. "The wind will come in and scrape everything away."

Jim turned to Ash and Austin. "Scientists projected that eruption and the outcome. Their calculations were overly optimistic. This data is grim."

"Rose colored glasses," Trevor said.

Neils held his glass high. "Might as well drink up everyone, we're headed the way of the dinosaurs."

"The things that were predicted since the late eighteen hundreds are indeed happening." Jim lifted his tumbler and considered the amber liquid in the cut crystal. "Just sooner than we expected. We thought we might have another hundred years."

"The domino effect," Neils repeated. "Increased heat begets

fires, which release carbon, which increases heat. The natural world is responding to the centuries of abuse."

"You can't blame Mother Nature," Pria said, "for swatting at the mosquito that carries malaria."

"What's the metaphor?" Ash asked. "The mosquito is man? The malaria is our activity?"

Tara, wanting to change the subject, said, "Before I came down to town for dinner—hoping to course correct from this morning's Dr. Masami exercise when I pulled the coyote card— I picked the eagle from my animal deck. What did you all get this morning?"

Pria focused on Ash and Austin to explain. "It's part of our required morning meditations as prescribed by our research group's guru of mental health, Dr. Masami." She hitched her thumb toward Tara. "The animal deck is the one that Tara likes. I use a different one, botanicals." She pointed down the table. "Jim uses a traditional tarot. Trevor isn't in the science group, but he plays along with us, using one that's gemstones. Neils uses a color deck." Pria caught Neils's gaze. "What color did you pick today?"

"Green."

Pria squinted her eyes at him and shook her head.

Tara thought there was a meaning that they both understood, but it was, thankfully, over her head.

"What does the eagle card mean to you?" Austin asked.

"I should keep my focus on the goal while I ride the air current. So, a kind of stay in your lane kind of card. My lane is to find doubloons. When I find the doubloons, I look for gold." She pointed down the table to Trevor, hoping to lighten the mood. "Trevor's lane is finding a huge cache of coins and precious gems, tomorrow."

"This is true." He smiled.

"Eagle seems apt for this moment," Pria said. "I got Stinging Nettle, go figure."

"That eagle focus is something we trained for in the military," Austin said. "We had a saying that 'there is no secret sauce.' It means that you can't trick your way to success. Success comes from focusing on a goal and figuring it out. Another thing you'll hear about is the 'three-foot world'. That's the space around us that we need to manage."

"Exactly," Ash said. "When we arrive at a disaster zone, it's complete chaos. Everyone needs help, stat. Life or death kind of help. It's easy to get overwhelmed," Ash said. "We pull our focus in tighter. We try to contribute to making one thing better. Otherwise—"

"The overwhelm sucks you down, like Tara's quicksand," Trevor said.

Pria wasn't looking well. She lifted her water goblet and held it to her forehead, muttering, "Now, isn't that the truth?"

"All right everyone." Jim clapped his hands. "This party is degenerating into a wake. What do you say we take a walk on the beach?" Jim suggested. "Get our bodies moving, shake this off. I'll sign the check. The Trifalgar is picking up the tab."

As everyone rose from the table, Tara turned her attention toward the ocean.

It was only June, the first month of rainy season in the Caribbean, and already, out at sea, thunder ominously rumbled the air.

17

Austin Mace

Saturday, Dominica

MACE AND ASH MIMICKED THE OTHERS AS THEY SAT IN THE white plastic chairs, removing their shoes and socks and placing them on the seats to collect later.

The men rolled their pants up to their knees.

Pria lifted the hem of her long skirt and looped it over the arm she used to clutch her purse.

As the party rambled down to the water's edge, Mace tried to stay close to Tara but not seem as though he was hovering.

He was definitely feeling the pull of her gravity.

Mace was thrown off balance by today. By how it felt when he stood near Tara, touched her hand. The kiss she'd planted on his cheek, when she returned his phone, buzzed his senses awake.

Like Rip Van Winkle blinking awake from his hundred-year sleep, Mace was disoriented by the shift in dynamics.

Throughout the dinner, Mace had been charmed by Tara's storytelling. The way she looked at him across the table, made emotions swim through his system. Things he'd never felt before.

Yeah, he just needed some time to get his bearings.

He wanted to call this nostalgia.

But nostalgia was what he'd experienced when he visited Mrs. Alvarez and saw his childhood home.

This wasn't nostalgia. He didn't have a word for these sensations.

But something magnetized him to Tara.

Hovering over all of this was the dark cloud of the reason for his being here in Dominica with Tara and her friends, Mrs. Alvarez's week of nightmares.

Mrs. Alvarez was the one person in his life that seemed to have a direct phone line to the ether. She kept her gifts to herself. But she pegged it *every* time.

Once, when Mace was on the naval ship, she emailed to tell Mace he should lay off his exercise routine for a few weeks and let his body heal, or he'd have a pain in the ass.

She didn't say 'ass'; she said 'bottom', on the right side specifically.

But he was newly branded a SEAL. Young. Fit. Invincible.

Mace was jogging the perimeter of the deck when his muscle detached in his right butt cheek. Surgery. PT. Had he listened to Mrs. Alvarez, he could have avoided all that.

He had hundreds of stories along those lines that he'd accumulated over the last decades.

Mrs. Alvarez had called him because of the nightmares. She was clutching at her chest.

There was a threat hanging over Tara, Mace was certain of it. He just didn't know what direction it was coming from or how to protect her.

Yeah, it was a damned big surprise when Mace found Tara singing and dancing in the clearing. That when he found her, she was perfect.

Perfect.

Perfectly fine, he amended.

He had been braced for the worst.

Mace hated that he was leaving in the morning.

Something had to be brewing, and he wanted to be here to stand in its way. To scoop her up like he had the day of the bee swarm and plunge into the cool waters with her in his arms.

He paused on that thought. Yeah, boiling it all down to the essence, Mace could stop with those last five words: *with her in his arms.*

Hell of a thought.

He'd work that out later. Right now, that guy Neils was buzzing Mace's antennae. Yeah, Mace remembered that name from stories shared by Matteo and Mrs. Alvarez. Both had seemed relieved when Tara had broken their relationship off.

It seemed to Mace, from watching body language, that Neils had moved on to date the best friend, Pria, and that Tara was fine with the shift.

Walking ankle deep through the waves, Tara stepped forward between Jim and Trevor, looping her arms through theirs. "Hey, why are you two being so cold to each other? Is everything okay?"

"Cold?" Jim asked.

"Usually, you two are very handsy. Lots of cuddling and smooching. Now, I find out from Pria that everyone has their own hotel rooms even you and Trevor?" She looked down at his left hand, then over to Trevor. "Where are your wedding rings?"

"We're in Dominica," Jim said in a hushed tone.

She shook her head, "I don't understand."

"People get arrested and charged with buggery."

The corners of Tara's lips dragged her face into a fierce scowl. "Is it a ticket and fine?"

Trevor sucked in a noisy breath. "Fines and prison sentences."

"What?" Her voice crawled up the scale. She dropped back down to a whisper. "What?"

"Up to ten years," Trevor said.

Jim shoved his hands into his pockets, which pulled Tara closer toward him. "We have to research very carefully the countries where we travel and conduct ourselves according to the laws."

"Even on the boat," Trevor added. "If we can be seen by binoculars in territorial waters, it's no-can-do with feeling my hubby up."

"While we're here in Dominica, Trevor and I have the same last name because we're cousins."

"Okay, good to know. But still, that's terrible."

"Prison is worse," Trevor said.

"So, if I grab you, Tara, and act like we're a couple." Jim tilted his head and caught Tara's eye. "You'll understand."

"Yeah, you can even kiss me if needs be. Just no tongues."

"Eww," Trevor said.

"Exactly," Tara said then sent a quick scan toward the hotel as if making sure that their conversation was completely private.

Mace grinned at their exchange. Those were companionable friends. Friends with a warm history.

Neils on the other hand, Mace had the unusual urge to slug the guy.

Especially now, as Neils fell in step beside him, distracting Mace from appreciating Tara's long legs, toned from her hikes up and down the mountain.

"So, do you like have PTSD and shit? Is that why you stopped—"

Quite the opener, this guy was smooth.

Mace sensed Ash moving up behind them, once a SEAL swim buddy, always a swim buddy. Ash must have read the body language. Mace was trained as a professionally violent man. He applied that violence to missions and necessity. He wasn't a brawler by any stretch of the imagination. Had never landed a punch unless it moved him closer to fulfilling his orders from Command. Neils might feel like an exception.

"Stopped what?" Mace asked. "Being part of the military?"

"Yeah. I mean…"

Tara turned around and shot the guy a look filled with daggers, "Neils!"

That she thought he needed her protection amused him on one level and filled him with a strange kind of joy on another.

"What? It's a simple question anyone would have." Neils's tone conveyed that "I'm going mano-a mano" crap that was part and parcel to bar scenes, when men thought they needed to take a SEAL down a peg. That PTSD jab was the opening note on an old song.

Mace decided to deescalate. "That's okay, I prefer people ask than just look at me sideways." He turned to Neils. "I left the military because my job seemed complete. I joined Iniquus straight off. At Iniquus, we're provided with ongoing support. We see a lot in our line of work."

"In battle," Neils said, "blowing shit up?"

"Look." Mace's voice was even. "I'm not talking with you about my time in the military. War stories are about real lives lost and destroyed. They aren't for sucking on like an after-dinner mint. It's disrespectful to my brothers. Not caricatures. Not characters in a movie. Real people who hoped and who suffered."

"Neils what is wrong with you?" Trevor asked in annoyance. "I hate it when you drink."

"I will say, though," Mace added. "I was in the military to serve a purpose. As ugly as it was, it was man made. Now, I deal with civilians that get hit by disasters that are mostly from nature. It's even more indiscriminate, elders, infants, doesn't matter."

Tara stopped, turning to face him, her eyes troubled.

His arms ached for her to step forward and for her to lean her head onto his chest.

He wanted her to look at him. To see that he was safe to have as a— He stopped that thought, dead in its tracks. Even in the privacy of his own mind, Mace didn't want to give volume to whatever his brain wanted to say there.

"Working in disaster zones is rough as hell. One of the things that makes Iniquus golden is that they understand it's a mental challenge to do what we do. So, they provide us with the support, and we're required—every single one of us—to participate. Sounds a lot like your system with Dr. Masami." He was watching Tara closely.

War had its toll. Rescue work, too. But so did life. He didn't know anyone who was unscathed. Heck, look at these scientists. He never thought that a lab rat would have issues like this. It never occurred to him that they were battling their own demons.

The highlighted information about ocean warming that he'd see resting on the stool in Tara's living room came to mind. The Tonga eruption. These people had clarity about the storm gathering on the horizon and what it would mean.

How hard had it been for Tara to be up on that mountain all by herself dealing with what she referred to as 'existential dread'?

She sighed and swallowed, like she could read his thoughts and was acknowledging the difficulty.

Mace fought against reaching for Tara's hands.

This was Tara, Matteo's sister.

Mace needed to queue up a different topic conversation. *This whole night had been—*

Tara blinked at him and exhaled. "Unusual."

Her timid smile warmed his whole being.

"I have another topic," she said.

Mace canted his head. Did Tara have her mother's gift? "What's that?" And if she did have that gift, had Tara heard his thoughts about her? *Shit.*

Pria caught up to them just as Tara pointed at the horizon where a bolt of lightning licked the water. "See the lightning dancing?"

Their group turned to watch.

"I'm not a fan. I love the thunder. Love it. I love it when it's warm like a blanket wrapping me in the rumble. Making my bones vibrate. And I love when it crashes suddenly and startles me, sending a shiver up my spine. But I am very much not a fan of being hit by lightning."

"Hit?" Trevor asked. "Wait. Did you just say you were you hit by lightning? What is that, like a one in a bajillion chance?"

"That explains so much," Neils said.

Mace felt his posture shift, his muscles tighten. Then he felt Ash clap a hand on his shoulder and give it a squeeze.

"Not exactly hit. Just sort of kinda hit. And it was hair-raising." And she laughed that tinkling happy laugh that Mace had wanted to illicit from her before he scared the living heck out of the poor woman, and he got bear sprayed. Ash and Bear had laughed their heads off when he got back to the hotel. The irony of a guy named Mace getting maced.

"Were you digging worms?" Ash asked.

"No, no, I was a kid. Maybe a freshman in high school? I can't tell you exactly, suffice it to say, it was long enough ago that my mom had a home phone with a cordless receiver. I was hanging out, talking to a friend of mine when ball lightning flew through the window."

Mace was aware that she'd trotted this story out to protect him from Neils's goading. Mace would pay attention to that, Tara used stories to deflect. A strategic tool. She'd done it with the bee story after she'd told Pria—and the whole restaurant—that she'd loved him.

Loved *him*.

As a preschooler, past tense of that verb, Mace reminded himself. Days gone by.

"What?" Pria squeaked.

"It looked like something in a superhero movie. It was literally a white-hot ball. It flew right past my face while I was talking on the phone."

Trevor wrapped his hand around the top of his head. "What did you do?"

"Screamed."

Mace nodded. "Sounds reasonable."

"The lightning ball hit the phone, and it exploded, then the lightning bounced off the antenna and angled into the kitchen and blew up the fridge."

"Wait, I vaguely remember this story. The fridge blowing up part of your story," Mace said. "I don't think Matteo told me you were hit."

"Not hit. It flew past my face. Close enough that it burned my eyebrows off, and I was blistered on my forehead. I smelled like burned chicken feathers."

"How would you know what those smell like?" Neils asked.

And Mace felt as Ash pat-patted his shoulder, again.

Yeah, something about Neils was a red cape in the bullring to Mace.

"In my imagination, I smelled like what I think burned chicken feathers would smell like." Tara's tone was even.

She could handle herself.

Mace was vaguely amused with his own Neanderthal reaction. Again, he blocked the part of his brain that wanted to say something possessive. That didn't mean that Mace wasn't fully mindful that those thoughts were gathering force in his system.

He was equally aware that they were meritless. *Not gonna happen.*

Three of Mace's brothers on Team Alpha had found their wives in the last year. Ares, Bravo's leader, had popped the question to his now fiancée just days before the team left for St. Kitts.

Mace was happy for them. But he watched the domestic lives of his teammates like a goldfish in a bowl on the kitchen counter sees what happens around it. They could inhabit the same space, those that breathed air and the goldfish that breathed under water. But no matter what, the goldfish would always be just an observer.

A committed relationship of his own was out of the realm of reality. Mace didn't have the background, didn't know how loving relationships worked other than vicariously.

And Mace would be damned if he was ever going to bring his own background into a life with someone he cared about. He consciously and strategically stayed away from all that.

In his relationships, if Mace thought things were getting serious with a girlfriend, he'd break it off, for the woman's protection.

What Mace brought to the table was an addicted mom and an asshole dad. Oh, and a wound collecting, narcissist of a step-mom. All his domestic habits were toxic.

Tara was *absolutely* off limits.

His hurting Tara would destroy his relationships with Matteo and Mrs. Alvarez and to lose all three of them would be hell.

"Did you have a cell phone to get help?" Ash asked, pulling Mace back to Tara's story.

"I wasn't old enough yet, according to mom. But the cops came to check on me. My friend told her mom that I was talking then screamed and hung up. Her mom called the police, then raced over. It was really sweet that she cared. They took me in the ambulance to the ER just to be extra sure that I was okay."

"Were you?" Jim asked.

"Depends on who you ask. Me, I think I'm okay. I kind of felt let down that I didn't achieve superpowers from the ordeal. I mean even being able to pick up radio stations in my dental fillings would have been cool. My brother, Matteo, claimed that when I was hit by the lightning, my soul flew out of my body and was replaced by an evil fiend floating nearby looking for a human experience. He insists I'm a fiend in a Tara skin bag."

"Sounds like big brother crap," Ash said.

"Even so. At that age, he scared the shit out of me. How could I tell if that happen or not? Does a demon know it's a demon?"

"How indeed?" Jim chuckled.

"Killer bees as a kid, quicksand, lightning strikes," Ash said. "What about earthquakes?"

"India."

"Volcanic eruption?"

"Iceland."

"You're a dangerous woman to be around," Ash said.

A big grin spread across her face. "Yeah, and don't you forget it."

"I take her stories a different way," Mace said. "She's like the guys out on patrol who lean over and tie their shoe just when a bullet whizzed by. When you meet a guy who just seems to survive the craziest things, what do you do?" he asked Ash.

"Hang out with him in the hopes his good luck is contagious." Ash added, "And you get the added bonus of some killer bar stories." He lifted his arm to point at an almost full moon that was painted tangerine. "Tara," Ash asked, "why is the moon that color?"

"We're just past the strawberry moon and that often has a pink cast to it. This is caused by atmospheric debris."

"From what?"

"I don't know." She turned to Jim. "What's going on with the weather?"

"Mildly concerning," he said. "I'll text Sammie."

Pria stepped forward and leaned on Tara, dropping her head onto her friend's shoulder. Tara wrapped her arms around Pria, and they stood looking out over the waters.

The group was silent, as the waves brushed warm and grainy over their feet.

Shortly after the text was sent, a reply pinged.

SAMMIE: **Things are rocking and rolling here in the Atlantic. Gathering energy. Concerning temperatures. We usually see these ocean temps in August. We're two months early in this hurricane season, which means a Cat 5 in June isn't out of the picture soon. Right now, our guy thinks the storm is heading toward Puerto Rico. You won't get that from the atmospheric guys. They're saying up the East Coast.**

. . .

AFTER READING that to the group, Jim's thumbs moved over the keyboard. Without looking up, he said, "I'm asking her how big."

The group huddled close.

SAMMIE: **Air is saying tropical storm. Water has a different tale. This looks like a monster. Stay off the boat, Jim. I'm serious here. This one has spiders crawling up the back of my neck. Make sure you have shelter planned just in case you get some of the outer ring.**

"BUT NORTH OF HERE," Tara said. "Puerto Rico, she said."

"Bad for those in its path." Jim caught Trevor's gaze. "I'm grateful it's not heading toward us." He turned to Mace and Ash. "You may want to take this back to your team and get a plan in place. Maria devastated Puerto Rico. They aren't a hundred percent yet. You know this."

Tara jostled Pria. "What's going on?"

"Darn it. You know what? I'm not feeling great."

"Emotionally? Physically?"

"Stomach. I think I ate some meat."

Tara turned a worried face toward Mace. "Pria has Alpha-gal."

Alpha-gal was a reaction to ticks that made people allergic to meat and animal products. In some cases, it caused anaphylaxis and death.

"I need to go back to the hotel and lay down," she moaned.

"I'll take you there now. Austin, could you grab our shoes, please?"

"We'll all go," Jim said.

"No, please don't." Pria held up a hand. "You won't be able

to help, and I'll just be embarrassed to have messed up the evening."

Mace turned and set off at a jog, quick enough to beat them to the hotel terrace, but not at a pace that would make people think this was a crisis and gather around to watch.

"I've got this," Tara said to the group. "I won't leave her alone."

"I'll knock on the door when we get in and see if you need anything," Trevor said.

"Ready?" Tara's voice was whipped away by the wind as Mace reached the chairs. "Pria, just in case, where's your epinephrine?"

18

Tara Alvarez

Saturday, Dominica

"You told them nothing from an animal." Tara had caught Pria under the arm and was propelling them back toward the hotel as calmly as she could. "You told them you were allergic."

Austin had jogged off to grab their shoes as asked. And Tara hoped he'd follow them up the elevator. Pria had never gone into anaphylaxis, but if she did, Tara didn't know how she'd manage it on her own.

"Sometimes people think I'm lying and that I'm a vegan by choice. Tick spray, always."

"I know you keep warning everyone. Rightly so. Who knew that a tick bite could make someone allergic to meat?"

"I miss meat!" She frowned, splaying her hands over her stomach. "And butter. And cheese. Ugh. When the doctor said 'Lone Star ticks' and 'Alpha gal' my first reaction was to laugh.

It sounded like the start of some superhero saga. Like your lightning ball story." She shifted her voice to sound like a film blurb announcer. "Bitten by the Lone Star tick, she became an Alpha gal! Able to bend steel with her bare hands." Pria stopped, filled her cheeks with air and blew out. "Instead, it bends me over a toilet."

"Maybe not. Maybe you're just tired from your trip. Or you're working on getting your balance after being out on the boat."

"Mmm. This feels like an Alpha gal reaction. It's usually worse when I exercise and drink alcohol. It's been a long day traveling, and I had the cocktail at dinner."

"You never said, do you have an epi pen?"

"The epi is on the counter in my bathroom. I shouldn't need it." She nodded at Austin as he arrived. His shoes already on his feet his pants rolled down. He handed off the pink sandals to Tara and knelt on one knee to help Pria with her flip flops.

Normally, that would be an absurd gesture—Prince Charming trying on the glass slipper to find the right fit—but Pria was swaying. And he had to catch her elbow to steady her, even with her hand on his shoulder.

"Sorry." She lifted the back of her hand to her lips. "My room, please."

Tara held Pria's hand, and she leaned into Austin's arms. "I thought I was improving. I haven't had a reaction in… I can't remember how long. Thank you both for your help. Since I haven't had any new tick bites, the researchers said my case was waning and might even resolve eventually." She stopped and huffed.

They took a step forward, letting Pria set the pace.

"We're almost to the elevator. Tell me what's going on, right now," Tara asked.

"Should we get a doctor involved? The hospital?" Austin asked. "Is this even remotely life threatening?"

"For me, no. Not so far, knock on wood." Both women reached out and knocked on the wooden table beside the elevator bank.

"Gastro-intestinal issues. I'm expecting a night of nausea and vomiting." She swung her attention to Austin as Tara dug the room key card from her friend's purse to flash in front of the elevator. "I've never had anaphylaxis. They gave me the epi in an abundance of caution."

The car dinged, the doors slid wide, and the three climbed on to too many mirrors for someone who was dizzy like Pria. She closed her eyes and dropped her head to Austin's chest.

Tara pressed the number four and cringed as the car jolted.

Tara wanted to keep Pria talking. Less brain space available to Pria for thinking about what was going on in her stomach seemed like a good idea. "I guess being out on the research boat is extra helpful in avoiding ticks."

"And that's the reason why I won't go up into the rainforest to see your house, sorry."

"For heaven's sake. It's a hut. It's cute and comfortable, but I can show you pictures." The elevator bobbled again as it stopped at their floor. The doors motored open, and they exited, turning left on the maroon carpeting with golden peonies. This hotel was indeed swanky just like Mr. Francis from the mailroom had said. Even better if they could get Pria to a bathroom before she messed it up.

Just three more doors before Pria's... "What do you think happened, Pria? You ate a dinner salad with shrimp." Tara swiped key card through the lock and pressed the door wide.

Pria stopped with her hand on the door frame, her head resting on her arm, shaking her head.

"What can I do?" Tara asked.

"Is the hospital a better plan?" Austin swept his arm under Pria's knee and effortlessly carried her over to the bed, where he gently lay her down.

Tara had never seen anyone do something like that in real life.

And she didn't think she knew any men who could pull that off with such grace.

Here was another vignette that Tara would later pull up to feed her sexual fantasies. Of course, in her imagination it would be she that Austin lifted and carried. And it wouldn't have anything to do with a life-threatening meat allergy or bowel-dissolving gastrointestinal pain.

Tara clicked on the light on the bedside table, and the room was bathed in warm light. Turning, Tara found Austin looking at her, kind, strong, ready to act for the benefit of others.

Tara held back the sigh that expanded her lungs, yes, she was definitely in the mood to fall back in love with Austin Mace.

Knowing from Matteo that Austin had zero interested in a committed relationship, those feelings were sure to stomp on her heart.

Careful, girl.

Who needed that?

Pria had her stomach settled enough for the moment to answer, Tara's question. "At dinner, cross contamination is always a risk. Austin, thank you, but unless I become dehydrated and need an I.V., there's really not much the hospital can do for me."

"So, electrolytes?" Austin asked.

"Yes, thank you. If you could find me a lot of something, please? I don't know what kinds of things they might have here in Dominica. If you can figure something out, I'll just go in and sleep on the bathroom floor."

"Shit," Tara said.

"Not usually," Pria said a glimmer of mirth behind her waxy complexion, "just puke."

"I'm spending the night with you," Tara said.

Pria nodded. "Appreciated."

Austin touched Tara's arm, and she stilled as buzzing warmth radiated through her body. *How did he do that?*

"I'm going to take her key card, so I can get back up the elevator and won't disturb you. Besides electrolyte replacement, can you think of anything else?"

"Something with salt? Crackers?"

With a nod, he was gone.

After the door shut, Tara turned to Pria who had thrown her arm over her eyes. "My god, Tara, you weren't kidding. That man is totally a mythical knight in shining armor."

PRIA, leaning back against the tub, had just swallowed the last of the drinks that Austin had brought up earlier.

He'd made Tara promise that she'd call him if she needed anything more.

Tara lifted Pria's phone to swipe, but she saw the time—eleven thirty. Ash said the team would be out running their dogs at the crack of dawn. She wasn't dragging Austin from his bed. He needed his sleep to catch up from his day up and down the mountain, and the bear spray in his lungs.

A picture of Austin—lying on his stomach, sleeping naked under the drape of a white sheet, one leg, muscular and relaxed, curled over the top—sprang into her mind. Tara blinked it away.

Austin wasn't for her.

Team Bravo was leaving out in the morning after they got back from running their dogs.

It was probably a good choice for Tara to head back up the mountain in the morning and miss any public goodbyes.

The place in her heart that had always been Austin's was feeling tender and in need of protection.

She'd mail a polite "thank you for your concern" note to Austin and consider it settled. She wouldn't see him again until Matteo and Bethany christened their baby. And then it would be another few decades before their paths crossed again.

Yeah, Tara really didn't like that her heart and mind were racing forward when she knew Austin was a very solid dead end. Better to course correct now, before impact.

Reaching out to squeeze Pria's ankle Tara said, "I'm going to see what's in the vending machine for you."

"Ginger ale, please, if they have it. And salty crackers. No chips."

"I'll be right back."

With the key card and change in her hand, Tara swung into the hall to find Trevor moving her way.

He wore yoga-styled pants with tropical fruit motif.

The outfit recalled one of their first conversations they'd had after Jim introduced Trevor to the gang. Trevor said that he wasn't a fruit. He was a vegetable. An asparagus to be exact. He'd laughed at his own joke in such an infectious way that Tara had been charmed.

Long and thin, Trevor's wasn't a painful thinness of jutting hipbone and visible rib. His muscles wrapped a narrow skeleton. His improbable dimensions made clothes shopping impossible. The off the rack stuff that was long enough was never thin enough. The clothes that buttoned and hung properly from his hips always looked like capri pants on him. Or bracelet-length sweaters. This left Trevor with two options. He had a tailor in

India that would sew a bespoke suit to fit him. That's where he got his dapper clothes, his go to eat in five-star restaurants garb. His everyday wear he made himself, having learned to sew as a theater major, taking costuming classes. He not only dressed both himself and his husband with flair, but Trevor and Jim always rocked Halloween.

Tara could just see Trevor delighting over the tongue in cheek joke of this print on the pants he would wear to bed.

"How is she?" Trevor asked when he reached Tara. He looked back up the hall to his room. "I couldn't get comfortable. I hate being in a bed all by myself," Trevor pouted. "I decided to come down and check on Pria again."

"No sign of anaphylaxis. She's out of that danger zone. She's pretty miserable though." Tara tipped her head toward the vending niche. "Come on. I'm getting her some soda."

As they moved down the hall together, the Ponytail man was moving up the hallway.

Tara sent him a tight-lipped smile of recognition. Tara cautioned herself to be careful of her conversation around the man, and in public in general, lest she get Jim and Trevor involved with the law.

What a nightmare that would be.

Scanning over the offerings in the machine, she dropped the coins in.

Ponytail man moved to the snacks machine. He smiled politely. "Did you have a nice meal?"

"We did thank you. And you?"

"Delicious. But maybe a little bit on the light side. I have the nibbles."

Tara was trying to place the accent and thought may South African. Maybe some European language that had been smoothed over with a stay in England or a good teacher. Hard to say.

Tara was quiet as he dropped coins into the machine, pressed the red numbers, and his chips dropped into the well. He bent to dig them out, then, with a nod said, "Have a lovely rest of the evening."

Trevor helped her gather the drinks, and Tara was able to find some salted crackers as requested.

When they rounded the corner, Ponytail was leaning against the wall, texting, his chips bag caught under his arm.

He didn't look up from the screen.

Tara wondered if he was out there in the hall because he'd found a spot with better bars. In Pria's room, Pria's phone barely got one bar. If things took a turn for the worse tonight, Tara would remember that spot.

Back in the room, Trevor went to the bathroom and sat on the lip of the tub. "You look like total shit."

"Love you, too," Pria mumbled, her cheek resting on the rim of the toilet.

One by one, Trevor unloaded his arms, setting the drinks within easy reach and looking at the garbage filled with bottles.

"As soon as it goes in, it comes right back out," Tara said.

"But it makes me feel better to do that," Pria's voice strained past painful vocal cords.

"The bubbles of the soda though, that's going to be like sandblasting the inside of your throat."

"It's been almost an hour since she last spewed. We think she'll be able to get to sleep here in a bit."

"I'm not moving until I'm sure. Vomiting in a hotel bed is the worst."

"Especially if I'm sleeping in the bed with you."

"Careful you don't say that outside the hotel room," Trevor cautioned. "Dominican laws being what they are. No need to borrow trouble."

No, not when trouble already seems to follow me around.

Pria reached out and her hand landed on Trevor's ankle. "Trevor, you realize don't you that there's no way it will be safe for me to dive tomorrow."

"Tomorrow is the only day that I have the permits," Trevor whispered. "No pressure, just disappointment."

"I know, so I was thinking that Tara could take my place. Shoot her from the back. I'll do the front shots a day when you're not under water."

"Take Pria's place? What? No. I can't do that. I haven't read the script. I wouldn't know the lines."

"You have diving skills," Pria said.

"But Pria is model beautiful. I…" She lifted her hands and let them drop. "I dig worms and hang out in a lab."

"I'm not touching that," Trevor said. "Look, your coloring is the same. Your bodies are similarly shaped."

"Pria has triple D boobs." Tara gestured at her chest. "I most emphatically do not."

"You'll be in a shorty wetsuit," Pria countered. "Who could tell?"

"Pria's right, I can splice her in. If I film you from the back, she can read voice-overs. I can do this. I just need you to be a little brave for me." He laced his fingers and looked at her with the innocence of a choir boy.

She sighed. "All right. I'll do it. But you'll be buying all the drinks when we get back at the end of the day, and I will be drinking buckets."

"Girl, you're a lightweight. One and done. But I've got you."

"I need go by my place to get my dive gear in the morning."

And this way, she could avoid seeing Austin again and avert the need to say goodbye.

Coward.

_____

19

Austin Mace

Sunday, Dominica

Mace stopped at Pria's door to check on her status and offer to bring the women anything they might need or could make them more comfortable.

A very hungover and very ripe Neils opened the door. A brief update on Pria ended with, "Tara's not here. She left crack of dawn for the worm thing." Then shut the door.

Mace looked down at Diesel. "Crack of dawn for the worm thing."

Diesel sat down waiting for his next command. His fiery eyes stared intently at Mace.

Tara was on the mountain. He'd admit it, that was a gut punch. He wouldn't see her before he left.

Was she avoiding him for some reason?

Diesel got up and wandered toward the staircase they'd just jogged up. Mace followed after him, perplexed by this turn of events. "She had to know Bravo wasn't going to be here tonight for their dinner, right?"

With a *cachunk* of the bar, Mace pressed the door wide, and Diesel padded through. Instead of climbing the stairs toward their room, Diesel headed back down the stairs.

Mace followed along, stunned. *Tara didn't say good-bye.*

"I mean, she doesn't owe me anything. I'm the one who showed up in her world. Ruined her day. I probably put her behind schedule, which is why she had to go up there this morning."

Diesel sat in front of the side door they'd been using for their potty breaks, and Mace held it open for him.

"And there might be a time of day that's better for worm collection than others, right? The early bird catches the worm? That's a thing. Maybe she thought she could get up there, do her collecting and get back in time."

Diesel turned away from the field where he'd been relieving himself and trotted over to the SUV where he sat expectantly by the passenger door.

Mace patted his pants' pocket. He had the keys. He could go up... "But for what reason?" he asked Diesel. And when he caught Diesel's gaze, he remembered he'd left his uniform shirt on the mountain. "Lame," he said. "But I'll take it."

The idea of flying away without one last opportunity to give her a smile and a hug didn't sit right in Mace's system. He loaded Diesel into the vehicle and trotted around to driver's side, swung the door wide, and climbed in. With a twist of the key, Mace backed out of the spot. He remembered the cold sweat of the nightmare that woke him up this morning. Nightmares weren't unusual for Mace. But in this one, Mrs. Alvarez was standing in her driveway, "Did you find her, Austin? Did you get her back? Austin, *where is she*?"

Panic—just sheer cold panic—raced through his veins and

sprang him from his bed. Mace had never experienced anything like it. He'd forced himself to go for his morning jog and wait for a reasonable hour to knock on Pria's door.

And he'd missed her.

He absolutely needed to see Tara again, whole, and healthy, and *safe*.

Having made the drive before, Mace was up at her door within minutes.

His knock brought no response. He made his way around to the back door. Again, it was unlocked. This time, the bottom screen was ripped.

Inside, the papers on her desk were disheveled and scattered across her floor.

His heart stuttered as he raced through the little house looking for more signs of violence.

When he got to Tara's room, Diesel's nose rested on her bed.

There lay her cards and her journal, same as yesterday. The day's date was neatly written at the top right. There was no quiver in her loopy script to show she was under duress. He wouldn't read it, though, without permission.

He glanced at this morning's cards. One looked like a turning wheel. One said, *Fork in the Road.* The third was a wasp. He had no idea what any of that meant.

But she had been here. And she had been fine at that point in time.

Diesel lay on the floor at Mace's feet, focused on something under the bed. "Diesel, bring." As his dog crawled forward under the bedskirt, Mace could hear his chuffing. Diesel wriggled his butt back out with Tara's shoe in his mouth.

"Good plan, let's do this." He reached down. "Diesel, give." After the shoe dropped into his hand, Mace held it out.

On command, Diesel sniffed the scent source.

"She can't be far," he told Diesel as the K9 sniffed the shoe and got the imprint of the scent he was to follow.

Just like yesterday, Diesel took his time finding the right trail. Unlike yesterday, Diesel took a few steps into the foliage, stopped, looked left and right, nose chuffing, perplexed. He ran to the left, forward, right forward, and so they continued in this odd zigzag that Mace couldn't figure out.

Eventually, Diesel sent up a sharp happy bark.

This was something he was trained *not* to do for a find. Making any noise at all would tune the bad guy into their location. Mace's stress dropped a notch from the tone of the bark, a play bark and not a growling, I'm ready to rumble vocalization. This was happy Diesel.

A moment later, Tara pushed past a screen of leaves.

"I thought that was you," she said to Diesel, then sent Mace a smile. "Hi there."

She was fine.

His heart reseated in his chest as she dove down to full body rub Diesel. No permission, but she wouldn't know the etiquette, and Diesel was thoroughly enjoying himself, peddling his back leg as Tara found his tickle spot.

"What a nice surprise." Tara looked up at Mace, her face bright with laughter as Diesel snuffled her hair.

"I came to say good-by before we took off. Are you working?"

"No, I was looking for my computer. It's pretty heavy."

"I'm not following."

Tara flipped over, butt in the air, then pushed to her feet. "The monkey that's loose on the island is part of a monkey thieving gang."

"And you're out of bear spray."

"Sadly true. I would so blast that monkey right now. I am furious with him!"

"Go back to the computer."

"Same story. The radio said that the monkey was trained to steal electronics from tourists. Friday, he stole my phone." She looked up at the tree canopy. "Though weird that he's moving that many miles up and down the mountain. Pria said she saw the monkey in the hotel lobby when they checked in." She brought her gaze back to Mace's "A very athletic monkey. And stronger than I would have supposed. A phone? Sure. A computer? Not so much."

Mace planted his hands on his hips and pulled his brows together, a silent ask for more information.

"I got back to my house this morning, and the screen at the bottom of my door was ripped out. So much for locks, right? The things on my desk were scattered on the floor and my computer was gone." She gestured a small rectangle. "It's just a little notebook sized thing. Not very big. And it has back up when I go down to town and am in internet range, so I didn't lose much in the way of data." She cast her gaze around the forest floor. "But still. I'd really like it back." She started walking. "I figured it was pretty heavy, so it shouldn't be far. The monkey was bound to have dropped it quickly. I've been walking in circles around my house, each circle a little wider out," she looked at her watch, "for hours now."

And that explained Diesel's strange search pattern.

She stopped and looked over her shoulder. "Hey, do you think Diesel could track it?"

"The monkey?"

She turned to him with a hopeful nod. "Or the computer."

"I'd have to isolate either of the scents to give Diesel the right information."

Tara canted her head. "What did you use when you were looking for me on Saturday?"

"Your shoe." He pulled the shoe from his side pocket. "And I used it, again, today."

"Ah. Yes, that would be a very personal scent signature." Tara started moving toward her house, and Mace fell in step just behind her, almost side by side. Their arms brushed as they walked, he liked the warm silkiness of her skin.

"As I was hunting the computer, I noticed that the air is different this morning." She reached out an open palm toward a bush. "The light on the leaves is strangely vivid."

"Like the moon last night?" Mace asked.

"I was thinking of Sammie's warnings. Since Pria's not going to be up to the shoot today, I'm taking her place. I came home to get my dive gear. That's when I saw the monkey issue."

"You're sure it was a monkey?"

She stopped and turned. "Do you have another explanation?"

"Way out where you live?" Mace considered for a moment then said, "Other than wildlife, not off hand I don't, no."

Tara kept walking. "From what Sammie texted last night, I figure we'll be fine today out on the water. We'll have to check the waves, of course. When I'm down at the hotel, I'll have Jim text Sammie for any updates."

"What's your plan for a storm? Your house seems problematic."

"Ha! You think? Yes, it's been a great house for me. But the trees around it are too tall, the roots too shallow. The wind in the foliage? They'll come down like bowling pins. I'm told that during Maria, the trees were stripped naked. But that was a category five." She took a few more paces before asking, "Since you know about Dominican emergency preparedness, I'll ask you. How well does Dominica do with hurricanes?"

"How well does anyplace do with hurricanes? It depends on

the size and strength of the storm, right? How fast it moves." He reached out and caught Tara's elbow to steady her as she moved over the log. "After Maria, a lot of governments rethought their architecture and systems."

"And you all, are you safe on St. Kitts?" She threw a worried look over her shoulder. "You're right there, half in the Atlantic half in the Caribbean Sea."

"We have an interior location on St. Kitts."

"Why St. Kitts and not say St. Croix, and American soil?"

"Proximity. Elevation. We're above any storm surge or tsunami."

"Tsunami?"

"St. Kitts has a sister island a few kilometers off its coastline."

"Nevis, where Alexander Hamilton was born."

"That's right. Both islands have lost land mass because of rising seas. That makes storm surge difficult." He looked down to check on Diesel who was happily sniffing his way down the trail. "Most of the people live along the outer ring."

"But not Iniquus."

"We're in the mountains where we have a barracks built on bed rock with a storage facility for our equipment. So far, it's worked. That might change with—"

"Climate. Yeah."

"Well would you look at that?" Tara stopped short and turned around, her face painted with wide eyed excitement. "You, Austin Mace are *very* good luck to me."

His heartbeat raced as she shined a bright grin his way. She turned away again, just as he reached out for her. And he let his hand drop.

Tara stood beside a plant, putting waypoints in her GPS to flag this location. "These are near extinct," she said without looking up.

Diesel padded up to see what the excitement was about. Mace had hoped it was her computer. Monkey…that was very strange. But what did Mace know about monkeys? He'd talk to Goose about it when he got back to the Iniquus compound. St. Kitts, Goose's island of origin, was rife with monkeys.

"Oh, hey! Austin, you'll want to keep Diesel away from them."

Mace patted his thigh, and Diesel instantly rounded to his side.

"The Dominican researchers asked me to be on the lookout for these. These and Mountain chickens. And this week, I've found both specimens. I'm going to get a gold star from their staff." Tara put the GPS back in her pack and pulled out her field notebook. Bending over to balance it on her thigh, she wrote, then lifted back up to read it to him:

"Today, on my Dominica adventure I found a heart of gold. I knew they existed. I'm looking for them as a constant. It was surprising, though, when it suddenly popped into my view, a treasure to behold. I thought they might have been a myth."

She put the notebook in her pack. And when she turned, Tara and Mace were a hair's breadth apart.

"I was surprised to find you gone this morning." Mace's heart beat against his sternum, his voice was gruff. "Neils is in bad shape."

She swallowed. "Yes, he is and none too pleased that I pulled him out of bed to watch Pria. But." She lifted a palm and let them drop onto Mace's forearms. "I had to get my things to help Trevor."

Mace took both of Tara's hands in his. "Neils said Pria was doing fine this morning, just worn out."

"Yes, poor thing," she whispered. "It was a pretty rough night."

"Are you okay to dive? Did you get enough sleep?"

"I never sleep any more. So, it doesn't matter."

Diesel shifted away, walking a circle around them, with a distracting whine.

"What time is Trevor getting going?" Mace stroked his thumbs over the backs of her hands, testing the waters. The air was suddenly much to heavy, much too humid, he couldn't get enough oxygen into his lungs.

Diesel pushed into Tara, making her stumble forward the last fraction of an inch. Mace caught her around the waist, feeling the softness of her breasts pressing against his chest. His hands fell to the curve of her hips. Mace immediately set Tara away from him before she could feel his dick roaring to attention.

With that move, Tara's face flamed pink.

"Sorry," he said and turned, patting his thigh to get Diesel into place. Diesel sent Mace a look that if Mace could give it words would be something like, "Dude, I got her where you wanted her. It was perfect."

Mace couldn't disagree. It was perfect just…this was *Tara*.

20

Austin Mace

Sunday, Dominica

MACE STARTED THEM BACK TOWARD HER HOUSE. "IT'S NICE OF you to help out with the filming. Trevor seems jazzed about it."

"Nice. Hmm. Well, the way I see it is: No one can do it all. All I can do is my little. But if a lot do a little, we'll end with a lot," she chanted.

"I bet you can't say that three times real fast."

"Don't tease. It's my mantra."

"My mantra is *Om*." He bent over. "Is this the kind of worm you want?"

"That's not a gold."

"What is it?"

She shrugged. "Earthworm?" She reached out her hand for his as she stepped over another log. And she didn't let go once she was on the other side.

"I can see why you'd need a mantra. Out here all day with

your thoughts churning through your head. No one's chatter to distract you."

"I'm low tolerance on chatter. It's peaceful out here. Nature is loud enough to keep my thoughts quiet. I think about the people who have gone to monasteries and taken the vow of silence. Years they don't speak. Can you imagine?"

"No." He turned his hand so he could lace their fingers together. "And when you go down to the village and reconnect to the outer world, you read the news, you download the scientific studies, you talk to your friends, and then what?"

"Then, I remember the existential dread. I have to put it back into my box and pull out my mantra."

"No one can do it all."

"But I can do a little," she said quietly.

"And that works for you?"

"It does. We don't have a lot of time. But we have a little. And we're making progress, in small ways—scientists, governments, average everyday people."

"As you said, small ways add up."

She rolled her lips in and bobbled her head, bird like and not fully convinced.

"What's it like to live out in the middle of nowhere alone?"

"Pros and cons—for example, without connectivity I can connect with other things. Nature. Hobbies. Myself."

"Come on, Diesel, catch up."

"In Maryland, I find social media addictive. I'm in contact with scientists all over the world. There's something of a dopamine hit when I get unexpected terrible information. I spend hours doom scrolling it. The worse it is, the more my brain is zapping around with excitement."

"Excitement?" Mace asked. "I saw everyone's faces when you found out about the underwater volcano erupting near Tongo."

"Yes, but then our brains were awake. The brain says, 'Hey, there's a threat! Pay attention.' Sizzle. Sizzle. Zap. Our brains are wired for that shit. I found that when given the opportunity to doom scroll through the different social media sites, I was zapping all the time. And it was addictive. I'd lose hours a day and come up for air with no time for real relationships. Conversations with others. Myself. I'm an introvert anyway. The social media meant I could feel connected without actually connecting to anything or anyone."

"But it helps with your job, right."

"It's necessary for my job. Also necessary for my job is finding doubloon plants and digging for gold worms. Here where there's zero connectivity, I'm forced into a place where I can't get that internet joy juice. It's good to reset."

"When your door was open, I went in and collected your shoe. I hope you don't mind."

She shook her head.

"I saw the meditation cards on your bed. They're like your mom's. For her they predict the future. Does that work for you?"

"Not for me... Mmm, that's not entirely true. They can be uncanny. They're *often* uncanny. For example. I have the animal cards. The day that I pulled the monkey card," her voice was painted with indignation, "an *actual* monkey leaped from a tree and stole my phone."

"Bananas."

"Ha." She looked down to get safely over a rock out cropping. "Yup. Of late. The cards have been ultra-accurate. Like I said, I don't—I haven't in the past—used the cards as predictive. Simply a lens with which to view the day."

"Monkeys and coyotes." And today was the wasp, Mace thought. That didn't seem good. If Mace could, he'd scoop Tara up and take her with him back to St. Kitts. He wanted to be right there if anything were putting Tara in harm's way.

"This week they have been entirely too literal for my comfort. I don't know if I like that."

Mace focused on the warmth that radiated from Tara's palm, up his arm, buzzing his elbow, climbing to his shoulder and around to his heart. It was one of the strangest things he'd ever experienced. Drug-like in the euphoria it spread.

He could see himself becoming addicted.

"When you were a kid, do you remember that Matteo and I built you a tree house?"

"That was like five feet off the ground? Yes." She laughed

"Your mother's directions. She said she wasn't worried about you falling out of the tree, being a tree frog was second nature to you. It was more that if you fell asleep, she wanted to be able to bring you a blanket and check on you. She didn't want to crawl up a ladder."

"Her hip," Tara said in a faraway voice.

"Yes."

"I love her." She smiled up at Mace.

"Me too. Your house reminds me a bit of that tree house, what was in my imagination anyway, when we tried to build it for you."

Last night, he'd thought that Tara's storytelling was a distraction strategy. And he was using her own tactics against her. It was helping. He was remembering what roles everyone played, he was Matteo's friend, soon-to-be godfather of his daughter. The honorary son of Mrs. Alvarez, the protector of this beautiful butterfly spirit.

Tara stopped and reached her free hand across to brush it over their clasped hands and looked down at their entwined fingers. "When I was little, after you left, I grieved." When she lifted her head, her eyes glistened with tears.

Mace softly swiped his thumb over her lashes.

"I found solace in the night sky. Wherever you were, we were looking at the same stars. I'm just going to tell you the truth, because what have I got to lose, right?" She stopped and held still for a long moment; a tremor moved through her. "I've been holding my breath since you drove away to move with your father. And when you walked back into my life yesterday on the mountain, I remembered how to inhale, again."

She was looking up at him with her beautiful brown eyes, soft and intelligent, kind. For the first time Mace saw tiny age lines etched around her eyes. A white scar near her brow. He brushed his hand through the length of her silken ebony hair, all the way to the ends, halfway down her back.

He leaned down and kissed her—a tentative brush of lips.

Mace rubbed his index finger over his buzzing mouth.

She stilled, her eyes excited and expectant.

Cupping her head between his splayed fingers, Mace found Tara's mouth again. He let himself get lost in the sensations of her full lips. The slick of her tongue invited him deeper.

Shifting, she rose up on her toes. Their bodies pressed together, his arms tightened, holding her in place.

And everything—the cacophony of wild things, even the "this is not for you" thoughts—everything that was not that kiss faded into the background.

When he lowered his forehead to hers so he could catch his breath and his heart would stop pounding so damned hard it hurt, she said, "I thought it would be like that."

Their gazes met.

"I'm never scared when you're near me, Austin. It's been that way all my life. When you're near, everything is soft and fluid. You're like a drug. The perfect stillness of my soul, like what I feel in the moments after I finish meditating. I remember these feelings very clearly from way back before you left me."

Mace shook his head. This was a lot. His whole world was shifting under his feet.

And damned if there wasn't a hook, dragging him away from this magic. In the back of his mind, he thought, *I just found my way back to her, and now this.*

Whatever the hell the "this" was, he had no clue.

But now he knew in every cell of his body what it felt to experience existential dread.

For Tara, he said, "I'm adjusting, Tara. I left a child leaping through the tall grass on a summer's night, catching fireflies for her jar. Matteo and I would sneak into your room after you'd fallen asleep to let them go free so they wouldn't die in the night."

"Sweet of you. I would have been devastated if I'd woken up with them dead. Thank you."

"It's been a shock to discover that you're a woman. My best friend's sister…"

"Makes me off limits, doesn't it?"

"My lips are still buzzing."

"Has that ever happened before?" she asked.

"That? No. No, it has not."

"No going back now." Tara's voice was rock solid.

"I think you might be right about that."

They turned and walked the rest of the way to her house in silence. When they got to her front steps, he kissed her again. And his reaction hadn't dimmed. "When can I see you again? We're in St. Kitts training through the summer unless we're called up for deployment to a situation."

"I'm finishing up here." Her arms wrapped tightly around his waist. "In the next week, I'll have collected enough specimens to head back to the lab."

"Which is in Maryland," he said. "I'm out of Northern Virginia, D.C. area."

"I'm Annapolis, so I won't be far."

"Do you think you could take a break between Dominica and Annapolis to come to St. Kitts? I'll be working. And it might be a bore to hang out on your own."

"Austin, I spend my days on the side of a volcano digging worms. I see people once a week when I go to the post office and buy my sandwich makings. I am not capable of being bored on St. Kitts."

There was a long pause.

"You're thinking of Matteo," she whispered.

"Crossed my mind. But I *need* to see what this is between us."

Her smile was radiant. "I'm brave enough, if you are."

21

Tara Alvarez

Sunday, Dominica

Tara reached the dock, dropping her SCUBA tanks next to the boarding ramp of the *Onward, Ho!* That comma placement still cracked her up. "Good morning," she called.

Neils looked up from his busywork with a line and looked back down.

Funny, since Austin's kiss, Tara had been floating on a cloud, nothing could bring her down. Not even Neils's sour attitude. She'd noticed that he was markedly crankier than the last time she'd seen him. Maybe he was pickled in the brine of too many months of salt air. Everyone had their limits when it came to confinement, she thought with as much generosity of spirit as she could muster.

"You're looking radiant today," Jim said. "Especially having been through such a rough night with our friend."

"How is Pria?" Tara asked before she went back to retrieve her next load from her side-by-side.

"Sleeping, poor thing," Trevor said spooning up what looked to be a perfectly ripe juicy strawberry. "Symptoms have been flushed down the toilet, and housekeeping was warned not to disturb." He popped the strawberry into his mouth and looked straight at Jim with a disappointed expression.

"I know. I'm sorry," Jim said, before turning and reaching for Tara's gear. "When we were docked for supplies in Jakarta, we met up with a scientist who's trying to figure out offshore farming. He speculates that the weather extremes will make land-based farming impossible sooner rather than later."

"Joy," Tara muttered sarcastically, releasing the tanks to Jim's grasp.

"But it was, though," Trevor said. "Absolute pure joy."

"Why's this?" Tara squatted, so they were eye to eye.

"The guy has biospheres about seven meters under water," Jim said.

"Water filled?" Tara asked.

"Air-filled spheres, hydroponic farming system. Right now, he's focused his experiments on basil and strawberries."

"And you should not eat them," Trevor said.

"Bad?"

"Opposite! They are the best things I've ever put in my mouth." He turned and gave Jim a sassy look. "Yes, you heard me. The. Best." He swiveled back to Tara. "Sweet. Juicy. They tasted like they were made by or for the gods."

Jim chuckled.

"You laugh," Trevor admonished him. "But I truly wish I'd never tasted them. Now, basil tastes like lettuce in comparison. And these berries? I don't think we can call them strawberries." Trevor closed his eyes and tipped his head back. "It's more like just the straw."

"Wow. I can see how that would make things difficult," Tara smiled and accepted the proffered plate of rejected strawberries, "the only strawberries you like coming from a single under-water farmer off the coast of Jakarta, and all." Tara bit into a ruby ripe fruit and thought it was delicious. She couldn't imagine what the ones that the Driscolls had experienced could do to top these.

"I think those berries need a new name, 'mana-berry', maybe, or 'ambrosia-berry'."

"Scholars believe that manna was simply trehalose, a white crystalline carbohydrate made of two glucose molecules joined together," Neils said. "It's a naturally occurring molecule and has some sweetness to it. Though, sweetness taste panels put the sweetness of trehalose at about half the sweetness of table sugar where artificial sweeteners are about six hundred times the sweetness. Manna might have kept folks alive if they found it in great enough quantity, but it certainly wasn't the end all beat all of tastes."

"Okay," Tara said, "fascinating. Thanks." And last night this man was ordering a drink because the rest of the table was a bunch of geeks?

"Neither word is right," Jim said. "Manna doesn't evoke the heavenliness of those flavors. And for me, at least, Ambrosia has a different connotation. Ambrosia in my world was my grandmother's go-to Easter recipe—crushed pineapple, mandarin oranges, coconut, and frozen whipped topping. I loved it as a kid. Last time Trevor and I were home, I got all nostalgic for my grandma and whipped up her recipe."

Trevor stuck out his tongue. "The whole thing tasted like chemicals and aluminum cans. With the name ambrosia, it was *so* disappointing." With a grimace, Trevor reached his hand out. "No offence to your grandma. A recipe of her times is all."

Jim laced their fingers together and sent Trevor a sympathetic smile, his eyes alight with mirth. "I'm sorry if my happy memory damaged your sensitive taste buds." Then Jim's eyes pulled wide, and he drew back his hand.

Tara stood to send a searching glance up and down the dock to see if anyone had witnessed that loving exchange.

Ponytail and his friends were on the deck of their cigarette-styled speed boat—two spaces down from Onward, Ho! — getting ready for their day. When she focused on him, Ponytail looked their way.

Tara lifted an arm in salute. And he returned it, then turned back to his chores.

When Tara felt reassured that the moment of tenderness hadn't put her friends at risk, she crouched back down to tell Jim that she had another armload to bring down.

Trevor was blinking grieving eyes at a fat rabbit of a cloud off in the distance.

And Tara knew exactly why.

When Trevor's parents rejected him as a teen, his grandparents took him in. They told Trevor to be whoever he wanted to be, do whatever he wanted to do. As long as he was being a good person, his grandparents promised that Trevor never had to worry about fitting in with the traditional world. And they made good on their word with a trust fund that offered Trevor freedom before their death and after. His grandparents had died together just after Trevor received his MFA. It was a suicide pack they'd put in motion when their health took a sudden turn, and they were done with life. They sent Trevor a note saying just that: *Life was good, and we want to go out without the suffering. So, thanks for being the perfect grandson. We'll be watching you from above, continuing to send our love. Do us a big old favor and live the life you want most, that's all we ask.*

Mentioning grandparents on a day when Trevor was living his life to his fullest—making his film with husband and friends in a glorious setting—yeah, Tara understood the look in Trevor's eyes.

She could also see that Jim wanted to move in and give Trevor a hug. Instead, he looked up to find Tara's gaze.

Tara quickly scrambled on board, to take Jim's place, wrapping Trevor in her arms. "They're here today. They're watching you. Don't let them down, okay? Let's make this spectacular, what do you say?" She had to rise high up on her tippy toes to plant a kiss on his cheek.

Travor swiped at his eyes. "Grief comes at weird times. A bucket of ice water dumped over my head." He hip bumped Tara. "They'd be so jazzed to see what we're up to." He turned to his husband. "Jim, are we ready? Let's get this show on the road."

A male's scream turned the four of them around.

A monkey was crawling up a man's back as he stood on the walkway near the dock, cell phone to his ear. As the man curved over protectively, the monkey stretched out its long hairy arm, trying to snatch the phone. The man shoved the monkey away, yelling at it to leave him alone.

Tara called out, "He's not rabid. He's just a thief." As the monkey scampered off to find a different victim, she pointed an angry finger at the monkey. "Hey, you, I want my computer back. Do you hear?"

22

Tara Alvarez

Sunday, Dominica

As their vessel rounded the island, Tara reached around to grab the long ribbon meant to make zipping up her shortie suit easy.

Trevor was taking pictures of her feet.

"I swear, Trevor, if I find those photos for sale on the internet, I'll kill you."

"I'm just doing this so I can remember to tell Pria to take off her pedicure polish. We have to make sure that your nails are cut the same." He lifted her hand and looked at it. "Pria will never agree to making her nails this raggedy."

Tara snatched her hand back. "I dig worms for a living. What did you think my nails would look like?"

"Here we are. I'm dropping anchor," Jim said, checking his instruments. "Yeah. This is the GPS coordinate where we're cleared for dredging." He turned to his husband. "I think we do that dive first, then we move on to clear waters where we haven't swirled up the sediment for the second series of shots."

"Agreed, Tara can hold the sword and the platter out of my shot here. Neils can be the one directing the uptake nozzle while I film him, since he knows how that works. And since it's only five meters, I can bounce up and down between underwater shots and surface level shots."

"You will *not* bounce up and down, Trevor." Jim was stern.

"I know, sweetie pie, figure of speech. I can," he put up finger quotes, "carefully control my ascent." He dropped his hands. "Lest the mere five meters give me the bends and my stomach pops out of my mouth like a blowfish jerked from the depths on a fisherman's line."

"Quite the visual. Thanks," Tara said.

Trevor turned back to Tara. "First, I have a few scenes to film with you on the boat." He held up a clip board. "They're all here so we can breeze right through them. I have to be careful of my daylight. I can't shoot the boat in the afternoon if it's the morning in the movie. Since the sun is almost overhead. That makes syncing things up a little easier."

"All right." Tara had been reading over Pria's script and had a fair idea about how this needed to go down.

Of course, Pria, Jim, and Trevor had entertained themselves at sea by making shorts. Little snippet films—little cinematic snacks, as Tara liked to think of them. Their ship had internet, so the group would post them to social media for their friends.

Tara thought they got better with time. Not necessarily from a script writing or filming perspective—that was always really interesting and thought provoking—but with practice, the actors had loosened up and honed their skills a bit. They were to the point that Tara thought they could pull off the acting in this longer project.

She, on the other hand, hadn't had the advantage of practice other than playing a pirate on the mountain.

And Trevor could obviously see her tension through the camera's lens.

"Tara, my love. Have you ever done something called Qigong?"

"Me? No…I'm…should I know that word?"

"Let's do a little body thing together." He set the camera down. "Feet hips distance apart. Good. Now bend your knees just a bit. Uh-huh. Let everything hang loose. Now bounce into your heels and let yourself shake loose."

"I feel ridiculous," Tara said.

"Good. I want you to be comfortable with that feeling. You're so uptight and unnatural."

"Wrong," Neils said. "Uptight is natural for Tara."

Shithead.

"She's not Tara. She's Gwen in this shoot, and Gwen is nothing if not comfortable in her skin. Enthusiastic about her future. Filled with joy." He focused back on Tara. "Gwen, pick up the binoculars and scan the horizon for any boats that might be out there."

"Lest they be pirates, ready to swoop in and steal our booty, arrr."

"That's the spirit. Only, uhm, could you kind of curl your fingers in so we don't see your nails?" Trevor moved around behind her, and now Tara could see him in her peripheral view focused on her other side. Tara turned her head to hide her face.

"Good, now, Gwen is scanning, scanning. Nice slow pan. Loosen the shoulders, you are the queen ready to pull the sword from the ocean."

"That's a big acting ask, Trevor. This is Tara after all."

"Okay, Neils, not helping." Jim clapped a hand on Neils's

shoulder. "How about you sit down, enjoy the view of the coast, and zip it."

And so went the morning.

Tara took regular shaking breaks between shots and did her best to embrace her inner "Gwen," expert in the treasure hunting universe.

Underwater, for sure, was easier. It wasn't necessary to act with a regulator mouthpiece between her teeth, and the diving mask obfuscating her face. Tara simply moved through the tasks, each clearly written, laminated, and attached to an O ring.

Trevor would flip to the next explanation, hold up the page for thumbs ups, and drop it back down to float from a tether on his belt.

The camera came up. Light went on. And…Action!

Brushing the sand and seeing the hilt, Tara reached down and pulled up a sword. She held it up triumphantly—though brandishing a sword underwater was a no go.

She did her required fist of victory.

Neils swam over to take a look at it and gave her a high-five.

That was the last of the task sheets.

And with a thumbs up sign and a returned okay gesture, the three carefully ascended to the surface where they floated until Trevor got in place to film them handing the discovered sword and platter to a very enthusiastic Jim.

Phew!

Lunchtime.

THE PICNIC that the hotel had packaged for them looked wonderful. Tara thought that food always tasted better when she'd been outside all day as compared to food when she had been hanging out indoors. She wasn't sure why.

The boat was rocking more than it had been earlier.

"The waters are getting unhappy, Trevor." She pointed out. "We may want to get the next shots done sooner rather than later. I don't have the skill level to fight the current if it gets any worse."

Jim stood, sandwich in hand and revved the motor, motoring another hundred yards down the coastline where he cut the engine and dropped the anchor.

"This morning I was pointing out the colors to Austin," Tara said. "Something in the air is making an odd filter. Are you seeing that through your lens, Trevor?"

"I am, and it's gorgeous. There's no way I could light this any better. Every hue is saturated with color and has a luminescence that makes everything, above the water at least, look wild and alive."

"Yeah, but looking in the direction of the wind, we have a bank of black," Neils said. "For once, I agree with Tara, down and then up."

"Two hours wait," Jim said. "You ate."

"I only had three mini-bites." Tara wrapped her sandwich back up as she looked over at Neils.

"Same. Well, four at the most."

Jim turned to Trevor. "I didn't eat a thing. I'm too excited about what I'm seeing through the lens. It's all going swimmingly." He offered up a broad wink, making his husband smile.

"Half an hour wait, then." Jim walked forward to sit near Tara. "I got in touch with Sammie. The way you asked."

Tara stilled.

"The storm has gone from a tropical storm to a cat one."

"Who is saying that, the air or sea predictors?"

"Air. And they are now putting the storm on the same pathway that Sammie told us last night."

"Uh-oh, that's the preamble," Neils said.

"Sammie thinks it's further south in its trajectory than does either the U.S. or the European models."

"As far south as St. Kitts?" Austin and his teammates should be there by now. They had a very safe complex built into the mountain, he'd said.

"Possibly. She's looking at land fall in the U.S. Virgin Islands. But she thinks the islands will be getting away lucky if it's only a category one."

Tara chewed her thumbnail. "Team Bravo will deploy north to help them." That meant Austin wouldn't be in St. Kitts—and probably wouldn't be for quite a while—depending on who they had in the area to move to safety and how much damage they encountered. Well, those "visit-Austin and the see where that kiss was taking them" plans might be out the window. Tara thought for a moment that she could go volunteer. But she had no training and surely the rescue groups required something even if it was just proper equipment and insurance. Those poor people. "What rating is Sammie projecting?"

"As of now? Three."

"Oh wow. Okay." Tara turned to Trevor. "Well, that explains the air, doesn't it?"

"Listen," Jim said. "I'm being quite serious now. I want you to come down from your mountain until this has cleared the area. I'm going to go stay with my cousin over there." Jim pointed to Trevor. "There are two king-sized beds in his room, and we will have the excuse of freeing up a room for a friend in need."

"Am I really in need? Or are you two really in need?" She popped her brows.

"A bit of both." Jim let a sly smile slide across his face, then dropped an ear toward his shoulder. "Mostly, I want you safe. Our hotel is rated for a category five, so no matter what Mother Nature has in store, on the fourth floor, we're in a safe place. And from the pictures of your house—"

"Which is totally cute, by the way," Trevor interjected.

"It's not a safe construction," Jim persisted. "And, you don't have any neighbors or communications channels."

"Agreed," Tara said. "When is it supposed to hit? Today?"

"No, not until tomorrow early afternoon. You can go home tonight, pack a bag, batten down the hatches, and plan to meet us for lunch."

"Late lunch," Neils said. "I plan on making up for the sleep I've lost taking care of the puke queen."

"Any time you want to get to the hotel is perfectly fine," Jim said. "I'm going to go to the store this evening and get some non-perishable foods and water for any worst-case scenarios. I don't know what the hotel has stored, but it never hurts to have backup."

"Tell me the truth." Tara leaned forward. "From chatting with Sammie, what does a worst-case scenario look like?"

23

Tara Alvarez

Sunday, Dominica

UNDERWATER AGAIN IN THE BEAUTY OF CORALS AND TROPICAL fish, Tara would admit it, the sea seemed angry.

There were three quick shots Trevor needed under the surface that were only necessary for Tara to do instead of Pria because Trevor didn't want to lose the atmospheric lighting as Tara and Neils came topside. Any other day, and Trevor could at least approximate the light quality to make his edits seamless. But today was a phenomenon.

Three that was it, and she was going up.

With the dredging done, this part of the filming didn't require permits, and Tara wasn't putting herself in danger's way when she could always shoot again another day, even if the footage missed the magic of the oddly vibrant coloration.

Better yet, Tara could watch them shoot another day, and Pria could be the Gwen.

Tara made a hand motion to say let's hurry this along and get it over with.

She and Neils—as Gwen and Kenneth—were supposed to have a loving moment enjoying the splendors of the underwater world.

They had grasped hands and had finned in a circle.

Now Neils—Kenneth—was supposed to discover something interesting to show her.

Neils searched around, his hand squeezing hers a little too tightly for comfort, then he pointed toward the rocks.

Tara could see lobster antennae peeking out from under the lip. Good find.

Hand in hand they swam over until Neils was positioned over the outcropping where he couldn't see the lobster at all.

She pulled him back, pointing below.

He pulled her forward, pointing at the top of the rock.

Tara had no idea what he was supposed to be showing her, but there was Trevor with his video camera. He dropped below them angling the camera upward. Tara decided to play along, get this over with, climb back on the boat, and eat her sandwich.

Neils reached out his hand, drawing a finger along the rock. When an eye spread wide, it was startling, like a horror movie where the monster had come awake.

Tara laughed to herself and pushed those images aside. This was hardly monstrous.

There, camouflaged with its chameleon coloration and its bumpy skin, was an octopus.

Though, not a reef octopus that she'd seen many times in her dives. This was way too big. Tara remarked that this octopus wasn't in her packet of indigenous species that she was given to catalog during her stay. From the size of the octopus's eyes, this specimen was nothing like what was supposed to be in the region.

Had it come in from the Atlantic? *Why* would it come in from the Atlantic?

Interesting.

And if it didn't belong here, the authorities might need to send divers out to remove it (or them). Invasive species, like the lionfish around St. Croix, could be extremely destructive to local aquaculture. Tara would get Trevor to give her copies of these frames to share with the authorities.

Neils reached out to stroke the octopus again.

Trevor had the camera right down, capturing the encounter.

Tara was dragging at Neils's arm to get him to stop pestering the poor thing, waking it up from its diurnal sleep.

One long tentacle reached out and wrapped along Trevor's arm exploring his diving suit. Another reached out and wound its way up Trevor's arm, curiously.

Tara leaned backward and finned out of its way.

Those tentacles had to be two maybe three feet long.

The octopus was acting outside of octopus norm. Usually, shy. Usually, nocturnal. Tara couldn't fathom why it didn't squirt some ink and swim away, other than it was startled awake or it had plans for those lobsters under the rock and didn't want to share. Maybe it was just bored and curious. She'd seen that before, too.

On a trip to the Mediterranean last summer, one of these critters climbed onto her friend's board, during a full moon paddle, Tara discovered that these highly intelligent creatures were inquisitive and would explore.

It seemed to Tara, that the octopus was dragging both men closer.

Where they had originally been amused by the octopus, Trevor and Neils were obviously changing their minds.

As Neils peeled one tentacle off, another slipped around another appendage. At the same time, the tentacle dragged at Trevor's camera strap that pulled Trevor in closer.

The octopus was pecking at the lens with his beak.

Now this part, Tara did know, octopi have beaks made to break through hard shells like the lobster below and to open clamshells, tearing the flesh of its prey.

Tara floated there stunned as she saw pieces of Trevor's camera break off and drift free.

The tide pulled Tara away, and she struggled to stay close while she formulated a plan to help them.

Sadly, she was coming up with nothing in the way of a strategy.

Trevor dragged the camera strap off to gain space, finning hard to get himself out of range in an explosion of bubbles.

The octopus put its full attention—and all eight tentacles—on Neils.

Tara maneuvered herself in close enough to help when a tentacle grabbed at Neils's breathing apparatus and tugged it from his mouth.

Neils fought to get it back as the octopus pulled off his face mask.

Neils was wide eyed with panic. Kicking off his fins, he used his feet to try to thrust the octopus away from him, flailing his arms, trying to find his breathing tube.

The mouthpiece bounced and danced with his erratic motions, pulling it away from Tara's grasp each time she reached for it.

One minute.

Neils had one minute before he'd start to black out.

Too far from the surface, it had to be air from a tank. Anyone's.

But a panicked Neils, still grappling with the octopus, made it impossible for Tara or Trevor to get close enough.

Feeling the seconds ticking, Tara, breathed in her air, then extended the mouthpiece out for Trevor to take a breath.

One breath, and they'd have another survival minute.

The octopus wrapped its tentacle out to her hair, then around Tara's neck.

The current was dragging at her.

The tentacle was tightening like a boa constrictor.

Tara's world became a nightmarish swirl of bubbles and the octopus's ink. The bulging eyes of a terrified Neils without air.

Tara had always felt safe diving in the crystal-clear waters of the Caribbean Sea. There was little to surprise her. She was always oriented and never felt issues with vertigo. But she was a clear water diver only. She had no experience in the inky darkness that swirled around her and she felt panic set in.

Panic killed divers.

The vertigo she was experiencing, in the inky dark with no idea of up or down, that too was deadly.

Tara too kicked off her fins hoping for more agility in the water as she pried the tentacle from her neck.

The suckers seemed to be sensing her skin, trying to identify her. Each circle stretched the skin on her neck in all directions. Not cruel, just curious. It had no idea the disaster it was creating.

This was nightmare fodder.

With a twist of her torso, Tara now saw Trevor pressing his mouthpiece to Neils's mouth.

Neils gripped and held it there. Tara was sure he was trying to process enough oxygen through his system so he wouldn't black out.

But Trevor, too, needed air.

The men were fighting for dominance over the mouthpiece.

Finally, Trevor got behind Neils and wrapped his long thin legs around Neils's torso, pinning his arms.

With Neils kicking and Trevor sculling with one arm while passing the air back and forth between them, the men were moving up to the surface way too fast.

And now, Tara was in the depths, alone—she and the curious octopus that was constricting her airway.

Tara sucked in thin reedy wisps of air.

And just like Neils, a veil of panic curtained off her logical brain.

That was when Tara suddenly pictured Austin.

She could feel him there with her. "You've got this. Slow down. Think."

And then like a gift, she saw the group sitting at the table last night. Tara was telling the quicksand story, and she mentioned the board game about survival.

An octopus attack was one of the questions in the game.

And the answer was all the things she'd already tried. Pull away quickly? Check.

Don't play dead. Oh, hell no was she going to do that.

Keep the octopus's arm from wrapping you. Way too late for that one.

Pull it away from the rock, or whatever else it has anchored itself to. That would be her oxygen tank. The octopus was anchored to her back.

Tara was in grave danger.

With Trevor and Neils out of view, there was no one there to help.

This was it. She was going to save herself or she would die.

She felt herself blacking out.

Just as the world closed in around her, Tara remembered the last thing on the survival card.

Turn somersaults.

Tara was back in the pond near her house as a kid, a mermaid frolicking in the water. She turned somersault after somersault as best she could with her tanks on.

And soon, with another squirt of ink, the octopus shot off into the distance and Tara was free.

Fighting every instinct in her body, Tara reached out to the floating strap of Trevor's camera so the octopus could be identified, then she made her slow, safe ascent toward the boat.

This whole event had been stunningly outside of Tara's experience.

When she surfaced, Tara spit her mouthpiece free, dragged the mask off her face and gasped at the air.

"Are you okay?" Jim grabbed at the wrist of her extended hand. He must have been pumping massive amounts of adrenaline through his system. With a tug, Tara felt her body rising from the water, then she was lying on the deck.

"What the hell happened down there?"

She shook her head as she took in Trevor and Neils. They were both in bad shape.

"They came up way too fast, we need to get them to the hospital," Jim said as he furiously worked to get the anchor up.

Tara crawled over to the radio.

Ponytail's boat had been near them earlier in the day. She'd spotted them through the binoculars when Trevor was filming. It could well be that they were still within close range, snorkeling. A cigarette boat could cut the time back to the dock in half if not more.

She had no clue of their call sign; she hadn't cared about the name of their boat when they were at the dock. So, she tried, "Cigarette boat. Cigarette boat. Cigarette boat. This is Forward, Ho!. We have a medical emergency. Come in."

She waited for the count of twenty and was about to press the button to make a broader appeal to any vessel that could move faster than their lumbering boat, when the radio crackled. "This is the Beula Mae, Forward, Ho!. We are a cigarette boat."

"Beula Mae are you the gentleman with the ponytail?"

"I am. I believe I have you in my binoculars. You're just over the reef with a blue hull?"

Tara moved out into the open and waved her hands over her head.

"I have you, Forward, Ho!. We're on our way."

Tara snatched up her binoculars and scanned the horizon until she spotted a broad plume of white spray churning in a tight circle.

The Beula Mae had put her throttle down and was coming full tilt.

Jim was cradling Trevor in his arms.

Neils leaned over the side of the boat gushing blood from his nostrils. The boat looked like a murder scene.

"Pinch down at the bridge of your nose, Neils."

"I am never going out on a dive with you again. Ever," he croaked.

"Me?" Tara was offended. She was the one that had wrestled his bulging-eyed, panicking self free of the tentacles.

"Tara is a walking disaster zone."

"I am not." Tara was filling a plastic bag with ice from the cooler.

"You're like a black hole." He reached for the baggie she handed him. "You suck all of the natural disasters toward you."

"Does that even make sense?"

"No, I guess it doesn't." He reached for a beach towel and smeared blood over his face. "I'll work on the simile."

"Do you have to?"

"For my safety's sake, I think I do." He was flexing his legs against the cramps, blood now soaking the towel.

And Tara wondered if anyone had ever bled out through the nose.

"Neils don't blame Tara, blame yourself. It's karma," Jim said as the Beula Mae pulled flush. "You ate octopus at dinner last night. Today, the species tried to pay you in kind."

"Not in the mood, Jim."

"Beula Mae, thank you." Tara reached out to the stick the ponytail guy extended and the boats bobbed side by side. "We had a SCUBA accident and two of our divers had to come up way too fast."

"The bends. They need the hospital."

"Yes, fast. And this boat isn't going to do it."

"Absolutely, let's get them aboard."

The other three men on the Beula Mae, climbed onto the Forward, Ho! to help move Neils and Trevor.

Ponytail focused on Tara. "Are you coming?"

"I don't want Jim out on the water alone. We'll catch up. There's an emergency managers office right across the street from the dock. They'll have equipment and transportation. Thank you so much," she called out.

And with that, the throttle was pressed down, and the Beula Mae was quickly out of sight.

Jim threw himself onto the couch and gripped at his chest. "I'm just too damned old for shit like this."

24

Austin Mace

Sunday, St. Kitts

BLASTED OUT OF ROCK ON A HIGH ELEVATION IN ST. KITTS, THE Iniquus Southern Control Complex was formed into the mountain that sheltered the north and east sides of the structure under almost a hundred feet of earth. On the south and west sides, the building was designed and constructed to meet the specs for the highest storm and fire protection.

The runway, placed on the west side, was short and a little tricky for landings, but Ash did a good job lining them up for decent.

Take offs were always much easier as the slope fell away quickly at the end, allowing the plane to wing out over the water.

Below the runway, stairs—chiseled from the cliff's side—connected to the dock below. If the operators anticipated a cycle of training or a were doing a quick turnaround, the team could land and tie up to the dock as they had in Dominica. Both the boats and the floatplanes could fuel up in the boathouse, a large cave Iniquus had blasted into the cliffside where the emergency vessels were safe from storms.

When things calmed down, Mace thought it would be a good idea for him to spend a morning working on both his water up and downs, but also navigating the very short runway that demanded focus and precision.

Mace knew what he *really* wanted to do was make another trip down to Dominica.

As Bravo was saying their good-byes to John John before their flight, John had said that the cable patch had failed. The momentary connections that had been establish Saturday night hadn't held. The island had celebrated too quickly. The government was depending on satellites as they monitored the news from off the island, including the encroaching storm.

John was worried.

All these years later, they were still coming back from Maria's devastation. And should a storm hit, his number two wasn't available to help. This was a significant setback on a small island with few emergency personnel.

Mace was thinking about his flight to Dominica yesterday, when he had taken off for his check in with Tara, filled with resolution and concern.

His worry was still a ball of pressure in his chest.

Despite everything else that had gone on over the last twenty-four plus hours, that clawing sense of alarm that he'd picked up from Mrs. Alvarez hadn't quieted.

And now Tara was out of quick reach.

Out of communications range on the mountain.

Tara had told him that since her phone—with her favorite playlists—had been stolen by the monkey, she had been fiddling with the little FM radio that came with the house. The single island channel that she could tune into was mostly the ghost of music floating behind a wall of static. She knew to be listening for information about the storm. She was a highly capable, highly intelligent woman. She'd been through her share of crises and always come out on top.

Trust her, his head said.

The "I need to be there" was his gut.

After years of war, Mace trusted his gut.

The fact that he couldn't reach Tara felt perilous.

With Pria or Tara's other friends without off-island cell phone connection. Mace had no one to check in with who could pass the phone to Tara unless someone happened to be within earshot of their sat phone.

He'd admit it; Mace wanted to hear her voice. The week or so that it would take her to wrap up her work in Dominica and come visit St. Kitt's seemed far away.

Too long.

Mace had never felt anything like this in his life. Tara was definitely messing with his head.

With a jolt as they touched down, Mace tuned his attention outward.

Ash was following the signal lights of a staffer as she directed the plane back into the cave that served as a hangar, housing their six other floatplanes with amphibious configurations allowing them to land on any flat stretch of land as well as in water. The number of planes was sufficient for the team to get in place, unload the blow-up raft, paddle to shore, collect their protectees and take off again, should commercial jets be unable to land. One after the other they'd gather their people, quickly evacuate them to an unaffected region, then return to the disaster site to lend a hand.

That the plane was directed to the hangar rather than the dock told Mace that the information he'd conveyed from

Sammie was being taken seriously, and Ares was preparing them to shelter from the storm.

On their approach, when Mace had looked out the side window, he noticed that the steel sea doors on the cave that served as the boathouse had been lowered.

"Batten the hatches, matey." Mace heard Tara's pirate voice in his head.

Funny thing. Just after noon, as they were tracing their way through the sky, Tara had come to mind. It was a strange three-dimensional image of her that formed in his imagination. She was struggling hard as if she thought she couldn't survive the next moment.

It was such a tense, almost other-worldly connection that Mace decided had sprung fully formed from his hyped-up concern. It made the small interior of the plane—filled with three over-sized men and three gassy K9s—claustrophobic.

He'd felt like a drowning man.

As a SEAL, in battle as panic gripped at him, Mace would counsel himself, "Slow it down. Think it through."

Mace believed his whole encounter with Tara was going to take a lot of thinking through, and that mantra would serve him well here.

He focused on how proud he was of her. How capable she was. How, even though she did difficult things under difficult circumstances, she was conquering the obstacles.

And just as suddenly as the suffocating sensations had wrapped his system, the claustrophobia lifted.

Now that they'd landed, there it was again, that tickle that said, *"Man, you're in the wrong place right now. Get back to her."*

But after that kiss? Who wouldn't be magnetized back to Tara?

∾

THE OPERATORS CLIMBED from the plane and unloaded their K9 partners.

"Ares is waiting for you in the conference room." The staffer's voice echoed in the damp cave where the darkness swallowed the illumination cast out by the fluorescent bulbs.

The men pulled their go-packs from the cargo area to take in and repack, fresh and ready for any reason they'd be called to jump.

If a siren sounded, the men leaped from their beds, yanked on their clothes, grabbed a leash, a dog, and a duffel, and arrived on the X, ready for a brief in less than five minutes. Ready to go and stay gone, the operator could live out of what was in that bag for a week. They and their dogs.

Dropping their gear outside of the conference room, Bear, Ash, Mace, and their K9 partners moved silently through the door.

Hailey Stapleton—newly engaged to Bravo leader Ares—was on the screen on a video call with the rest of their team: Goose, Red, and Knox. Hailey had left her previous employer to take a logistics position with Iniquus. With her ten years of field experience working for an NGO, Iniquus was glad to have her organizational expertise.

The conversation was paused as the men took their seats.

"Hi there," Hailey said. "I was just telling the team that Logistics will be headed to your region, possibly to the Southern Control Complex. We'll wait in Atlanta and watch landfall. But you should know, our team is in full force. The semi-trucks were loaded this morning and are driving to Georgia. We'll be jumping on the same flight as Team Alpha. Logistics will hold at an airport hotel until we get the necessary reports. Team Alpha, though, is changing planes and heading to

St. Kitts. They'll be on island in the next eight hours. They'll get rested, oriented, and ready for duty before the storm hits tomorrow."

"What is Noah saying about the storm?" Ares asked.

"At this point, it's a coin toss, but we should be prepared for a bad time, all hands on deck." Hailey checked her watch. "It's best if you speak directly to him. I'll make a note for Noah to call in. Quick take, Puerto Rico looks like it's going to duck a direct hit."

"St. Kitts?" Goose asked.

"Is gonna get breezy." She shuffled through a pile of papers. "Okay, here we go. I have lists of our protectees in the Caribbean region. There are two hundred adults spread throughout the islands, ten minors." She looked up. "Luckily, many of our lists cleared for a few weeks as the spring semester finished, and the university students haven't made their way out for summer abroad sessions." She put her finger on the list. "Our biggest corporate concerns are in Barbados where ALM is hosting a corporate retreat. And there's an executive planning meeting going on in Martinique for QualityPlus. With Mace, Bear, and Ash in Dominica, they'll be positioned for either or both, depending."

Ares turned to the men. "Bob and I decided to turn you three back around. You've already developed rapport with the Trifalgar group and reconnected with John John. We're concerned about their lack of communications through their sea cable."

Mace was jazzed by this news but maintained a stoic expression in front of his team.

"Yes," Hailey said. "We'll be waiting for any information you can pass us about how things look from the ground. It'll help us with our planning the best route for getting our supplies in, be it cargo plane or boat if needs be. And if things stay in good shape there, you'll be closest to assist in Barbados or Martinique." She took a sip of water. "Side note, this is an interesting ride for me. This will be my first storm season with Iniquus. I already see I'm going to learn a lot about how the commercial side of rescue works. For right now, my team is contacting and personally speaking with each person on our list. We're mapping their locations and documenting room assignments and asking them to stay put until we've made contact post storm, whether they experience adverse weather or not. We're emailing checklists and suggestions for gathering some supplies for the time when they might need to wait for our teams to get to them. We cannot reach the Trifalgar group, obviously. But we have documented that they are, at least, aware of the storm."

"Other than Trifalgar, how are those phone calls going?" Ares asked. "Are they taking this seriously?"

"Mmm. Sounds to me like the executives in Martinique are planning on making buckets of "hurricane" cocktails to drink for a watch party. They're headquartered in Louisiana, so this isn't their first rodeo. I've checked on their hotel. It's only three years old—so updated construction requirements. And their rooms are all on the west side of the building with a privacy walled courtyard. And while we have no communications link to Trifalgar, I did check on their hotel, and it's one of the structures that was built with international funds. It's the gold standard."

"Speaking of which, Hailey," Ares said. "I need you to find a way to communicate with Blue Horizon and get three rooms for our team."

"I have a boat captain with a satellite phone who has allowed us to pick up his hotel tab to be our communications conduit when Bravo operators were down there. I'll ring him as soon as I'm off this conference call."

"Well done," Mace said.

"Thank you.

Ares pressed back in his seat; arms crossed over his chest. "I also need you to get in touch with a man named John John—"

"John John, is that a last name? First name?"

"Both. It's "Captain John" when you speak to him for the first time. He's the director of emergency management in Dominica. His headquarters are about a block up from the Blue Horizon. Tell him Bravo is heading back his way for an assist. As soon as our guys get checked in at the hotel, and have communicated with our clients, they'll head to his headquarters to lend a hand. Make sure you advise the hotel that the working dogs are coming in. They may balk because of the storm and the difficulty of taking care of dogs under such circumstances—"

"I'll just explain that the dogs are coming in for search and rescue should it be needed. That should smooth it over."

"Hailey, I'd like to get the plane space in a boathouse if that's possible," Bear added. "West side of the island."

She scribbled notes on her pad. "I'll work on it."

"Whatever you can manage under these circumstances would be appreciated."

Mace waited for Hailey to look up again. "Hailey, Tara Alvarez is also a Trifalgar scientist, she wasn't on your list?"

"Ares told me that your friend was down there. I checked for you when that name didn't come up on the computer. Tara Alvarez's contracts don't include the hazard intervention insurance through DARPA."

And so went the back and forth, lining everything up, looking for the holes, getting them plugged.

After the conference with Hailey concluded and the screen went blank, Ares stood. "We have a plan. Gentlemen, I need you to go and pack enough gear to sustain you and your K9 for a week. Everything you might need to support an urban search." He gestured between Ash, Bear, and Mace. "Once Trifalgar personnel are out of danger, your job will be clearing houses and finding people in the rubble until we know you're needed for our contractors."

"Sir," the men responded.

"You'll leave out in the morning. I'd like a little more information about the storm and to make our plans with Team Alpha once they set down."

When the men stood to leave the room, their dogs yawned and stretched then trotted alongside them.

Ash, Bear, and Mace threw their go bags over their shoulders and started back to their personal quarters.

Ash adjusted his bag on his shoulder and let his hand drop onto Hoover's head for a quick scritch. "What's up with you and Tara?"

"How do you mean?" Mace asked.

"I thought I saw sparks flying between you two during the dinner. And I thought I was going to have to haul you off that guy Neils."

"Nah, he was a gnat, that's all. I had a nice time catching up with a family friend. My best friend's little sis."

Ash chuckled. "Uh-huh."

"What 'uh-huh.'?"

"Glad you had the opportunity to catch up," Ash said. "She's led a damned cool life. I like listening to her. She could go toe to toe with a lot of operators in a bar story contest."

"Good that we're going back to check on her, though," Bear said. "Her up on that mountain like that with no one around? That takes *cajones*."

When Mace didn't say anything, Bear added, "Look, man, Tara's traveled the world and has been fine without you. She can navigate this. She'll check in with her friends. Pria will insist Tara come down and stay in the hotel."

"Yeah, it's just a tickle in the back of my throat. It feels like I have mission orders in my hand, and I need to jump now."

"Okay here's what'll happen. Ash and I will check that the scientists are comfy and prepared. Then we'll go sit with John John and his team. If Tara isn't already down from the mountain, you go get her, stick her in your room. Then join us over at the Emergency Center."

"Yeah, man. Sounds like the right plan."

Bear was right, Tara was an intelligent, practical woman. The best choices were really a no brainer. Under normal circumstances, he'd assume a good outcome.

But as he rounded into his room, a text message pinged his phone.

MATTEO: **Hey, buddy, two things: First. Bethany just gave birth. Everyone's fine. You're a godfather.**

MACE: **Huge congrats, man. I'm stoked!**

MATTEO: **The other one was Mom.**

Matteo: **She had another nightmare about Tara. She's climbing the walls. I mean, I had the doctor give her a sedative kind of climbing the walls. It has to be that storm. The cable fix didn't hold. We looked it up on the internet and they said that they're working on it under adverse conditions whatever that means.**

. . .

MACE: **Okay. Tell your mom two things for me. One. Pria and the gang are in a cat-5 rated, storm surge protected hotel. Tara slept there last night. I am certain with a storm coming in, they will insist Tara stay there with Pria.**

MATTEO: **Good news.**

MACE: **And I will personally check that's true. My team is headed back to Dominica in the morning. We'll be there in time for me to check on everyone's safety before we get to work.**

MATTEO: **Thanks man. Truly appreciated.**

MACE WONDERED if Matteo would be as grateful if he knew about *the* kiss.

And about how Mace now felt about Tara. This time when Mace went to check on her, it wasn't for Mrs. Alvarez's benefit.

Tara was *his* to protect.

25

Austin Mace

Monday, Dominica

THE WIND WAS ALREADY A PROBLEM.

It was Bear's turn piloting, and it was like wrestling an alligator all the way south.

Mace would admit it, there were more than a few gut-tightening drops. The flash of an image came and went of the three men and their K9s trying to ride out a hurricane in the Caribbean Sea in a floatplane.

Ridiculous.

It didn't help that the interior reeked of dog puke. Not one of the three dogs thought this was cool.

Ash was sitting back with the crates, and when Mace turned to check on him, he was holding a plastic bag at the ready, a little green around the gills himself.

They landed onto choppy waters on the far side of the island.

Taxiing to the marina, where Hailey had secured a space for their plane, they'd found that she'd also arranged for three offroad vehicles to be waiting for them there.

Things couldn't have gone more smoothly, at least as far as logistics was concerned.

Comms were still out.

The guy stacking sandbags outside his office said that the storm had taken a sudden turn. "Better you get where you're going."

That confirmed what Ares announced over their radio when they were about halfway to Dominica. "Get in and get zipped up. They've elevated this to a cat 4. It's a monster. And it's heading straight for you."

Even now that they'd landed, Diesel was feeling the effects of the rollercoaster flight. His body was lax, and his head hung down, as he panted, tongue dripping.

Mace decided to head to the hotel and get his search gear and medical pack inside. That would give Diesel a distraction and some time to adjust. Mace would see if Diesel could shake this off before making any decisions about next steps.

When they arrived at the Blue Horizon, Mace said, "I'm dropping, checking, and if needs be, rolling out."

"Sounds good." Ash slammed his door shut on his all-terrain. "What are the chances these vehicles are still here after the storm?"

"Depends on the storm surge." Bear had Truffles in his arms like a big baby.

"How's she doing?" Mace asked.

"Eh, she'll be okay. I'm going to give her some water and let her rest in my room while we do our welfare checks on the good scientists."

"I think I'll leave Hoover in there with her," Ash said

throwing a pack over either shoulder, and grabbing a third bag by the grip handles. "They can commiserate."

The men grabbed their keys from the reception desk and headed for the elevators.

Diesel had already perked up.

With a quick run to his room to drop his search gear, the next stop was Pria's to check if Tara was already in place.

Pria opened her door. "Well, hey there."

Mace said, "Hi" as he turned his attention to Ash and Bear, rounding the corner.

"The men weren't answering their doors," Bear said, looking to Pria for an explanation.

"No," Pria confirmed. "Jim went up to the hospital about twenty minutes ago to pick up Trevor and Neils."

"Hospital?" Bear asked.

"Diving accident. Neils lost his mouthpiece to an octopus attack. He came up too fast, buddy breathing with Trevor. They both had mild decompression sickness. Their good now. We have lunch reservations in an hour if you'd like to join us."

Octopus attack? In the Caribbean?

Ice rushed through Mace's veins. "Tara?" Her name was barely audible.

"Is fine. In the water yesterday, she came up at the right pace. We had dinner together last night, and she went home to pack her stuff and shut up the house in advance of the storm. The radio just said we're lining up with the eye, and it's a four. That's unnerving. I've never been through a storm this size."

"This hotel is the safest place to be," Bear reassured her.

Pria pulled her shirt away from her chest and let it fall back into place. "Tara will be staying in Trevor's room. And Trevor will be staying with his cousin Jim. You okay, Mace?"

"Rough ride in, no big deal," he managed. He looked over at Bear. "What's your play?"

"Depends." He turned to Pria. "What preparations do you have in place. What with the accident yesterday that might not have been—"

"I gathered food and water for all of five us for a week," Pria said. "Tara's bringing things down from her house, too. My stuff is mostly snack foods. There wasn't a lot left on the store shelves." She skated her hand out. "Oh, and I unloaded what food there was on the Forward, Ho!. Jim moved the boat to the other side of the island last night. It's in a cove."

"Good," Bear said. "Why don't we have lunch with the scientists and go over a few things, then head over to John John's headquarters. How about you?" Bear rocked back on his heels. "Are you waiting here for Tara to show up or are you going up the mountain?"

"I'll go up and see if she needs a hand with anything. I'll be back by lunch."

"MOLTKE SAID that no plan survives contact with the enemy. Now, isn't that the damned truth?" Mace asked Diesel.

They'd made it three-quarters of the way up to Parrot's Perch when he stopped at a tree laying across the road.

Huge trunk, bigger root ball, it was one of the first soldiers to fall to the gusts that intermittently gathered then roared down the mountain.

Tara wouldn't be able to drive around this. And there was no way she could jog herself to safety before the full wrath of Hurricane Alvise struck.

"Good thing we decided to get on up here, Diesel."

Mrs. Alvarez was batting a thousand.

Mace did a three-point turn to have them facing in the right direction and left the keys in the ignition.

"Ready to go find Tara?" Mace didn't need to wait for a response, Diesel bounded out of the vehicle and leaped the tree trunk. "Dude, wait for me." Mace grabbed his go pack, slipped his arms through the straps, and scissored his legs over the trunk.

Diesel matched Mace's pace as they sprinted up the mountain.

"Two kilometers up. Two kilometers down," he told Diesel. "A little over a mile should be easy for her. But I don't know how fast Tara runs, so let's get on this."

As the wind snatched at his clothes, they pressed harder.

The sky was bruised with splotches of green and purple.

Ahead, through the swaying banana leaves, he could see Tara's lights glowing bright.

As they curved into her clearing, Mace didn't stop to knock, he burst through her door.

There she sat splay legged on the floor, shoving equipment into a pack. Her head jerked up to assess the intrusion.

"Shit, you did come." Tears sprang to her eyes, and Tara covered her face.

Mace was over to her in two strides. Scooping her up, he crushed Tara in his arms, pressing a hard kiss on her mouth.

He could taste her anxiety, and a breath of relief.

Still panting from his race up the mountain side, Mace said, "Quick, do you have the bag you were taking to Pria's?"

She pointed.

Without another word, he snatched it up and strapped it to his front.

Grabbed her hand.

Dragged her out the door.

Tara came to a full stop on her stairs, eyes scanning. "How did you get here? There's a tree in the road."

"We ran. And we're going to need to keep running. Two

kilometers, full tilt, okay? More trees are going to come crashing down. It's too dangerous out here." His voice rode the wind.

And they took off with the gusts at their backs, pushing them toward safety.

Mace held her hand on one side, keeping her steady. Diesel pushed her back upright when she teetered on the other.

The three of them raced toward the all-terrain.

This was the push, then they'd just drive that last bit to the hotel and safety.

He could tell Tara was challenged by the pace. But that was the requirement here.

Do or die. There was no special sauce.

When they reached the tree with the vehicle sitting ready just on the other side. Tara put her hands on her knees and gulped in deep breaths, while Mace pulled off the packs and set them on the other side of the downed trunk.

Tara was spent. Wrung dry from the pace he'd set.

Since she was a foot shorter than him, Mace decided to just lift Tara over the trunk rather than ask her to climb.

Bending, Mace slid an arm around her back, then under her knees. He cradled her in his arms as he stepped forward.

Tara slid her arms around his neck. When he looked her way to explain next steps, she kissed him.

She tasted salty and sweet. He buzzed from head to toe, standing there not wanting the moment to stop.

With a wrenching wooden shriek in his ears, Mace intuitively dropped to the ground, curling protectively around Tara, calling Diesel in tight. He hoped if a tree fell their way that the first downed soldier would keep it from crushing them.

Crunching, whining metal had Mace closing his eyes.

Tara jostled out of Mace's arms, swiveled, and gasped, "No!"

"Tara Alvarez," he caught her chin, "you are a good luck charm. If I hadn't wanted to kiss you so bad, we would have been climbing in the vehicle when that tree hit."

She grabbed her stomach. "I think I'm going to puke."

"You can do that later. Right now, we need a plan. You were packing when I burst through your door. Where were you going?"

"Okay." She gave herself a shake like Trevor had taught her yesterday on the boat shoot. "Okay," she started again. "There were basically two options. The Josephs' own a car. They're about two miles from here. But I wouldn't think they'd stay in their house. They'd surely go to a shelter, which means no car. I don't think we have enough time left to run all the way to the hotel."

"You're right about the hotel. I don't think I saw a car as I drove up. But I was focused on getting to you."

"My next thought was to go to the waterfall."

"The one where I washed my eyes clear?"

"No. no. That would be much too far. And not helpful. This one is up the mountain on a different path, only about two hundred yards from my house."

"Why there?" They remained crouched there by the trunk, talking between the wind gusts that stole their words.

"There's a cave just above it," she said. "High enough that if there's a deluge of water coming off the mountain, it should still be safe. I thought I'd shelter in there until it was all over."

"Big enough for all of us?"

"Yes." She nodded. "Yes, absolutely."

Mace grabbed her hand and dragged her up with him. He fished up their bags, strapped them on, and with Tara's hand in his, the three started back up the mountain toward Parrot's Perch. Even that rickety structure was better than standing in the open. "We'll work that plan. Let's get back to your house and pick up the gear you were packing." He lifted her hand to his lips. "How are you doing? Do you think you can run?"

26

Austin Mace

Monday, Dominica

As Tara collapsed on her steps, then crawled to her front door, the trees arched in improbable ways. Like a stick that he broke over his knee at a campfire, Mace thought they would snap and drop on their heads.

Or the limbs would become javelins and spear through them.

The assault was like going up against a prize fighter. Strategic lulls in the wind force would extend long enough for them to feel a bit of complacency, like they had this wrapped.

Then a gale would hit them across the chest.

There was so much air that Mace couldn't seem to get enough into his lungs. Like a man dying of thirst, chomping at the end of a fire hose to swallow a single drop.

Diesel had hunkered low to the ground. There seemed some

joy in the way he'd look up at Mace. Of course, Diesel liked to hang his head out the window when they were powering down the highway at seventy miles an hour. This was his jam.

Tara was about a hundred pounds lighter than Mace, and she had had to bend in two using her head as a driving tool, carving a space in the air for her body to follow.

When Tara extended her arms toward the ground as if she were going to drop down next to Diesel and crawl the rest of the way, Mace tucked Tara behind him with her fists wrapped into the waistband of his pants, so he could use his body to shield her from some of the onslaught.

At least they'd made it back to Parrot's Perch, a resting spot on this treacherous journey.

Now, Mace was second guessing himself. If he'd stayed the hell away. Stayed at the hotel. Tara would have gone to the cave by herself. She'd already be hunkering down and would have missed the last hour of extreme effort.

Where Tara was the lucky charm, had he become the jinx?

Mace forced those thoughts away. There would be time to assess his actions with his brothers in the hotwash. Everything that was done and not done was owned up to, presented to the brothers to assess, and the team would make plans to do it better should that scenario show itself again.

There was no way to know that the tree would be down.

And then a second one.

In an emergency, you roll with the punches. No time to waste on this now.

His hand gripped the doorknob.

Tara held out her keys.

When he got the door open an inch, the wind ripped it from Mace's hands and banged it against the wall, shattering the glass.

Tara and Diesel staggered inside.

Mace had to press his body weight into the door to get it shut again.

The thought of another two hundred yards trek through the rainforest was daunting. And Mace felt complete responsibility for Tara and Diesel's wellbeing.

As safe as it felt here, comparatively. It was like running from the Taliban, holing up in a compound, knowing that compound was a target for an incoming RPG.

As intimidating as it was to face the enemy, the shelter was a mirage.

"Time to go," he said.

"One more minute."

"No, Tara. That one more minute might be the very minute we needed to survive this."

"Seriously, it can't get much worse, can it?" She lifted her palm. "This is sort of what it looked like on the weather channel when the reporters are out in the worst of it being buffeted around."

"Tara, my team was told a hundred and forty mile an hour winds. We're only up to sixty-seventy miles an hour now with faster gusts."

"Are you kidding me?"

"These are just the outer bands."

"*Just?*"

"We can't stand up against what's coming. This *house* can't stand up against what's coming. We've got to get in that cave now. And by now, I mean five minutes ago." He reached out his hand for hers and pulled her up. "I know you're tired. I'll help you. It's two hundred yards then safe, right? The cave is good? It's deep?"

A look crossed her face that made him doubt this plan.

"It's deep enough for safety?" he pressed. "High enough of an elevation to handle thirty inches of rain?"

"It is deep enough. We'll be safe from the water." She was holding something back; he could see it in her eyes. But there was nothing she could say that would make him change his mind. At this point, there was *nowhere* else to go.

"What's in your pack that you need to survive the next five hours in the cave?" he asked.

Tara looked where he'd dropped the pack.

"That one was clothes and food for the hotel. Nothing in that one." She looked at the pack she was shoving together to get herself to the cave an hour ago when Mace crashed through her door. "This one was cave survival stuff. Camping gear to keep from hypothermia sitting on the rocks. Like a camp stove."

"I have that. Is there anything that you can think of that you need to add for survival's sake. Lighter is safer."

Tara hustled to her room and came back a moment later with rain pants over her shorts, and a hiker's raincoat. She tugged at the storm cord at her waist that would tighten the bulk of her rain jacket and keep the wind out. From her pocket she pulled her GPS gadget and extended it to Mace. The cave pin was already on the screen. "We won't be able to find it otherwise. My trail will be destroyed by the downed foliage. The last thing I want to do is get turned around and lost in this."

"Good move."

She stopped in front of him, looking up. Her eyes were brown velvet and filled with trust. "Ready."

In the time that Tara was getting into her raingear, Mace had pulled on his headlamp with the high lumen lights, then his ball cap, and finally his own storm jacket. He'd cinched the hood down tight around his face to keep the wind from dragging away their light source. Like the GPS, this was a piece of life-or-death gear.

With a deep breath and determination, out they went.

Again, the door was whipped from his hands. Mace struggled to get it shut, then just abandoned it. The chances of the roof staying intact was remote. Shutting the door would do no good.

Tara hunkered against the wall.

The green had left the sky and the violent purple seemed to pulse above them. It was going to get dark fast.

Mace signaled Diesel between his legs, a place where Diesel trained to follow every move that Mace made while they were engaging with the enemy.

And Mother Nature—as beautiful as she was—was nothing if not a formidable adversary.

Mace reached a hand to Tara and pulled her around, pressing her hands back into his waistband like before.

There was no way to speak or be heard anymore.

At least they had SCUBA hand signals in common.

The GPS was clenched in his left hand. His right arm moved up and down with quick martial arts blocks to throw off the flying debris.

They stepped.

Then stepped.

Then stepped.

Each time they moved forward they stopped to balance between their feet. Mace conjured pictures of the astronauts on the moon.

It felt that way out here.

Gravity-less.

Weightless.

Ready to be blown from the surface and fly into outer space.

Mace reached out to press a hand into a trunk to steady himself, and the tree went down.

That was the last time he'd try that.

When they got to the cave, he'd make some joke for Tara about being so strong that he could topple a tree with one hand.

But right now, there was nothing funny about the time and effort it took to go a mere twenty paces.

27

Austin Mace

Monday, Dominica

IN A LULL, THEY SCRAMBLED UP THE HILL, FAR ABOVE THE waterfall, and into the opening of the cave.

Once he got Tara and Diesel inside, Mace searched for rocks that he then piled inside the entry.

Speed was his goal.

Tara had Diesel between her legs as she sat with her back against the stone surface. She rounded down over him, panting, her limbs visibly quivering from her exertion.

Mace, too, had had to dig deep.

That two hundred yards was the kind of thing Mace could imagine as part of Hell Week for those trying to make the cut and join the SEALs.

He dug a light out of his pack and moved farther in to hand it to Tara.

"What's that smell?"

"Wet dog? The pungent one is guano. We're not alone in here."

"Bats? Is that what you weren't mentioning earlier?"

"Yeah. Some people don't like them. Vampire nightmares and what have you."

"You?" he asked, turning his back as he began to build his wall against the winds at the cave opening.

"I'm indifferent as long as we are respectful of each other." There was a moment of silence before she added. "Oh look, not just bats."

Mace didn't look around; his focus was on this next crucial task. "Tell me."

"Boa."

"How many snakes?" Vampire bats? Cool. He could deal. Snakes, though…

"Just the one that I can see, but the cave is pretty deep. With the rough rock and the cold temperatures back there, it's probably just the one."

"Do you know anything about boas? I mean I can wrestle it out of the cave if necessary." Mace really *hated* snakes. And the thought of following through on that action? He'd rather go hand to hand with a jihadist.

Diesel caught Mace's gaze. There was that laughter, again.

Diesel had to be "snake trained" to avoid rattle snakes in the mountains of Virginia. Diesel learned to avoid them, but not from fear.

And Mace didn't "fear them." There was just something about snakes that sent a whole-body tremor of repulsion through him.

"Throw the boa into the storm?" Tara asked. "No, you won't. Besides if a snake wants to find a way in, the snake will find a way in. Mmm. Looks like she's eaten. Her belly is full."

"What do you know about boa behavior?" Mace asked.

"Apex predator. Top of the food chain. Not known for being super aggressive."

"How long do you think it is?"

"The snake? Maybe, ten feet? Hard to tell coiled up like that. Could be longer."

He placed the last rock that sealed them in. There were more stones in the interior he'd move into place.

"Hmm, she moved."

He braced. "Moved or is advancing?" Mace tried to keep his tone neutral.

"The temperature dropped precipitously. The snake is cold blooded. I'd say we're not in danger of Betsy."

Mace grinned at Tara, "Betsy is…?"

"Oh, I named the snake. She's less scary that way. Usually, I'm okay with snakes, but these are weird times. I just had my phone *and* my computer stolen by a monkey and tangoed with an octopus so…"

"It's a she?"

"Shes are less scary."

"Ah. Betsy the Boa then. And she's too cold to want to squeeze us to death." Mace was really hoping Tara was going to tell him some science-y fact that lowered the cringe factor on the snake. Naming it Betsy wasn't going to do it for him.

"Did you study boas in SEAL school?"

"In the Navy I did water and desert. I never did jungle training. Boa constrictors never came up in demolition school."

"K. Don't mean to wig you out—or me for that matter, but we're 98.6 degrees."

"Inside not out," he said.

"Still, we put off heat."

"Betsy might crawl up looking for a warm mat?" Yeah, that was going to be a nope from him. Mace reached in his go bag and tugged out the medical kit.

"I'm not sure that would happen. It's cold blooded so it might just stop. I think with what I've already told you about the bats and the boa, I've exhausted my bag of facts. It's not my area of expertise. I do polystyrene."

"Which under the circumstances—"

"Isn't a huge help." She pulled Diesel around, so his head was lying in her lap. "I thought they put you through jungle school and stuff."

Diesel turned to check if that was okay with Mace that he was lying on Tara. Mace gave Diesel a nod. He was probably helping to calm Tara's nerves.

"Only if we're deploying to the jungle. I was in the desert."

"Which right now isn't a huge help." She leaned in. "What have you got there?"

"Heating pads for minor injuries. They last eight hours. I thought I might try to keep Betsy comfortable back there."

Could be a help. Might just wake Betsy up and make her inquisitive. Only one way to find out. Mace shook the bag to combine the chemical, creating the reaction that produced heat. "I have a tent. I'll set it up in a minute, and we can zip it closed. A snake that heavy might be a problem, but mostly I want to keep the bats away. A round of rabies shots is no joke."

"Agreed." She scrunched her fingers into Diesel's ruff. "You'll tell me when I can be helpful?"

Mace thought that yeah, she could go back and deliver the heating pads to Betsy but decided that wasn't a good look. "I have a system. It's easier for me to do it."

He clenched his stomach muscles as he reached toward Betsy. "Good, girl. Gooood, girl," he whispered as he slid the pads nearby, but not so close they might burn her.

He backed out of the space, working on getting his game face back in place.

The next task on his list was to get the floor of the cave

cleared as much as possible for the tent, adding the loose rocks to his barricade.

The wind was finding its way through the cracks and crevices left in Mace's design.

More time and a thicker wall... Well, he'd made do with what he had. And right now, he was damned grateful for the cave. Damned grateful that he had Tara and Diesel with him and safe. "I have a friend named Remi Taleb—"

"The war reporter? You know her?"

"Yeah, we've crossed paths. She and her friend Hailey Stapleton—"

"Oh, I know that name, too. Ash told me at dinner, that's Ares's fiancée. They got engaged last week?"

"That's right. Remi and Hailey have a group of friends who call themselves the Wombats," he said as he worked.

"Wombats are totally cool. My friend Elisa told me the male wombats have heart-shaped penises no, heart-shaped testicles." Tara stopped to offer up a self-conscious laugh, probably for bringing balls into the conversation. Though, truth be told, Mace had been thinking entirely too much about dicks—his dick—since he'd walked back into Tara's life.

And her beautiful mouth saying "penis" made his cock jump to attention— "Me? Are you talking to me?"

Tara recovered from her embarrassment with, "The magical thing about wombats is that they poop square poops." She handed him a sizable rock. "And they stack them up. While it would smell terrible, I'd imagine, a wall of wombat poop might be a good wind block."

"Oh, yeah. You probably know all this."

"Tell me anyway." She handed off another rock.

"Remi was telling us how when there were the fires in Australia the wombats allowed all the other animals down in their dens and helped protect them."

"Why were you around a war reporter recently? Was she with the company you were helping to move out of the war zone? The one you told us about at dinner?"

"Right. Bravo was in Nezdolannyy effecting an extraction of the workers in an American company headquartered there. We had hunkered in the subway during a bomb siren."

"Oh, wow." Tara reached down and kissed Diesel, hugging him around the neck. "I'd make a terrible wombat," she told Diesel. "I'll hole up with the boa and the bats, but otherwise, I'd like to keep the cave to ourselves. Wouldn't you, Diesel? You're such a patient good boy. Thank you for helping me today." She planted another kiss on Diesel's head.

When she caught Mace looking at her, she said, "I'm thinking of the people who are facing their own kind of storm over in Eastern Europe. Man's inhumanity to man. And man's inhumanity to planet. We kinda suck."

"Very pessimistic."

"We're at the front end of a hurricane, lying in a cave with a 10-foot boa at our feet and possibly rabid bats over our heads."

"I've had my shots. I'm setting up a tent for you. I need to keep you safe."

"We'll hang a sign around your neck saying that you're the buffet, and they should leave me alone."

"Our light will keep them asleep. They're nocturnal."

"Maybe," she said with a curl of her lip. "I don't know."

"Truthfully, I don't either." He spread the ground tarp and smoothed it flat.

"So, you think I'm the pessimist? Tell me something optimistic to think about."

"There's a group of scientists called the Trifalgar Working Group, and they travel the world, digging up worms, searching out algae, and doing whatever else they can to right the ship."

"Very Navy of you to use that phrase."

"Truth, though, even in the time I've been with Iniquus on Cerberus Team Bravo. There's been an uptick in natural disasters. Each year, we go out on more and more missions. They're more dire. They last longer."

"How do you deal with it?" she asked.

"One mission at a time. One day. One life saved." He leaned in and kissed her. He rubbed his lip. "Just checking."

She raised her brows. "And?"

"Electricity. I think when you were struck with lightning, you became a superhero."

"No doubt. Can I whisper a deep dark secret?" Tara asked.

"Always." Mace stilled. His heart pounding.

"When I'm with you, I feel like I'm back in my body." Her eyes searched his. "Like I'm grounded again and not floating somewhere nearby. I'm safe again. Just like I felt with you way back when I knew you before."

He felt her trust.

Felt her conviction.

And it scared the living hell out of him.

28

Austin Mace

Monday, Dominica

THE WIND LIFTED ITS VOICE IN AN OTHERWORLDLY HOWL, AND Mace thought about the phrase, the wolves at the gate.

It had been over an hour since things had really kicked up out there.

So far so good in the cave.

He'd done everything possible to get them safe and secure, and hopefully, comfortable.

Right now, he had two MREs heating in their sleeves to buoy their spirits and warm their bodies. The temperature had dropped sharply.

With the lamp glowing inside their tent, Mace could focus for the first time on Tara's wellbeing. "Pria said you had an octopus adventure yesterday." He reached out to draw the pad of his finger over the welts it had left, strange looking circles along a strip that had coiled her neck twice. "Does this hurt?"

"Octopus hickeys? I had other things on my mind. I'd forgotten about yesterday's disaster. The misadventures seem to be coming fast and furious."

"This looks like you went through something pretty frightening."

"Yes." She sipped at the air.

He wondered if she'd had an opportunity to process the event with Pria. "Better out than in" was an Iniquus saying. They talked things out as much as needed to purge them from their systems and protect themselves from PTSD. "The tentacle wrapped your neck."

"It did."

"Did it choke you?"

"It startled me. It made me claustrophobic and fearful," she said quietly. "I didn't get the impression that it wanted to hurt me, us. It just felt curious. It wasn't like it was on an octopus rampage or anything." She was petting Diesel as she spoke. Dog medicine. "I mean, we are the visitors in the octopus world. We were the aggressors in that way. And if one could call it an act of aggression, it was Neils who started it. His fondling the octopus without consent nearly got him killed down there on the sea floor. I was the first responder of sorts."

"That's…unexpected. Octopi are usually pretty shy."

She shrugged. "So are monkeys. Go figure."

Mace followed the marks around her neck with his finger, gently, watching her face to make sure that there was no sign of discomfort. "I'm having trouble imagining…" He let the sentence fade.

"Its curious tentacle dragged Neils's breathing apparatus off, then his mask, and in the bubbles, Neils couldn't find his air supply."

"Shit." Mace sat back and imagined the scene.

"Pretty much. Trevor dropped his camera and was buddy breathing with Neils, and I was—"

"Fighting off the octopus."

"Two hands to eight. It wasn't a fair fight. But eventually we called a truce, and both swam away. Did you know that each tentacle can act on its own as if it had its own brain and its own task? Highly intelligent, if only they could communicate with each other, they'd be masters of the world. We would all bow to our octopi overlords."

She'd brushed right by the danger.

Trevor might be right about Tara leading the charmed life of a cat. How many of her nine lives had she used up?

"Don't you dare think that." She scowled.

"Think what?"

"No wonder Mrs. Alvarez is terrified about Tara."

He held up both hands with splayed fingers and a shake of his head, the hint of laughter wiggled at the corners of his mouth. "I didn't think that."

Up arched a single suspicious brow. "But something close."

Mace let that conversation fade, by fixing up their dinner plates.

"Kind of romantic, don't you think?" Tara asked.

Mace chuckled. He'd never met a woman who would think this particular setting and these particular circumstances were romantic.

"If I had invited you out on a date—which I plan to do on St. Kitts when this is over—I'd probably pull out a tried-and-true dating question."

"I'm not sure I know what that means."

"Dating questions?" he said, handing her a plate. "You know, like, if you could pick someone dead or alive to have dinner with who would you choose?"

She dangled her spork over the stew. "I always found that particular question useless."

"How so?"

"The question says you're having dinner with them. That means you're eating together. It says nothing about conversation. Perhaps they're fatigued from being dragged back from the great beyond. Maybe even disoriented. And all they want to do, in that moment, is to sit very still and very quietly as they get their bearings, with absolutely no interest in the food or a conversation."

Mace tucked his chin as he laughed long and hard.

When he finally sobered, she said, "The question should be more direct. Like, 'if you could spend three hours enjoying a cocktail and an intimate, openhearted conversation with anyone from anytime period who would you choose?'"

"Who would you choose?"

"Mmm. Right now, I'd like to chat the guy who started Patagonia. A billionaire, he just gave his money to the Earth."

"How's that?" Mace asked then bit into his cracker.

"All of his wealth—and the future wealth of the company— is going to Earth saving projects."

"Wow. Billion? Yes, I'd like to meet that man."

"And you?" Tara asked as she read the ingredients on the package on the cheese spread with a look of disgust.

"I'd like to talk to my mom. I'd like to understand some things about her. Things I wasn't mature enough to question while she was alive, and that I didn't have the world experience to consider."

"You were thirteen." She slipped her hand onto his knee.

Yeah, moving along. "Another dating question—since you brought up the billionaire guy giving his wealth to the Earth —what do you think about when you hear the word 'wealth'?"

"If one has to pick a way to be wealthy, I guess I prefer wealth of knowledge."

"Over money?"

"I'm not big into money. I mean. It's convenient, sure. But I have other priorities. You do too or you wouldn't have made a career in the military."

"I do okay." He looked over to check on Diesel who was chowing down on his dried kibble. There was a bowl of water for him in the corner of the tent.

"They pay you well at Iniquus?"

"They treat us with the utmost respect, in all ways, including our finances."

"That was very diplomatic way of saying they're paying you hand over fist for your skills. That's a form of wealth, too, isn't it? Respect."

"I think so."

"You're back on the island because Iniquus thought this is going to be a disaster zone? I mean, obviously it is. But they had to think that in advance to send you, right? I mean, the storm turned and time wise, you would have had to have been in the air."

"We're lending support to our friends who are in bad straights because of communication with the internet down and to be boots on the ground to describe the outcome. Team Alpha is in St. Kitts with the other half of Team Bravo. Besides Trifalgar here, we have two large groups of protectees we're monitoring on islands south of Dominica."

"Rescue is dangerous work. Is it more dangerous than when you deployed—but for different reasons?"

"We call it 'deployed' when we're sent on assignment by Iniquus Command. To explain that—each Bravo operator is paired with a trained working dog. That pair is a 'working team'. Okay? On Bravo, we have six working teams. Of those six, me and Diesel, Ares and Judge, Ash and Hoover—are cross deployed. The other three Bravo working teams are strictly search and rescue, like Bear and Truffles."

"Cross deployed means?" She held her eyes stiffly wide, a pump of anxiety flickered there.

For him?

That did crazy things to his insides.

He liked the sensation. But he didn't want to add Tara's worries.

Mace tried to lighten his tone. "When one of the operation forces at Iniquus goes out, and they need a K9 force multiplier, we get lent out."

"Like a library book?"

"Sort of. I like my work." Mace brushed a finger down her face waiting for the rumble of thunder to pass. "You didn't seem at all surprised to see me when I showed up today."

"No, actually, I was kind of wondering why you were so late."

"I was hitchhiking, and no one would give me a ride."

"I hate surprises," Tara says. "I can't imagine a life like yours when you can get a call at any time. You're up and running with no idea what country or continent you'll be on tomorrow. I think you have to have a brain that enjoys that. A surprise for me? I just find it confusing. I want to step back. Take some time to assess. My brain doesn't click, click, click into place, like some brains do. It can make me feel…slow and confused."

"You? You're brilliant. You've got a Ph.D. Big brain madness."

"Yeah, but I'm not the person you want to choose if you're playing a game of Trivial Pursuit or, you know, need to pull something up quick. Sometimes it takes a little while to get information to bubble to the surface. When the octopus surprised me with its behavior today, that's exactly what happened. It took some time for my brain to bubble up somersaults."

"Somersaults?"

"An anti-octopus attack strategy."

"I'll have to remember that. Share it with the team."

Tara took a bite then waved the spork in the air. "I remember one time, I went back to my apartment after a day in the field. I was filthy from head to foot and looking forward to a shower. I opened the door, and my living room was filled with my friends all dressed up. I had no idea what was happening. I thought maybe I had invited them a while back, and it had slipped my mind. I simply couldn't fathom what was happening. I excused myself to get cleaned up. There was nothing written on my calendar. I was so confused."

"So, what was happening?"

"My birthday was that upcoming Tuesday. It was a surprise party."

"And you didn't clue in when they shouted surprise?"

"That's the way it is on TV. You turn on the light, they yell surprise. There are decorations and such to orient the person. None of that was part of this scene. Just friends, potluck, and wine."

"How long did it take you to figure it out?"

"Until the birthday cake was brought out. And then, whew! What a relief. I was at the end of a project with a lot of data floating around in my mind. I could totally see myself calling out an invitation that then vanished from my mind before I got it on my schedule.

He grinned at her.

"What?"

"The other day I thought I spotted a pattern with your storytelling."

"And what does that pattern tell you?"

"That you're nervous as hell. I promise, Diesel and I are going to keep you safe from this storm."

"Oh, ha-ha, the storm isn't the only thing that has me nervous."

"Just so you're not surprised, I'm going to kiss you." He leaned in and kissed her softly. Their lips held. Finally, he tipped his forehead to rest against hers, breathing in the essence of Tara and whispered, "If it's not the storm, Tara, what are you afraid of?"

She shook her head against his.

"Well, I'll tell you that *you* scare me, Tara."

"Same," she whispered.

"What about me scares you?" He sat back so he could read her eyes in the dim pink light cast by the chem-stick.

"Matteo says you start relationships and don't stick around."

"That's right. I'm not family guy material."

"Why would you say that?"

"I just don't have any good experiences associated with it."

She stilled.

Mace could see the cogs whirring, and he gave her the space she needed to process.

Diesel rambled over to rest his head in her lap. Obviously, he sensed she needed him.

Tara's brow pulled together as she said, "So you moved with your dad, and he was terrible. You had a stepmom, though, right? Did she stick up for you?"

"She wasn't a pleasant person. She wore her victim status like a uniform. She felt everyone owed her. Granted, her father died when she was twelve. She had a younger sister who was seven. A younger brother who was a year and a half. Her mom was a teacher. I think they had enough, she went to private school through high school. The childhood pictures I saw, she was nicely dressed. Makeup. Hair. She seemed to have, financially, a stable middle-class life. She had few stories about her childhood."

"Do you remember any of them?"

"One was about her father. She was on top of a wood pile."

"Bad choice."

"Yes, but that's the story. She was on top of the woodpile and her dad yelled 'Jump!' and she did."

"Did he catch her?"

"That wasn't part of the story. I'd assume he did."

"So, why'd she tell it?"

"She didn't know why he yelled jump. She just trusted him."

"The sound of his voice was the warning, I'd guess."

"Yeah."

"And she jumped because?"

"Bee."

"One bee?" Tara flicked her hand through the air. "Psh, that's not much of a story."

"It was meant to show her utter trust in her dad and that when she says something we don't need a reason or explanation, we just hear and do."

"Huh." She reached around and stuck her hand down the back of her shirt to scratch the itch between her shoulder blades. "That's the opposite of science."

"True, but it prepared me for the military."

Tara tapped Diesel. When he lifted his head, she moved over to sit between Mace's legs and cuddled in.

I want her here always was Mace's thought, but he quickly pushed it to the side.

"Did you know your mom offered to take me in?" He

dropped a kiss into her hair. "She told my dad that she would raise me in your family. I wished for that so hard."

"Did she? That sounds like my mom. But your dad wanted you with him, surely."

"For my dad it was pride, not love."

"I'm sorry." She wrapped her arms around his waist.

"Your mom invites me for the holidays every year. Every year. I'm always included. I appreciate that so much."

"Mom never said."

"She wouldn't, would she?"

"No, she prays in private. She loves for love's sake. She doesn't need anyone watching and approving of her kindness. It's who she is. She's my rock. Now, that I've had time to consider your worldview about you and relationships, I'd like you to consider my dear friends Jim and Trevor. Trevor had a hellacious childhood. I mean his parents were vicious toward him. But a more loving supportive couple would be hard to find." She lifted her head and sought out Mace's gaze. "And some of that comes from Trevor having supportive grandparents. And now, I'm going to point out the obvious, since you *clearly* haven't put it together. My mom doesn't take in strays. She isn't a collector of human sorrow. She loves you like a mother. You said yourself that she tried to take you in so she could do that every day. When she couldn't, she did what she could from afar. She found you an auntie, in your neighbor Mrs. Tate, who was willing to conspire, so you would have birthday cake in your life."

Mace was holding his breath.

"My mom called you and asked you to fly to a different country to help her. Do you for one nano-second think that my mom would do that if she didn't think of you as family? Maybe not bloodline, but family of the heart. You have a loving family, my mom as your mom, a brother in Matteo. But not me." Her face became stern. "Let's be clear. I wasn't involved in any of that except peripherally and for sure my feelings for you are *not* sisterly in any way shape or form."

And just like that, Tara broke the fishbowl. Mace wasn't a goldfish that would swim around observing others having what he wanted for himself.

Man, Tara outright rocked his world.

She threw him off balance.

Yeah, he was going to have to work on his sea legs around Tara.

"What do you want for you, Tara?"

"More specific, please." She must have made her point because she tucked back into his arms.

"In a long-term relationship."

"I'd like to be married eventually. I think there's a lot to be learned about making that commitment and seeing it through. I love to watch Jim and Trevor, they role model that kind of 'we're in this together, might as well make it an adventure' quality that I love."

"Do you want kids?"

"I don't know." She paused as Mace stroked her hair. After a while she said, "Let me rephrase. Yes, I want kids. But I'm not sure I'm that selfish."

"I don't follow." His fingers caught in a snarl, and he gently worked it free.

"Do I want to bring them into a world of suffering? Famine and drought? Seems like a cruel thing for a mother to do."

"It's that bad?" Mace felt himself tensing against her.

"It might be. It wholly depends on what humans decide to do."

"And if science can figure it out. I mean worms, right?"

"'If' is a prickly bed to lay an infant on. I guess, I'm just not optimistic enough right now. Occupational hazard."

"I get that. I deploy to the disasters. I see what it does to children, babies. I wouldn't want to have a child born into war either. And you're right, it takes an enormous amount of hope and optimism to have a child."

They held each other, listening to the cruelty of the wind outside.

"Tara, come tuck into the sleeping bag. I need you to rest."

She looked up at him.

Oh, those beautiful liquid brown eyes... What wouldn't he do to keep this woman safe?

"When the wind stops," he said, "we need to go. And I mean fast."

29

Tara Alvarez

Monday, Dominica

THE ENTIRE DAY HAD BEEN SURREAL.

She had begun the day with a bit of anxiety, more for the Dominican peoples and for what was surely going to happen to flora and fauna on the island.

All of these years after Maria and the island had not yet recovered.

Things of that magnitude take time.

Her own little house at Parrot's Perch had needed to be rebuilt. The Josephs' home in its bowl of land had needed repairs. They lost their barn and livestock, and that was never replaced.

As Tara had packed up her rucksack to head down to ride out the storm with her friends, Tara had thought that it was quite possible that the islands of the Caribbean would never recover. That the rising seas, and destructive storm cycles would hit with such frequency that what had been could never be again.

She was preparing to mourn what she would see tomorrow.

She wasn't prepared for what happened next.

The violence of the outer bands of wind was completely surprising to her.

She'd been headed down to safety. Easy enough.

That a tree had already toppled, unfathomable.

That the tree blocked her escape route, terrifying.

A quick calculation told her to figure out a backup plan.

And the cave came immediately to mind.

Tara had been hiking the mountain side one day when she'd come upon it. She'd moved into the cool interior to rest from the sun and have her lunch. As she'd laid there on her tarp with her daypack as a pillow, watching the foliage blow in the wind outside the cave opening. Tara had thought if she needed to escape, she'd come here to the bosom of the mother and find peace. The reason for escape hadn't been defined. But it had been remembered. And she'd put it as a flagged waypoint on her GPS and filed it under favorites.

In her first trek down the mountain in her vehicle, when she discovered that a tree had already collapsed, she'd considered running for the hotel. But quick calculations that took into consideration the wind speeds, and her sucky jogging pace, she'd shifted gears to Plan B.

Actually, Plan B was that Austin magically showed up out of nowhere with Diesel.

Again, there was no reason to have that thought, but when they burst through her door, she hadn't been surprised.

That didn't mean that she wasn't quickly gathering a camp bag, ready to rough it alone in the cave for days if necessary.

Plan B meant Austin's ATV.

Boom. Destroyed as they kissed.

And then on to her back up of a backup plan, this cave. *Thank you, Mother Earth, for as you destroy, you have also given us protection.*

Truth be told, Tara had quite enjoyed this turn of events. Enjoyed kissing Austin, cuddling, and listening to the vast power as they talked earnestly.

The bats had stayed in the back of the cave. Betsy hadn't crawled up the tent.

It had been lovely.

But now it was time to go.

"We're leaving everything here. I'm taking the essentials, just water and a first aid kit. Whatever you need to do to be ready. This is it," Austin said.

She knew the next step, as soon as the eye passed over them, they were running again.

Her hips and feet ached from the last efforts. In the eye, they'd find calm. Blue skies, still air.

Dangerous, nonetheless.

All the trees and limbs that had been ravaged by the wind would now be collapsing.

The path would be littered with debris.

Austin unzipped the tent, tossed the rocks to the side. "Ready?" he asked, extending his hand to her.

No. She most certainly wasn't ready for what she saw.

Even thought she'd seen pictures of the island's destruction in Maria, with its naked trees stripped of everything, this was surreal.

She emerged and stood, wide-eyed in stunned silence. Her brain hiccoughing and not processing.

Austin had, during their time in the tent, worked the topo map to figure out a way to get down the mountain without crossing water. Easier said than done on a tiny island with almost four hundred rivers.

But he'd developed a path that kept them out of the drainage and down to the Josephs' house on the off chance that they were there, had a car, and by some miracle the road below was clear. Austin thought it was possible since the trees and foliage were much shorter down there.

He might be right, but after seeing this?

Austin grabbed her hand. "We need every single second to survive this. The wind changes direction on the other side of the eye, and it will be going directly into that cave. There aren't enough rocks to build protection for that. We can't survive here."

That was a piece of information Austin had held back.

Sure, Tara understood how a hurricane worked. She just hadn't put it together. Hadn't realized that the cave took the wind from aft. But after the eye it would come straight at them.

Unsurvivable. He was absolutely right.

And getting down the mountain in time? That depended on a bunch of things. Mostly, how wide was the eye? How much time would Mother Nature allow them?

Adrenaline powered her system and the three of them jetted down the mountainside, following the little red line on her GPS that was their *only* hope of getting to safety in time.

30

Tara Alvarez

Monday, Dominica

Austin's expression was set with a fierceness that Tara found conflicting. Austin usually had black eyes that glittered with intelligence and amusement. He normally held his body loose and relaxed.

This Austin was highly focused. Fierce.

Here, Austin seemed to have his awareness on everything at once, to absorb it into his brain, process it, and the output was their next move, aware of every rock, every branch.

It was daunting.

Tara decided that what she had to do to make this easiest was to have no opinion and no thought. She wouldn't try to discern or conceive. She was a sail that was being directed by an expert sailor. Bad metaphor. Right now, there was no wind. And if they weren't to the shelter of the hotel by the time the wind came, no amount of mastery could save them.

He said, "put your foot here," that's where her foot went.

Diesel the wonder dog trotted directly in front of Austin.

"Diesel, lead" was the command. The information from the GPS seemed to go into Austin's eye, filter through his brain, and flow down the leash to Diesel. Because when Tara caught a glance of the tool, their little trio was slip sliding right along the red line.

Tara had no idea that her body could do what her body was doing. She'd had no reason to try. But her ankles and knees had grown stable from the daily climbs up and down her research area for the last seven months. Had she been asked to do this last December, she'd be on her butt.

Even in Tara's limited understanding of how dog handling worked, she could tell that Diesel, like Austin, used every sense and all his training to move them at breakneck speed down that mountain.

Diesel led them around holes and rocks. He avoided overhead limbs. And interestingly, Diesel seemed to pace himself for her benefit.

Tara was under no illusion; she completely understood that she was the dragging anchor that endangered both Austin and Diesel.

The thought that they'd be in harm's way because of her—they were here and in harm's way because of her—was a burden that she desperately tried to leave on the side of the mountain lest the horror of it steal her breath or the weight of it slow her in any way.

Tara could hear Diesel chuffing the air. He turned his head. To look over his shoulder. And Austin and his dog did some weird mind meld communication thing.

"What?" Tara gasped, so winded she could hardly be heard. And then she saw it for herself. "Smoke," she exhaled. "That's the Josephs'."

Somehow, she had more to give.

Somehow, she became superhuman.

If she had adrenaline for herself and Austin, the adrenaline that flowed through her body now, thinking of that beautiful family, the children, in danger. It was as if she snapped her fingers and she transported.

The next thing she knew, she was standing in Mrs. Joseph's garden, Austin grabbing her hand to stop her forward momentum. With flames licking out from between the slats of the storm shutters, the bottom floor was engulfed.

"Stop!" Austin shouted.

He dropped his ruck. "Wait here unless you hear me call."

Tara's foot didn't listen. It stepped forward as if to bolt in.

"Tara, I need you on the outside. This is your position. How many are in there?"

"Possibly five. Two women and three children."

"Wait here." He pointed at the ground. "Diesel, seek."

Diesel leaped onto the porch and through the door. They disappeared behind a wall of smoke and flame.

Tara heard screaming at the back of the house, and she ran to get eyes on the situation. To see if there was anything at all she could do.

There was the Josephs' car.

She ran toward it.

Inside, the keys dangled from the ignition. Maybe she could drive it under the window and climb up on top.

Of course, that was a no.

A car, after all, was filled with gas. Talk about adding fuel to the fire.

The window was thrown open.

Austin leaned out, yelling, "Tara!"

"Here! Here!" She waved her arms and tried to catch his attention.

"I need you to catch the children. We can't get them down the stairs."

"Catch?" *What if she missed?* "No! there has to be some other way."

"Now, Tara. Now! Get under the window. I'll hand them out, oldest first. He'll dangle. You don't take his whole weight. Your job is to try to grab him under the arms and hug him to slow his drop. Ready?"

He trusted her.

She didn't trust herself.

But here came the oldest boy. Eight years old. The tallest.

He clung to Mace's hands as Mace bent at the waist lowering the boy as far as possible.

When Tara reached up, her finger tips could just brush the soles of his feet. But now she could see how this was doable.

And she would do it.

She would.

"Ready!"

"Three. Two. One."

Tara was not ready. There was no way in this world that she could have been ready. This was not part of her world.

It happened fast. And heavy.

Tara heard "one." The next thing she knew she was in the grass with a child in her arms. They both laid there, stunned.

"Tara, get up! Fast! Come on!"

She was on her feet, leaping back into place. Now Tara knew why Austin picked this order. The second child, five years old was going to be a harder catch and Tara needed a little experience.

"Ready?"

"Yes!" *No!*

This time, Austin had put the child into the center of a sheet and tied it at the top. Like a stork delivering a baby well past its delivery date. Even in the sheet, the child was just out of her reach.

"Three."

Please, God, help me!

"Two. One."

The five-year-old in his bundle slipped like and eel through her arms with velocity. Tara threw herself backward to use her body to break that last bit of fall.

His brother moved up as Tara untied the knots.

The boys hugged and coughed, wiping their wrists over smoke-blinded eyes.

"Tara! Now!"

"Ready!" The baby was next.

The baby!

After almost losing the last child. How was she going to catch a baby?

"Tara, drop down with the momentum. You have to ease the baby down. We don't want to stop the momentum suddenly. There's a cushion to help you."

She didn't know what that meant until out of the window came another sheet bundle, bright blue flowers, vibrant green leaves. Squared at the bottom. This must be a cushion of some kind forming a bed for the two-year-old to lie on.

"Three. Two. One."

As Tara reached for the cushion, she felt it fold like a burrito around the baby. And again, she dropped to the ground.

The baby was fine. He didn't even cry as she handed the little one off to his brothers.

Tara was a mess.

Her limbs shook like spaghetti noodles, barely holding her up.

Mrs. Joseph was up there. Tara could see the elderly woman standing in the open window.

How would they all get down?

Mrs. Joseph was lowered in a contraption that Austin had MacGyvered together, Austin held all of the weight. Tara just needed to guide her down and unknot her as quickly as possible.

"Mrs. Joseph, is your daughter in the house?"

Coughing, Mrs. Joseph shook her head then waved a hand at her oldest grandchild.

"My mom is at work at the hospital."

With a nod, Tara raced back under the window as Diesel was lifted through the opening.

A sheet tied was to the handles of his tactical vest. When Diesel was at the length of the sheet and just over Tara's reach, Austin commanded, "Tara, sweetheart, I need you to stay back."

The scorching heat from the house made her skin feel blistering. She stepped clear, then Austin commanded, "Diesel, jump."

And Austin let go of the sheet.

Diesel dropped his front legs toward the ground, and with a few bounds that dispersed the energy, he raced back to Tara to get the sheets off.

"That's all the sheets I had," Mrs. Joseph gasped out from where she sprawled on the ground.

Austin!

Even Tara knew he'd break his legs if he tried to drop onto this incline. She watched horrified as he climbed out of the window, perching on the sill.

Then, instead of jumping down, as Tara had feared, he went up. Which honestly didn't make sense to her.

Standing on the windowsill, he reached up and grabbed the roof. He did a pull up that got his hips balanced on the edge. He threw one leg up, then the other, rolling onto roof then racing up the slope.

Tara rounded to the front, trying to keep her eye on him.

Holding onto the roof he lowered himself to the porch roof, jumping the short distance. From the porch roof, he shimmied down a post. And then he was there beside her grabbing her hand, running to meet up with the family who were coughing and gasping.

"Get them into the car, Tara."

Tara ran to the car, jumped in the driver's seat, and drove to the family. She wasn't sure they had enough oxygen to walk. Bag, dog, four Joseph family members, and Tara crammed into the passenger areas, Austin behind the wheel driving that beat up old rust bucket for all it was worth.

"Closest hospital, Tara."

"At the bottom of the mountain road turn left." And then Tara squeezed her eyes for the hell ride down the mountain, slipping sideways in the mud, winding around debris, wheels screaming as they tried to find their grip. It was vertigo. It was fast. And Tara thought that at any moment they'd just go end over end.

She held her breath until Austin squeezed her knee.

They'd made it this far.

They unloaded the family to get the care they needed. Then he floored it as he drove back to a building near the dock. "Stay here," he told her. "I need to let my brothers know we're off the mountain. Then I'm taking you to the hotel."

31

Tara Alvarez

Monday, Dominica

THE WIND STARTED UP AGAIN WITH A VENGEANCE.

Now night, the sky was already pitch black.

In the front of the hotel, metal storm curtains had been lowered.

Tara didn't see a way in. No welcome mat was set out for them. No doorbell to press to get assistance.

Austin drove around to the side of the hotel protected by the rise of land, parking right next to the door. And still, getting to the building was a full-body experience.

The wind snatched the air from her lungs.

Diesel had his belly almost to the pavement as he squatted low.

Someone saw the three struggling for the door and threw it wide for them.

Tara staggered in with Diesel, Austin and the guy who had

296 | FIONA QUINN

helped them dragged the door shut. Austin threw the bolt that went into the ceiling and the floor. If the guy hadn't been there, they might not have found a way in at all.

"Thank you," Tara gasped out once she had enough breath.

Austin stuck out a hand and the men shook, then the guy moved on down the corridor.

Tara waited for Austin. He had taken the burden of their survival onto his own shoulders and now that they were safe, she figured he needed a moment to gear down.

The lights were dim; the hotel was probably running on generator.

Austin adjusted his pack on his back and took her hand. "Ready to eat, Diesel?"

Yeah, he was. His tail wagged. He'd been happy through this entire misadventure.

Unfathomable.

Austin had to pull out his headlamp to navigate the black staircase. They climbed to the seventh floor.

"Pria and the others?" she managed.

"Everyone on your team and mine are fine. The Trifalgar group are in their rooms. Bravo is at Emergency Management preparing a response."

"Do you need to be there?"

"I'll be there when I'm needed. We have hours yet until anyone can get out."

"The Josephs?"

"Their kerosene lamp knocked over. Mrs. Joseph couldn't get to a door downstairs. She thought if she got upstairs, she'd have time to figure out a plan."

"A plan? Like what?"

"The sheets for lowering the children. She had all her sheets ready when I found her."

"But then she…"

"Would have died from the fire. And the kids would have died from the storm. With no storm, she would have saved them. She told the eight-year-old to get into the car, and they'd be safe there."

"She might have been right. It was parked in a place that a tree couldn't fall on it."

"The direction of the wind after the eye would flip it."

"A miracle of a day. An absolute miracle."

Austin opened his room door, extending a hand so Tara would go in first. She clicked the lights, but none came on.

"Emergency use only. I have glow sticks in my pack. Just step farther in."

Seconds later and the room was bathed in pink.

"It's been my experience," Austin said as he moved into the bathroom.

Tara heard the water flowing from the faucet.

"Yup." He came out with a grin. "It's my experience that in a storm no one uses the hot water. But the hot water is still hot in the tank. This is probably your only chance to soak and get comfortably cleaned up until the electricity is restored. You'll be home before that happens."

Tara yanked off her boots and bent to tug at her socks. "That sounds marvelous." She peeked into the bathroom and the couples-sized tub. "You're going to join me to soak, right? Ease our muscles." That was such a lame way to ask a guy to get naked with her.

She tugged off her coat and shirt as he stood there looking very funny in his indecision.

Tara was fairly sure that indecision had nothing to do with his desire for her but everything to do with his desire to protect her.

"Throw caution to the wind," she said with a smile, dropping her pants.

298 | FIONA QUINN

"Okay, you go get in. I need to get Diesel situated, and I'll be right there."

He was stalling, and she knew it.

In the bathroom, she took off her bra and underwear. There were leaves and debris in both. Pieces of sticks.

Austin had leaned the light against the mirror to increase the brightness, but still the room maintained a romantic cocoon.

Naked, she pulled the elastic from her hair as she looked in the mirror, picked up Austin's comb and dragged it through the snarls.

This was going to be a task getting the knots out.

Looking over her shoulder, she saw the tub was almost filled. She took the comb with her as she climbed in.

The temperature was perfection.

Oh, the bliss of a hot bath.

Still no Austin.

He'd have to make his own decisions about what was right for him, no matter how hard Tara wanted this.

The door opened.

Tipping her chin up, she could see Austin's reflection in the mirror.

Naked, Austin quietly slipped into the bathroom.

He slid into the tub behind her extending his legs on either side. "Is this what you were thinking?" he asked.

"Exactly," she said as she leaned back pillowing her head on his chest. Resting her arms on his athletic thighs. Thighs that didn't quiver from exhaustion like hers did.

She set the comb in the soap dish and made an ungainly turn in the tub until she was kneeling as she faced Austin.

She traced her fingers over his skin, looking for any place where he'd been hurt. She lifted his arm where the flames scorched the hair off. Tara lifted his arm to her nose and sniffed. "Burned chicken feathers."

"You would know." He grinned back at her.

That grin undid her.

All of it. All of the surprises and joy, the shame and horror, the terror and desperation from the last few days flooded into her system at once. Tara covered her eyes and swiveled her body trying to find some position that would relieve the pressure.

She pressed into the tub and stood.

She didn't want to get out. She couldn't figure out a way to stay in.

She just wobbled around looking for relief.

Austin reached out his hands. "Hey, hey, hey. Come here. I've got you."

Tara let herself sink back down to cradle her head against his chest.

"I've got you," he crooned.

And in a sublime act of trust, Tara did what she'd never done before, she sobbed in front of someone.

"That's right. Good. Cry it out. All of it."

It was long and ugly.

It was the splotchy red eyed, snot snorting, hitched breathing kind of cry, and it felt so good.

It ended with her closing her eyes and falling into a kind of stupor.

"That's adrenaline. Days of it." He kissed her hair. "You've been a warrior goddess. A mountain queen. I am *so* proud of you."

Tara had a little drool running out of her mouth, a little snot running out of her nose, and she did nothing about either, as she rested her cheek on Austin's chest, curled in fetal position between his legs.

"Adrenaline does this to the best of us. My team has learned to deal with it over decades of experience. That you're handling everything this well is amazing."

Tara didn't care what Austin was saying, she wasn't really registering his praise. His tone was a balm to her spirit. This was what she wanted for herself. Someone who would chase into the storm for her, someone who she could talk to for hours on end, someone who trusted her to be a partner, someone who could be a resting spot.

What did Austin want for him?

That was the question that hung in the balance.

AUSTIN REACHED FORWARD and took the comb from the dish.

Starting at the ends, he worked to get the tangles out of her hair. This was another of his practiced moves. He'd done this before.

But so had she.

They were both the sum of their life experiences.

Even after the last snarl slid smoothly through the teeth, Austin continued to comb her hair until the water grew cold.

With her toes on the handle, Tara had topped off the water with more hot, twice.

Now, the water came out cold. They'd exhausted the heater.

Austin pulled himself from the tub and quickly dried off while Tara watched, his hard cock dancing with his moves.

"Such a lovely show you put on, Austin."

He smiled at her and held out his hand. When she stepped from the tub, he took a fresh towel and did a very thorough job of drying her off and wrapping her up.

God how she ached. She'd never experienced this kind of pain before. She winced with each step.

Austin snagged his Dopp kit and led Tara into the bedroom.

There, she looked over to where Diesel had curled up on the

comforter nest that Austin had made for him. He was deep asleep softly snoring.

Reaching into his kit, Austin pulled out a bottle and held it up. "I think I can help with the aching muscles."

The thought of Austin's calloused hands exploring her body sounded like Nirvana.

"That would be so welcomed, thank you." If Austin had looked like he was in any way in need of his own ministrations, Tara would decline. But Austin seemed to take on this day like it was part of his everyday world.

Tara laid down on her stomach, pulling the pillow to her chest to keep her breasts from crushing and to let her head fall forward so he could work the muscles in her neck and shoulders.

Austin poured oil onto his hands then warmed it between his palms.

The first strokes over her back and shoulders were light.

She relaxed into the sensation.

Another slide up the muscles in her back, avoiding her spine, a little deeper. Very assured. He knew what the hell he was doing.

Of course, he did, this was Austin.

"Okay?"

"Yes. Thank you." When she tucked her head down, Austin moved to splay her thighs. *Here we go*, she thought. What was it going to be like to have Austin inside of her?

But that was not what followed.

He knelt between her thighs, adding more oil to his palms, he kneaded her bottom, slid the heels of his hands up her back, slicked gently into the crook of her neck.

He worked every kink out of her thighs and calves until she stopped whimpering at the tender points and was almost comatose with relaxation.

He slid down to her feet, bruised and strained from running.

But now, he was pressing his thumb into different points on her foot.

Tara fell asleep.

Naked Austin or no naked Austin, how could she not fall into a stupor with his magic hands?

She felt him wiping the oil from her skin then tucking the blanket around her.

She had just enough awareness that she caught his wrist before he went away and grunted as she tugged at him. So not sexy—absolutely nothing like her fantasies—but *he* was the one that melted her brain.

Austin complied with her demand by sliding in beside her.

Once again Tara curled into Austin's arms, pillowing her head on his chest.

This time her hand explored.

She was not Austin Mace; she didn't have his capacity to heal and restore.

Honestly, she barely had the capacity to move her arm, she was so relaxed.

But it was lovely to feel his skin under her fingertips. To follow the ridges and valleys that defined the planes of his biceps and chest.

She twirled her hand over his abdomen, then swirled her finger around his navel and discovered the head of his cock, just there, lying expectantly. She wrapped her hand around the velvety shaft.

This was a wrinkle in time. There was no clock ticking. No before and no after.

There was just the surreal soundscape of the storm that stood counterpoint to the soft pink glow of their room.

The safety she felt in Austin's arms was more than a counterbalance for Mother Nature's wrath.

There was nothing to do in the blacked-out hotel in the middle of a hurricane than to enjoy the sensations.

She stroked her hand up and down Austin's shaft, getting to know its length and width, eliciting a deep moan from Austin that made Tara wet and needy.

With a swirl of her thumb along the ridge just under the head of his cock, she lifted up to move the weight of her leg between Austin's thighs, and he pressed into her giving her something to grind against.

When he reached down, Tara pressed his hand away. "It's my turn to play."

"Oh." He leaned back into the pillow.

Pressing the head of his cock into her palm, Tara slowly rotated her wrist until she felt Austin's stomach clench and quiver. He lifted up to drop a kiss into her hair.

Sliding down until her head rested on his hip, Tara lazily kissed and lapped at the length of his shaft. Slowly exploring the ridges.

Austin was petting her hair as she explored.

His dick was growing hotter, thicker, harder. His breathing was coming in staccato bursts.

Salty slick pre-cum was on her tongue, bringing a moan of desire to her lips.

"Austin, a condom?"

When he tensed, Tara lifted her weight onto her elbow. "No?" She shook her head in surprise.

"It's not that, lightning bolt woman." His brows drew together with concern. "It's just that when you kiss me you make my lips buzz. I was lying here imagining what might happen if I was inside you when you orgasmed. I might be afraid for my life." His hand came up to touch his heart.

Hearing Austin talk about her orgasming made Tara's whole body jolt. She was slick with desire.

"See that?" Austin asked. "Can a man survive that?"

She tipped her head. "Are you brave enough to find out?"

Much to Tara's surprise, Austin reached to the table where a condom lay next to the bottle of oil.

He must have been waiting to see if she asked.

Gentlemanly.

But equally lovely that he'd thought it through and was ready for this.

Tara ripped the foil package open and as she painted the condom over the length of his cock, he hissed as if even this much was a pleasure to him.

That sound left Tara panting for breath.

On top, she thought, where she could best watch his face.

Up on her knees, he held her hand as she positioned over the top of his head and used her other hand to guide him in.

A low moan and a slow smile rewarded her. "Perfection."

Yes, yes it was.

He pressed the pad of his thumb against her clitoris, making slow circles as she rode him.

Three, that was the number of strokes he allowed her before wrapping her in his arms and turning so she was lying on the bed. "I don't want you doing any of the work. You've done enough for today. This is for me to do for you. Relax. Let me take care of you."

His mouth found her breast.

And with a gasp of pure hedonism, Tara let Austin take her to a place far, far from the howling winds of destruction, raging outside.

32

Austin Mace

Tuesday, Dominica

THERE WAS A POUNDING ON HIS DOOR. "MACE, YOU IN THERE?"

Mace pulled himself out of the near coma he'd fallen into after Tara and he had orgasmed the third time.

"Mace?"

"Yeah, man. I'm coming." He looked directly at Tara as he said it and gave her a wink.

She whispered, "You're coming? I thought you said you were out of condoms." Then offered up that pretty little pout that made his cock throb to be in her.

No more condoms.

None for now.

The sensations of making love to Tara? It was like nothing Mace had experienced in his life.

Did he want more?

Mace couldn't imagine ever having his fill of Tara.

Throwing himself out of the bed, Mace dragged on the clothes he'd prepped in case he had to jump and run.

As he zipped up, he realized the storm had quelled. The roar of the winds had stopped.

He combed his fingers through his hair and made sure Tara was tucked under the covers before he opened the door where he found Bear with Truffles and Ash with Hoover.

"Have you got any of the scientists with you?" Ash asked.

"Tara Alvarez."

"That's it?" Bear asked. "Not Pria or the others?"

"What's going on?" Tara called. Mace could hear her pulling on the extra shirt he'd set out for her.

Mace blocked the door so his teammates wouldn't see in.

"We're getting ready to head out and assess," Bear said, "see if they need the dogs on any of the structures looking for people. But we needed to make sure the scientists were secure first."

"And they're not in their rooms?" Mace asked.

"Uhm, I have Pria's key." Tara hustled into the bathroom and grabbed the shorts and panties she'd been in as they escaped to the cave. She jumped into them. Sitting on the floor pulling on her socks and boots, Tara said, "I bet she's just asleep. The anxiety from the storm was exhausting."

Tara was winding an elastic band around her ponytail and her ponytail into a bun as she moved into the hall. Mace's shirt she was wearing was longer than her shorts.

Mace signaled Diesel, and the group moved down to Pria's room on the fourth floor

Tara knocked and called, "Pria? Pria are you and Neils in there?" She knocked louder and called again, "I'm about to open your door, so if you and Neils are, uhm, *busy,* please call out." She put her ear to the door.

She caught Mace's gaze and shook her head, then held up the card for the battery-operated doors to flash green.

What they found made no damned sense.

None at all.

"Were the windows open?" Tara shifted to run into the room, and Mace held her back.

"Give us a minute," he said, pulling her from the doorway.

Tara frowned up at him.

Mace put Diesel in a down-stay, and then to give Tara a role, he handed her the leash. Careful not to touch anything he walked in. He stood in the middle of the room, turning slowly. "Tara, without coming in tell me, was Neils ever violent around you?"

"Violent?" There was confusion in her tone.

Mace saw Bear brace an arm across the door to stop Tara from going in. Knowing that was covered, Mace paced the room, looked behind the curtains, looked in the bathroom. Shook his head.

When he came back out, he hooked his thumb toward the room. Bear and Ash put their dogs in down-stays and went in making the same moves as Mace had.

They came back out.

"No clue, man," Bear said. "Could have been a temper tantrum? Could have been shutters needed adjustment and the wind blew things up. No blood. Nothing broken."

"Seizure?" Ash asked Tara. "The Alpha-gal. Could Pria have had a seizure from eating meat again?"

"I...I haven't heard of that," Tara said. "But yes, I guess she gets dizzy and," Tara waved her hand by her head, "disoriented."

The men nodded, looked in the room, considered.

Mace offered, "Someone who was having a reaction in the dark might be further confused by the sounds of the storm and stumble about knocking into things. One of her friends might have discovered her and taken her to their room?"

"No one's answering their doors," Bear said.

"Taken her to a safe place?" Ash tried. "Maybe there's a doctor in the hotel? Wanted her somewhere there was a light source?"

Mace went back into the room and through the bathroom door. He verified that Pria's epinephrine shot was on the counter and unused. He fished a sock off the top of her dirty clothes pile under the sink. This time when he came out, Mace shut the door.

He wasn't sure if it was a medical scene, a crime scene, a nothing-to-worry-about scene. It needed to be as pristine as possible until they had some answers.

Mace signaled to Diesel, and tail wagging, he came to sniff the sock.

As Diesel snorted his way toward the vending machines, Tara said, "I know where to find you. I'm going to run down to the front desk and see if someone's on duty and if they have any information. There may well be a group of folks who decided to party through the storm or something."

Mace hesitated. He didn't want her leaving his side.

But before he could think of a valid reason to stop her, Tara took off for the stairs.

33

Tara Alvarez

Tuesday, Dominica

TARA FLEW DOWN THE FOUR FLIGHTS OF STAIRS CARRYING THE pink glow stick she'd brought from Austin's bathroom.

It was eerie going, and she didn't want to stay in the stairwell for a second longer than necessary. She had the willies.

She burst through the lobby door with an exhale of relief.

As she rounded the columns, she saw the ponytail man. "Oh! Hey, there!" she called out. Since this man saved Trevor and Neils, he would recognize them as they moved around the hotel. And he didn't look like he was wandering around, he was definitely headed somewhere.

Maybe the guests had gathered in a safer room?

Joined together in a meeting hall to give mutual support?

"There you are," Ponytail said with a smile. "Your friends have been frantic."

"Safe!" She grinned. "I was looking for the gang. Do you know where they are?"

"We're hunkered together in the kitchen. My friends from the boat are with me," he said. "You saw them when we were helping Neils and Trevor after the SCUBA accident."

"Oh, yes. Yes. Thank you so much for all you did." She held out her hand. "I'm Tara. I made the SOS call."

"Pleased to meet you."

She thought he'd offer his own name so she could stop referring to him in her mind as Ponytail. But his gaze was searching the room and the stairs.

"I'm so sorry, did I stop you from something?" She took a step toward the dining room. "I know where the kitchen is."

"I was coming to look for you."

"What?" Tara stopped. Something had shifted about the man's posture and the tone of his voice.

He pulled a hearing aid from his ear. "I was listening, so I'd know when you came to check on your pals. Radio waves still work. The staff I've seen are using walkie talkies."

Tara shook her head and stepped back to give herself a chance to figure this out. It felt all too much like that sucky surprise party. He was listening for her? Did that make sense? But why? How?

"Tara," his voice was low and even, "come along now." He reached for her arm, and she moved out of reach.

She looked toward the main stairwell that took guests to the ballrooms, thinking maybe she should go up there away from this man until someone else was around.

Sweat dampened Austin's shirt under her arms.

"Jim and Pria were worried you weren't safe. They expected you before the storm."

She backed another step. But he advanced.

"They didn't know if you were safe. They thought perhaps you were with your security force friends."

"I was with friends." And for some reason she felt compelled to lie about Mace. "Yes, I was taking my friends to the hospital. I came from there to here during the eye of the storm."

There was a shift as he reached behind him.

Tara looked down, registering that he had a gun in his hands.

Guns are dangerous, deadly even, she thought. And yet there was something preposterous about this situation. Her brain couldn't grasp what this gentlemanly stranger with his bows and good wishes, with his altruistic help in a crisis would be doing pointing a gun at her. To have a hearing aid thingy in his ear listening for her.

Did any of that make sense?

Why would this man suddenly be pointing a gun at her?

No, she concluded, this made no sense at all. "I don't under-stand," she said lamely.

The gun came up to her temple. "Move."

Into the dining room they went, her friends weren't there.

Through the empty kitchen.

Through a storage room.

Was this a rape? Was this…no she had no idea what was going on.

With hand on her shoulder, keeping her from turning around, Tara pressed through a curtain of heavy carpet strips into a room filled with pipes and mechanical units. There, Pony-tail directed her around the machinery to the back corner where her friends sat in their pajamas on folding metal chairs, bound.

Tara simply could not process the improbability of this scene.

In her head she screamed at herself to get it together. This was no time for brain stutters.

She couldn't figure out what her body should be doing. Cooperate? Run? Fight? Pretend to pass out?

Tara had no experience at the end of a gun—or the vicinity of a gun. The closest she'd been to a weapon was the one's she'd seen on TV.

Matteo told her that nothing worked like it did on TV or in the movies. She should never rely on those fixes. That was fiction.

And this was…

Surreal.

She looked at a table where one of Ponytail's friends stood. There was her computer. And her journal and field notebook.

"Do you train monkeys?" Tara asked. Was this the set of thieves that was stealing from the tourists on St. Kitts?

As she looked around at the four men with their blank, confused looks, which had to mimic her own, she discounted their connection to the monkey.

But then how did they get her computer from the monkey?

And her journal? Why would anyone want her journal of gratitude and daily meditation card picks?

Tara focused on Pria. She had cuts and bruising on her face.

Austin! Tara screamed in her mind. *Diesel, help!*

"First, you will open your computer."

"Yes, of course." Tara moved to the table and opened it. When the home page came up, she put in her password and spun the computer to Ponytail.

He pointed to a chair, and she went docilely over to sit.

The others were bound. If she were calm and cooperative, could she avoid that?

Ponytail sat in a chair and started going through her files. He'd be finding a lot of chemical equations. He might come upon her governmental documentation that used the codes given to her by the Dominican researchers. It would all be meaningless.

Rather than try to figure out what he was searching for, Tara tried to think like Austin.

If he were here, how would he use this window?

He'd look for opportunities, Tara was pretty sure. Okay, first, this place made sense.

Sure, there were no doors coming in here, just those weird carpet strips hanging from the ceiling. But what was this place? The mechanics of the hotel. No one would be down here until the electricity came back on, and that could be weeks.

Why the weird carpet things dangling? Noise absorption. And yes, as she looked at the ceiling and walls, they were covered with materials that would soak up the sounds waves of the cooling units—the sounds of the hotel operations so the guests wouldn't be disturbed.

Screaming wasn't going to help.

Even in here, when Ponytail spoke to her his words seemed to disappear in the air before they reached her ears.

That wasn't her fear, the way she'd first supposed, that was a function of the acoustics.

Well, maybe—probably a bit of both.

This was a time game, though these guys may not know it. She wasn't sure about what training Hoover and Truffles had, but Diesel had tracked her down twice already.

Austin and his teammates had skills and they were actively looking for her friends.

But they had no guns.

Did she want them to come in and try to save them? Ponytail had the only gun she'd seen yet. Four men against three operators? Not a problem. But a gun with three bullets could do the job quickly and efficiently. And in this room, probably silently.

"Here," Ponytail said. "You reference the doubloons you've found."

"Yes."

"And the gold that you pack into treasure chests to send back to the United States."

Shit, Tara thought. It's all fun and games until some goon misinterprets what he's overheard and wants a fast buck—or chest of gold.

"You've found diamonds." He raised a questioning brow.

Should she explain the mistake? These men thought there was treasure at their fingertips. If they were disappointed, what would they do? Their faces seen, surely the next step would be lethal.

How could it not?

"Yes, diamonds," she said.

Pria was shaking her head, her eyes pleading.

"And you have this all mapped out?"

"Yes, there in the computer. But those are general GPS points it will only put you in the vicinity of the actual spot."

"But you know where all of this is located."

"I do."

"And you will show us?" He turned the pistol toward Trevor. "For your friends' lives?"

"Of course," Tara said.

Pulled forward, and thrust into a seat facing Tara, Trevor looked at her with horror.

He, too, was badly bruised.

The gun went to his head.

"Let's start with this," Ponytail said. "How much gold have you found so far?"

"In pounds?" Tara asked. "That's documented in the file."

Slow. Slow. Slow. Cooperative but slow. Team Bravo needed the chance to swoop in and save them.

What that looked like in terms of time or action Tara hadn't a clue. They didn't even know she was among the missing.

But they were tracking Pria…

"Why did your friends here try to tell us you were looking for worms?"

"I was, and still am. I was going to work until the end of the week. Hurricane season and all. I thought I'd come back after the wet season was done to do more." Tara glanced at Jim.

His face was almost purple, and Tara feared for his heart.

"They're right," she finished. "Worms."

"Worms?" Ponytail slid his hip onto the table. "Seriously?" His finger moved from the side of the gun to the trigger.

Trevor squeezed his eyes tightly closed, bracing his shoulders.

"Well, worm is a word I used. The gold is in the shape that made me call them that."

"The gold was in the shape of a worm?"

"More or less."

Tara wasn't great with this high-adrenaline shit. Her lungs banded so tightly that she preferred her time in the sea with the octopus.

"Not coins."

"By coins you probably mean the doubloons."

"Doubloons and worm shaped gold." The finger was off the trigger, but his voice was skeptical.

"Basically."

Ponytail pulled her journal over, putting his finger on a word that he'd circled. "And it says here that you found a 'heart of gold'. How big was it?"

"Mmm." She held up her hand and spread her fingers wide. "About like that?"

"It was affiliated with the church do you think?"

Tara blew out a breath. "I'm sorry that's not in my line of expertise."

"But doubloons and gold worms are."

"Yes." She nodded. Still surreal. She still didn't have her balance in this situation. How did Austin and his team face shit like this? *Did they face shit like this?*

"And you brought it off the mountain?"

"The heart of gold? No."

"Why not."

"I put the coordinates into my GPS, and I thought I'd go back. Someone was with me when I found it."

"I see. And the post office guy?"

Tara slid to the edge of her chair. "Is he here? Did you take him, too?"

"No. I went to his house, and it isn't the type of house someone lives in if they have better resources."

"I pay him to make the shipments. He doesn't ask for much. He only knows what I'm sending, so it can be insured."

"That's brazen."

"Isn't it?" Could he be changing his tune a bit? Did it feel like they could cooperate? Time. She needed time. "But I figure I need to be as legal as I can and declaring the package for its worth protects all of my hard work gathering the worms."

"Gold," he said emphatically.

"Exactly."

"Same with the diamonds? You left them? Why would you do that?"

"I seem to be the only one who's discovered them, right? Though, after this storm and the amount of water coming off the mountain. Everything's going to be changed. Have you seen it outside?"

He sat there staring at her for a long while.

Tara thought that he shouldn't be able to detect any signs that she was lying. She hadn't lied. She'd obfuscated and hadn't corrected, but that was different in body language tells, right?

Suddenly he leaned forward, swinging the gun to point at Jim. "Your friends said that they were merely filming a movie and the sword and the platter that we saw on Forward, Ho! when we were offboarding your friends were merely props."

Oh, shit. "That's true."

"Props." The gun touched her forehead.

"Sorry." Her voice squeaked as her shoulders came up to her ears.

34

Austin Mace

Tuesday, Dominica

Diesel had stopped his search. His body became rigid with concentration.

A low rumble rolled from his chest.

Mace had never seen Diesel like that, more wolf than dog in that moment. He looked wild and savage.

Bear and Ash back peddled, dragging their K9s away from Diesel.

Mace squatted. Goose bumps covered his flesh. The hair at the nape of his neck tingled up and over his scalp.

With a slow hand, Mace reached out and slowly unclipped the lead from Diesel's collar.

Mace trusted his dog.

Whatever this was, Diesel knew better than he.

Diesel's glowing ember eyes swung to look at Mace,

sending him a message, *danger*. He paced forward a step and stood paw in the air. Not sniffing, sensing.

He looked at Mace again and took off for the stairwell.

"Tara," Mace said to clue his team in. Only Tara would make Diesel act this way.

They were running.

With a push of the door, Diesel flew down the stairs.

Mace would leap a hip onto the rail and slide down to the landing run a few steps and leap onto the next railing, trying to keep up as they went down to the lobby.

There, Diesel waited at the door for Mace to catch up.

His brothers were right behind him.

Mace signaled to Diesel to wait. Though, he'd never seen Diesel like this, and he wasn't sure if they were partnered or if Diesel was going to go full tilt.

Diesel caught Mace's gaze and that concern faded.

Mace slowly opened the door. Clearing a pie wedge at a time, Mace assessed and opened more.

The room was empty.

With a release signal, Diesel dashed into the room and sniffed at the pink glowstick that lay by a potted plant. Tara had been carrying it when she went down to ask for information.

Tara.

Not just Tara. Now Team Bravo had five missing scientists.

It hadn't been the hurricane that Mrs. Alvarez had been dreaming about.

Mace remembered his own dream. Mrs. Alvarez was standing in her driveway, "Did you find her, Austin? Did you get her back? Austin, *where is she*?"

Mace had never felt this level of terror.

Diesel was chuffing, scenting the area. Finally, he latched onto a trail. Nose to the ground, he headed back through the dining room, back through the kitchen, he traced through a storage room when he laid flat at a wall of carpet strips, the kind used to block noise.

Mace reached out a slow hand and pulled the strips wide.

Diesel didn't move. He was telling Mace not to advance.

"You're lying to me!" a man yelled. And there, the sound of fist to flesh.

"Pria!" Tara yelled. "Don't do that! It's not necessary. I'll tell you whatever you want to know. My friends have nothing to do with what's on this island. Absolutely *nothing*. I'm sorry you thought there was real treasure they were digging up. They weren't. It was acting on their part. They got the whole idea for the screenplay from what I was up to on the island."

"I don't believe you," the man growled.

Diesel's lip quivered like he could taste the man already.

"Stop with the gun! I'm cooperating," Tara cried.

That was the magic word. That was why Diesel laid flat, the signal for explosives. That signal didn't normally look like what Diesel performed, but Diesel was trying to convey a lot of information. It was Mace that needed to catch up.

Mace slowly let the carpeting slide back in place. He squatted down and put his hand on Diesel's ruff, scratching his fingers in, giving him the signal of job well done. Standing, Mace backed to where his teammates positioned out of sight.

"Gun," he whispered.

"Scientists?"

"At least two. Pria and Tara."

Bear shook his head, hands posted to his hips.

Mace leaned closer. "It sounds like someone thinks that Trevor's treasure hunt was the real deal, and they want in on the action."

"How many tango voices?"

"I heard one," Mace said. "I can't imagine that's the headcount."

"No other way in. No other way out." Bear looked at Truffles. "I'll tell you what, Truffles isn't any help in this situation. I'll take her across to John's and leave her there. I can see if they'd be willing to hand me some fire power and body armor."

"That's a stretch," Ash said.

"Under the circumstances, they can't handle another crisis," Bear said. "They might be willing to point a finger and turn a blind eye."

Austin Mace

Tuesday, Dominica

BEAR WAS OFF.

Mace and Ash knew that even if he brought back weapons, they couldn't just barge into a hostage scene.

In their job as SEALs, they had equipment that could slide into place, optics and sound. They could map the site. Place the good guys and perps. Wait for a green light and pull the trigger.

Here, they had nothing.

No management or fire services to provide schematics even.

They had their skills and their dogs.

It was better than nothing.

But it wasn't enough.

None of the team really thought Bear was coming back with equipment. But it was worth a try.

"Diesel and I are going to get eyes on."

Ash looked toward the curtain, then slowly nodded his

head. He scanned the room. "Hoover and I'll watch your back. Signal if you want us in there."

A fist bump and they parted. Ash to stand in the shadows on watch, Mace with Diesel between his legs moving as a unit.

Mace pushed the carpet just out of his way at the corner of the opening. "Slow is fast," he reminded his body. He imagined himself to be liquid as he slid into the shadowed corner.

Crouching low, the team followed the sound of voices, making their way back toward the open area between pipes and machines that the tangos used as their interrogation space.

There, Mace found a spot where he could count heads.

He got all five of the scientists, four bound. Somehow, Tara had kept herself untethered. Mace hoped that situation continued.

He saw the man with the ponytail who had sat behind Pria at dinner the night of the bear spray. Mace remembered thinking that he'd pushed his chair impolitely too close to Pria's. He cast his mind back to review the conversation from the point of their entry. What would he have heard? He probably missed the part about the script and just heard about the expedition.

That was the man on the boat that saved Trevor and Neils after their diving accident. Tara said she'd seen them through her binoculars throughout the day.

That hadn't sounded off to Mace, Trevor had picked his filming spot for the marine life. And snorkelers would look for the same kinds of underwater experiences. Now, of course, that information filtered through a different lens.

The man with the ponytail held the gun. Tango One.

Tango Two was about Mace's height, maybe twice his weight. A linebacker of a man. He looked like he'd be hard to put down.

There was a lull in the discussion as Tango One looked at

Tara's computer. "You said you put the coordinates into a GPS device?"

"Yes, that's right."

Diesel vibrated with anger at the sound of Tara's voice. But stayed between Mace's legs. Mace could feel his K9 assessing, strategizing. They were a team and if Diesel sensed an in, Mace hoped he took it.

Right now, there was no space to maneuver. No way to encircle. And he had just counted Tango Three.

"Where is the GPS?"

"In my room." Tara's voice quivered.

"Give me your key card. Glenn." He wiggled his hand to bring Tango Four into the picture. "Go get the GPS."

Tara stood, lifting the edge of Mace's shirt, she was wearing, and patting her pockets. She pulled out a key card and looked at it.

Mace could feel her indecision.

That was Pria's key. It wouldn't get them what they wanted.

He understood her indecision.

But if she handed it over, they could take out one of the tangos. Three was easier than four.

Do it, Tara. Do it! In battle with his brothers, he could mind meld. He could send silent thoughts out, and they seemed to catch them in the wind. It wasn't best practices, but sometimes that's all you had.

Tara held the card out with trembling fingers and gave Mace's room number on the seventh floor.

Good job, Tara.

Quickly, Diesel and Mace slid back along their path, exited the room and signaled Ash: Four tangos. One approaching. Silent takedown.

Ash held up a boning knife.

Too much blood. Not enough information. They just needed

this guy to go night-night so they could tie him up and lock him up.

With Diesel in a sit stay, Mace waited for Tango Four to round the corner. Leaping on his back, Mace wrapped his arm around the man's neck, grabbing his wrist with his free hand, Mace pushed his hands toward his own shoulder.

This move squeezed the tango's carotid artery, depriving his brain of blood.

The count of twelve, and he passed out.

Ash was ready with cordage to hog tie him. "We can put him in the refrigerator, the electricity's off. He'll be cold but not hypothermic."

"Good. I'm heading back in."

Ash grabbed the guy's feet and dragged him across the tile floor.

Mace and Diesel moved to take up their spot.

When they got back in, things had turned volatile.

Neils was standing by the desk. Tangos Two and Three had him by the arms. Tango One gave him an uppercut that sent Neils's head flinging back.

Pria and Tara were whimpering. Out of commiseration or from their own wounds, Mace didn't know.

They dropped Neils to the ground and Number Two kicked Neils out of the pathway.

"I can do this all day long. All. Day. Long." Tango One threatened. "Until you tell me what I want to know."

DIESEL'S HEAD came up sniffing. His eyes searched above Tango One's head. Diesel stilled, then locked onto something.

Mace followed Diesel's gaze but saw nothing.

He softened his focus and looked in the shadows. There he thought he saw a flick of long and thin.

Snake?

Boa?

It flicked again. And now Mace could make out Tara's monkey thief.

Mace hadn't believed her when she said a monkey had stolen her computer. But there was the monkey. And there was her computer.

Did that make any sense?

Tango One reached under the table and pulled out a cooler. "I bet you're getting hungry about now, huh Pria? No food. No water. No bathroom breaks. You could have all of that with a little cooperation."

He opened the top, looked inside. "So many delicious, *moist*, tasty foods. Look," he said pulling out a plastic bowl with mango spears. He put the fruit in front of where Tara and Pria were sitting. "Mmm. Mango." He had his pistol in one hand, and he lifted a piece of mango with the other, sliding it slowly into his mouth.

Diesel was intent on the action. He moved out from between Mace's feet, backing up, his muscles primed.

Something about this scene was going to be a go.

Watching Diesel, Mace moved to the side, ready to race forward if there was an opening. A word would have Ash and Hoover in the mix, and they were formidable fighters.

The gun was the problem.

He didn't know how many guns were in the room.

"Oh, the best," Tango One crooned. "So wet and sweet." He lifted another and tipped his head back.

The monkey leaped from the machine to the tango's head, a hairy arm reached down and grabbed the bowl, and just like *that* he disappeared into the pipes and machinery.

It was the split second that Diesel needed. He

Diesel leaped through the opening, jaws wide, saliva flying, all the righteous anger that he'd been brewing in his system powered him forward.

"Hoover up!" Mace called.

Diesel's jaw clamped down on the gun arm.

Tango One's scream was long and loud as Mace pressed passed him to grab at Tango Two.

The Tango's arm lifted, and just in time Mace saw the glint of a blade.

There was a scrape of claws against tile as Hoover flew through the air and clamped on to Two's weapon hand.

Ash and Mace turned to Tango Three who hunkered, horrified by the anguished screams of his co-conspirators. Hands up. Eyes shut. "Sorry. Sorry. I'm sorry!"

Tara Alvarez

Tuesday, Dominica

IF TARA EVER NEEDED TO KIDNAP SOMEONE, THE TIME TO DO IT was during a cat four hurricane.

The chances of someone catching her would be near zero.

Bear and Ash ushered the bad guys to the jail. The emergency workers were all busy saving lives. There were no police to take a report.

There was no space in the hospital to have doctors check out her friends. Though, they did see the Josephs, and everyone was fine, thank goodness.

Dominica crushed. Everything stripped and broken.

While five Americans being kidnapped would probably make international news on a normal day. It was low on the news radar on a day like today.

Austin was doing field medicine in his room on the scientists and Trevor.

Everyone was stunned into silence.

To Tara, there had never been a moment more beautiful than when Diesel flew into the room. There was never a moment more poignant than Austin gathering her in his arms and just staring into her eyes.

"I *love* you." His voice was gruff with emotion. "Promise me you won't ever do that again."

Tara nodded. "No more kidnappings for me."

He *loved* her.

A day of horror turned instantly to a day of joy. She cuddled into his arms, feeling Austin's solidity. This was where she had always belonged. Where she'd found peace those many years ago. Where she found her home now.

With Team Alpha and the rest of Team Bravo, moving out of St. Kitts, headed down to check on the other clients affected by the storms, Austin, Bear, and Ash would stay here.

In this moment, Austin was waiting for the rest of Bravo to get back from the jail, then she'd have to let go of him. Tara hoped the others took a very long time getting back.

Tara wasn't ready to step out of Austin's arms.

Before Team Bravo went out to help the Dominican Emergency Force, Austin and Tara would use a sat phone to call Tara's mother.

Her mom. Tara's mom had put *all* of this in motion.

Without her mom, Tara would have gone to the cave and stayed in the cave.

The cave was death.

Without her mom, if Tara had made it to the hotel the kidnappers would have grabbed her. And Tara was sure, sure down deep in her bones, that they would have put her on their speed boat, driven her out into the Caribbean, and thrown her into the waters to die with no repercussions for the bad guys, ever.

She would simply disappear.

There was no scenario in which Tara would have survived this week without her mom being crazy protective and calling Austin in a panic.

And no scenario in which Tara could have survived had Austin shrugged off her mom's call.

That was years in the making.

Her survival was only because of years of love and care.

"Don't cry, Tara," Austin whispered. "I have you. You're safe. You don't need to be scared."

"I'm not scared, Austin. I'm just so grateful."

EPILOGUE

SIX YEARS LATER

The noise level in the yard at Austin and Tara's Maryland home was glorious.

Halfway between Austin's work at Iniquus and the research Tara was conducting in Annapolis, this location made whole family gatherings easy and frequent.

And safe.

They'd built this house to withstand any known assault—human or nature. No tumbled down Parrot's Perch for them.

Dogs and kids, rock music, laughter, and family—both blood family and family of the heart.

Tara balanced a cake platter in her hand, a purple coned hat on her head, singing happy birthday. Her other hand protected the single candle from the wind.

Everyone turned and moved to form a semi-circle around Austin as he bounced Mini-Matteo up in the air to make him shriek with giggles.

"Happy Birthday to you!" The song ended.

Mini-Matteo reached down and grabbed a handful of blue icing and shoved it in his mouth as Tara quickly blew out the candle.

Austin leaned down and kissed her. "Who needs more wishes when you have all this?"

Mrs. Alvarez came over to rescue the cake platter and to go slice and serve.

"Thanks, Mommy," Tara said.

"Talk about a mini-me." Mrs. Alvarez lifted her chin toward Hope.

Now four years old, Hope was pulling a giant toad from her pocket. She lifted it high to show Bear, who was enjoying the shade of the oak tree, talking with Neils and a very pregnant Pria, Jim and Trevor.

"What are you doing with those frogs, Hope?" Bear squatted down to tickle her. "They might get squished in your pockets. That's not nice."

Hope looked at the toad and looked back at Bear. "If I find enough frogs, and we all jump at the same time, I bet I can jump all the way up onto the roof." Her little finger pointed up.

"Because?" Bear asked.

"Because we all have our energy at the same time."

"Oh, is that how it works?" He rubbed his chin, looking up to the roof as if contemplating that scene.

When he looked back at her, Hope nodded, her black pigtails swinging.

"Are you going to be a scientist when you get big, like your mommy?" Bear asked.

"No, sir, I'm gonna be a frogman like my daddy." She pressed the frog toward Bear so he could see.

Austin, overhearing, yelled out, "That's my girl."

Tara reached out to rest her hand on Austin's arm.

There they were. A family. A big fat, *loud*, loving family.

Tara had come to believe that with love and kindness, there would always be a chance for good things to come.

A bright future for their children.

～

Keep reading for more from Fiona Quinn

Readers,

I hope you enjoyed getting to know Tara, Austin, and Diesel. If you had fun reading Rescue Instinct, I'd appreciate it if you'd help others enjoy it too.

Recommend it: Just a few words to your friends, your book groups, and your social networks would be wonderful.

Review it: Please tell your fellow readers what you liked about my book by reviewing Rescue Instinct.

Discuss it! – I have a SPOILERS group on Facebook. (www.facebook.com/groups/fionaquinnsspoilergroup)

Stay up to date with new releases!
Sign up to Fiona's Newsletter at www.fionaquinnbooks.com

If you're following the **Cerberus Tactical K9 Team Bravo series** or you're reading the Iniquus World in chronological order, the next book is: HERO'S INSTINCT

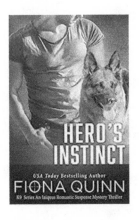

If you want to learn more about Remi and the wombats read: DANGER ZONE

If you want to find out more about Reaper, their trainer, read: FEAR THE REAPER

If you are new to Iniquus and want to start at the very beginning, turn the page for an excerpt from Book One in the Iniquus chronology, WEAKEST LYNX.

Turn the page and let's go!

1

THE BLACK BMW POWERED STRAIGHT TOWARD ME. HEART pounding, I stomped my brake pedal flush to the floorboard. My chest slammed into the seat belt, snapping my head forward. There wasn't time to blast the horn, but the scream from my tires was deafening. I gasped in a breath as the BMW idiot threw me a nonchalant wave—his right hand off the wheel —with his left hand pressed to his ear, still chatting on his cell phone. Diplomatic license plates. *Figures.*

Yeah, I didn't really need an extra shot of adrenaline—like a caffeine IV running straight to my artery—I was already amped.

"Focus, Lexi," I whispered under my breath, pressing down on the gas. "Follow the plan. Give the letter to Dave. Let him figure this out." I sent a quick glance down to my purse where a corner of the cream-colored envelope jutted out, then veered my Camry back into the noonday DC gridlock, weaving past the graffitied storefronts. I recognized that the near-miss with the BMW guy probably wasn't his fault. I couldn't remember the last ten minutes of drive time.

344 | FIONA QUINN

I watched my review mirror as a bike messenger laced between the moving cars on his mission to get the parcel in his bag to the right guy at the right time. Once he handed over his package, he'd be done—lucky him. Even though I was handing my letter off to Dave, the truth was that wouldn't be my endpoint. I wasn't clear about what an endpoint would even look like. Safe. It might look like I was safe, that I had my feet back under me. But that thought seemed like it was far out on the horizon, and right now, I was just looking for something to grab on to, to keep me afloat.

When I finally parked in front of Dave Murphy's mid-century brick row house, I sat for a minute, trying to regain my composure. I'd pushed this whole mess to the back burner for as long as I could but after last night's nightmare... Well, better to get a detective's opinion. Dave had handled enough crack-pots over his time with the DCPD that he'd have a better grasp of the threat level. Right now, even with all my training, I was scared out of my mind.

I glanced down at my hands. The tremor in them sent the afternoon sunlight dancing off my brand-new engagement and wedding rings. I felt like an imposter wearing them—like a little girl dressed up in her mother's clothes. *I'm too young to be dealing with all this crap,* I thought as I shoved my keys into my purse. I pulled my hair into a quick ponytail and stepped out into the February cold. Casting anxious glances up and down the street, I jogged up the stairs to bang on Dave's front door.

The screen squeaked open almost immediately as if he'd been standing there waiting for my knock. "Hey, Baby Girl," he said, stepping out of the way to let me in. Dave had been calling me Baby Girl since I was born because my parents couldn't decide on my name, and that was how I was listed on my hospital ankle tag.

"Glad I found you at home." I walked in and plopped down on the blue gingham couch. It had been here since I could remember. The fabric was threadbare, and juice stained by his five-year-old twins. On a cop's salary, fine furnishings ranked low in priority. Right now—edgy and confused—I appreciated the comfort of familiarity.

Dave shifted into detective mode—hands on hips, eyes scanning me. "Long time, no see."

"Where are Cathy and the kids?" I asked.

"They've got dentist appointments. Did you come to tell us your news?" He lifted his chin to indicate my left hand and settled at the other end of the couch, swiveling until we were face to face.

"Uhm, no." I twisted my rings, suddenly feeling drained and bereft. What wouldn't I give to have my husband Angel here? The corners of my mouth tugged down. I willed myself to stay focused on the reason for the visit. My immediate safety had to take priority over my grief.

Dave raised a questioning brow, waiting for me to continue.

"Angel and I got married Wednesday. I'm Lexi Sobado now." My voice hitched, and tears pressed against my lids. I lowered my lashes, so Dave wouldn't see. But his eyes had locked onto mine, and he never missed much.

"Married? At your age? No introduction? No wedding invitation? Why isn't he here with you now?" Dave angled his head to the side and crossed his arms over his middle-aged paunch. "I'd like to meet the guy," he all but snarled.

Dave probably thought I'd come here because my husband screwed things up already. I pulled the pillow from behind my back and hugged it to me like a shield. "I'm sorry. I should have let you and Cathy know what was going on—I was caught up, and I just..." I stopped to clear my throat. "Angel and I got married at the courthouse, and no one came with us. Not even Abuela Rosa."

"Angel Sobado. He's kin to Rosa, then?"

I gave the slightest tip of a nod. "Angel is her great-nephew. I couldn't bring him with me today because he deployed with the Rangers to the Middle East Thursday. That's why everything happened so fast. He was leaving." The last word stuck in my throat and choked me.

Dave leaned forward to rest his elbows on his knees. Lacing his fingers, he tapped his thumbs together. "Huh. That's a helluva short honeymoon. Married Wednesday. Gone Thursday." Dave's tone had dropped an octave and gained a fringe of fatherly concern.

His compassion gave me permission to break down. But those Angel-emotions were mine. Private. Right now, I needed to hold myself in check long enough to get through my mission of handing off the letter. I shifted my feet back and forth over the rug as I glared at my purse.

"Might even explain the expression on your face," Dave said, narrowing his eyes. He slouched against the arm of the overstuffed couch.

Stalling wasn't going to make this any easier. I reached a hesitant hand into my bag, pulled out a plastic Zip-loc holding the envelope, and held it up for Dave. "The expression is because of this," I said.

Dave took the bag. After a brief glance, he hefted himself to his feet. Over at his desk, he pulled on a pair of Nitrile gloves, then carefully removed the letter.

DEAREST INDIA ALEXIS,
   O my Luve's like the melodie

That's sweetly play'd in tune!
As fair thou art, my bonnie lass,
So deep in love, am I:
And I will love thee still, my dear,
Till a' your bones are white and dry:
Till a' your veins gang dry, my dear,
And your skin melt with the sun;
I will luve thee until your heart is still my dear
When the sands of your life shall no more run.
And fare thee weel, my only Luve,
And fare thee weel a while!
And I will come again, my Luve, so I can watch you die.

DAVE READ the words aloud then stared at me hard; his brows pulled in tight enough that the skin on his forehead accordioned. "What the—"

"Someone shoved the poem under the door to my room, and it's scaring the bejeezus out of me." I gripped the pillow tighter.

Dave peered over the top of his reading glasses. "Last night? This morning?"

"Wednesday morning." I braced when I said it, knowing it would tick Dave off that I didn't bring this to him immediately. Ever since my dad died, his buddies had stepped in and tried to take over the fathering job, even though I'd be turning twenty in a few days.

True to my expectations, Dave was red-faced and bellowing. "*Wednesday?* You waited two whole days to tell me you've gotten a friggin death threat?"

Yup, this was exactly the response Dad would have given me.

Dave jumped up, pacing across the room. Obviously, he

didn't think this was someone's idea of a joke. Fear tightened my chest at his confirmation. I had hoped he'd say, "No worries —someone is having fun pranking you," and then I could go on about my life without the major case of heebie-jeebies that tingled my skin and made me want to run and hide.

"It was our wedding day." I worked to modulate my voice to sound soft and reasonable. "I only had a few short hours before Angel had to take off. So yeah, I decided to focus on us instead of this." I motioned toward the paper in his hand.

Dave took in a deep breath, making his nostrils flare. "Okay." I could almost see his brain shifting gears. "When you first picked up the letter, did you get any vibes?"

"You mean, ESP-wise?"

He nodded stiffly; his eyes hard on me.

Vibes. That wasn't the word I would have chosen to explain my sensations. "I didn't hear anything. It was more like an oily substance oozing over me." I tucked my nose into the soft cloth of the pillow and breathed in the scent of cinnamon fabric freshener. "I vomited." My voice dropped to a whisper. "It felt like evil and craziness, and I can still smell that stench." A shiver raced down my spine.

Dave's lips sealed tightly; he was probably trying to hold back a litany of expletives. Finally, he asked, "That's all?"

"Yes."

"Did any of your neighbors notice anyone unusual lurking around? Did you check with management and run through the security tapes?"

"Dave, didn't you hear? My apartment building burned to the ground three weeks ago. I assumed you knew. It was on the news."

Dave's eyebrows shot straight up.

"I've been living in a motel the Red Cross rented out for all the families displaced by the fire. But to answer your question, no, nobody saw anything, and there were no cameras trained on my motel corridor." I curled my lips in to keep them from trembling. I was used to holding my emotions in check. I trained myself to present a sweet exterior, a costume of sorts, but right now, I was filled to overflowing, and my mask kept slipping out of place.

"Shit." Dave ran a hand over his face. "I had no idea. I'm letting your parents down. Apartment burned, married, husband gone, and now a death threat." His eyes narrowed on me. "Do you think that about covers all of your surprises for me today?"

I paused for a beat. "Yeah, Dave, I think that's it for today." Okay, even if he was like family, the way Dave was talking pissed me off. I was frightened. I wanted a hug and his reassurance. What I was getting was… Dave's brand of love. He wouldn't be this red-faced and agitated if he wasn't worried about me. Tears prickled behind my eyelids, blurring my vision.

"Hey, now. Stop. We'll get to the bottom of this. Did you already let Spyder McGraw know what's going on?"

I wiped my nose with the back of my wrist. "Spyder's still off-grid. I have no idea when he'll get home."

"Were you assigned a different partner while he's gone?"

"No, sir. I only ever worked for Spyder—he sort of wanted to keep me a secret." I still couldn't believe Mom had sat Dave down and told him all about my apprenticeship with Spyder McGraw. Under Spyder's tutelage, I was following my dream of becoming an Intelligence Officer, learning to out-think and out-maneuver the bad guys trying to hurt American interests. And like anyone heading toward a life in the intelligence community, my skills needed to go under the radar. Now that my mom had died, only four people—Spyder, the Millers, and Dave—knew that side of my life. I would prefer Dave didn't know.

"Still, did you consider bringing this to Spyder's commander? Iniquus would probably give him a heads up. Get a message to him."

"Iniquus is my last resort. Sure, Spyder told me to talk to them if I ever found myself in trouble." I sucked in a deep breath of air. "Bottom line? He never wanted them to know I worked for him, well, for them. Safety in anonymity and all that." My fingers kneaded the stuffing in the pillow. "Besides, I guess I was hoping this would all just go away."

Dave's eyes were hard on me. "You know better. Once some psycho's caught you on his radar, you're stuck there until someone wins."

"Okay, so I make sure it's me who wins."

"Exactly right." He considered me for a minute before he asked, "You've kept up with your martial arts training?"

"I have a sparring partner who's pretty good. We rent time at a Do Jang twice a week."

Dave lowered his head to read over the poem again. He put the letter and envelope back in the Zip-loc and placed it on his mantle. Pulling off his gloves with a snap, he looked down at them. "I hate these things. They give me a rash. Look, I'm going to take this down to the station and open a file. If you get anything else, I want you to bring it to me right away. Understood?"

"Yes, sir."

"This is the only poem, letter, communication of any kind you've gotten?"

I nodded. For the first time since I walked into Dave's house, I became aware of sounds other than our conversation and the thrumming blood behind my eardrums. A football game played on TV. I glanced over as the announcer yelled some gibberish about a first down, then moved my gaze back to Dave. "You must have taken graveyard shift last night," I said.

He picked up a remote, zapped off the TV, and sent me a raised eyebrow.

"It doesn't take a psychic. You look like an unmade bed."

Dave ran a hand over his dark hair, thick on the sides, sparse on top. He hadn't used a comb today or bothered to shave. He was hanging-out-at-home comfy in jeans and beat-to-hell tennis shoes. It looked like the only thing I was interrupting was the game re-run.

"Double homicide. Turned into a long night up to my ankles in sewage."

"Yum." I tried on a smile, but it was plastic and contrived.

Dave narrowed his eyes. "We need to move you. Pronto. It's priority one. You need to be someplace secure where I can keep better tabs on you."

"I've been looking since the fire, but I haven't found anything."

"Would you consider buying?" he asked.

"Yes, actually—I'm looking for a low-cost fixer-upper I can work on to help me get through this year without Angel." I followed Dave into the hallway. "Diversion, and all that."

"How about here, in my neighborhood? I could keep a better eye on you—and you won't be showing up at my door with a suitcase full of surprises." He grabbed his coat from the closet and shrugged it on. "I'm taking you over to meet my neighbor. She has the other half of her duplex on the market." He looked over his shoulder at me. "You shouldn't be running around without a jacket." He handed me an oversized wool parka that smelled like raking leaves. He kicked a Tonka truck out of the way, and we moved out the front door.

On the front porch, I slid into the shadows and took in the length of the road—no cars, no barking dogs, everything quiet.

Dave glanced back. "Coast is clear."

I tucked the coat hood up over my ponytail. Screened by

Dave's broad back, I started across the street. Down the road, a car motor revved. I reached under my shirt and pulled out my gun.

∼

Enjoying the read?

FIND WEAKEST LYNX IN EBOOK, PAPERBACK AND NOW HARDCOVER.

THE WORLD of INIQUUS

Chronological Order

Ubicumque, Quoties. Quidquid

Thorn (Uncommon Enemies)
Ours (Kate Hamilton Mysteries)
Cold Red (FBI Joint Task Force)
Even Odds (FBI Joint Task Force)
Survival Instinct - (Cerberus Tactical K9 Team Alpha)
Protective Instinct - (Cerberus Tactical K9 Team Alpha)
Defender's Instinct - (Cerberus Tactical K9 Team Alpha)
Danger Signs - (Delta Force Echo)
Hyper Lynx - (Lynx Series)
Danger Zone - (Delta Force Echo)
Danger Close - (Delta Force Echo)
Fear the REAPER – (Strike Force)
Warrior's Instinct - (Cerberus Tactical K9 Team Bravo)
Rescue Instinct - (Cerberus Tactical K9 Team Bravo)
Heroes Instinct - (Cerberus Tactical K9 Team Bravo)

Coming soon, more great stories from the ex-special forces security team members who live, work, and love in a tightly knit family.

FOR MORE INFORMATION VISIT
WWW.FIONAQUINNBOOKS.COM

ACKNOWLEDGMENTS

My great appreciation ~

To my publicist Margaret Daly

To my cover artist, Melody Simmons

To my editor Kathleen Payne

To my Beta Force, who are always honest and kind at the same time. M. Carlon, E. Hilder, S. Megdal, S. Miller, and K. Schup. Thank you, ladies!

To my Street Force, who support me and my writing with such enthusiasm and kindness.

To the real-world K9 professionals who serve and protect us.

Virginia K9 search and rescue teams for their work in our community, their dedication, and professionalism. Every time I search and train with you, I'm inspired.

To all the wonderful professionals whom I called on to get the details right—

Please note: This is a work of fiction, and while I always try my best to get all the details correct, there are times when it serves the story to go slightly to the left or right of perfection. Please understand that any mistakes or discrepancies are my authorial decision making alone and sit squarely on my shoulders.

Thank you to my family.

I send my love to my husband, T. We have been through so many storms together, I'm so happy that we're holding hands through it all.

And of course, thank *YOU* for reading my stories. I'm smiling joyfully as I type this. I so appreciate you!

ABOUT THE AUTHOR

Fiona Quinn is a six-time USA Today bestselling author, a Kindle Scout winner, Amazon Top 40, and an Amazon All-Star.

Quinn writes suspense in her Iniquus World of books, including Lynx, Strike Force, Uncommon Enemies, Kate Hamilton Mysteries, FBI Joint Task Force, Cerberus Tactical K9 Series Alpha and Bravo, and Delta Force Echo series.

She writes urban fantasy as Fiona Angelica Quinn for her Elemental Witches Series

And, just for fun, she writes the Badge Bunny Booze Mystery Collection with her dear friend, Tina Glasneck, as Quinn Glasneck.

Quinn is rooted in the Old Dominion, where she lives with her husband. There, she pops chocolates, devours books, and taps continuously on her laptop.

Visit www.FionaQuinnBooks.com

Find & Follow Fiona Quinn on Social Media

facebook.com/FionaQuinn.52

twitter.com/fionaquinnbooks

instagram.com/fionaquinnbooks

bookbub.com/authors/fiona-quinn

goodreads.com/fionaquinnbooks